MW01128009

DUKE OF DEPRAVITY

Sins and Scoundrels
Book One

Scarlett Scott

Copyright © 2018 by Scarlett Scott
Print Edition

Published by Dragonblade Publishing, an imprint of Kathryn Le Veque Novels, Inc

All rights reserved. No part of this book may be used or reproduced in any manner
whatsoever without written permission, except in the case of brief quotations
embodied in critical articles or reviews.

Books from Dragonblade Publishing

Dangerous Lords Series by Maggi Andersen
The Baron's Betrothal
Seducing the Earl
The Viscount's Widowed Lady

Also from Maggi Andersen
The Marquess Meets His Match

Knights of Honor Series by Alexa Aston
Word of Honor
Marked by Honor
Code of Honor
Journey to Honor
Heart of Honor
Bold in Honor
Love and Honor
Gift of Honor
Path to Honor
Return to Honor

Beastly Lords Series by Sydney Jane Baily
Lord Despair

Legends of Love Series by Avril Borthiry
The Wishing Well
Isolated Hearts
Sentinel

The Lost Lords Series by Chasity Bowlin
The Lost Lord of Castle Black
The Vanishing of Lord Vale

The Missing Marquess of Althorn
The Resurrection of Lady Ramsleigh
The Mystery of Miss Mason

By Elizabeth Ellen Carter
Captive of the Corsairs, *Heart of the Corsairs Series*
Revenge of the Corsairs, *Heart of the Corsairs Series*
Shadow of the Corsairs, *Heart of the Corsairs Series*
Dark Heart

Knight Everlasting Series by Cassidy Cayman
Endearing
Enchanted
Evermore

Midnight Meetings Series by Gina Conkle
Meet a Rogue at Midnight, book 4

Second Chance Series by Jessica Jefferson
Second Chance Marquess

Imperial Season Series by Mary Lancaster
Vienna Waltz
Vienna Woods
Vienna Dawn

Blackhaven Brides Series by Mary Lancaster
The Wicked Baron
The Wicked Lady
The Wicked Rebel
The Wicked Husband
The Wicked Marquis
The Wicked Governess
The Wicked Spy
The Wicked Gypsy
The Wicked Wife

Highland Loves Series by Melissa Limoges
My Reckless Love
My Steadfast Love
My Passionate Love

Clash of the Tartans Series by Anna Markland
Kilty Secrets
Kilted at the Altar
Kilty Pleasures

Queen of Thieves Series by Andy Peloquin
Child of the Night Guild
Thief of the Night Guild
Queen of the Night Guild

Dark Gardens Series by Meara Platt
Garden of Shadows
Garden of Light
Garden of Dragons
Garden of Destiny

Rulers of the Sky Series by Paula Quinn
Scorched
Ember
White Hot

Highlands Forever Series by Violetta Rand
Unbreakable
Undeniable

Viking's Fury Series by Violetta Rand
Love's Fury
Desire's Fury
Passion's Fury

Also from Violetta Rand
Viking Hearts

The Sins and Scoundrels Series by Scarlett Scott
Duke of Depravity

The Sons of Scotland Series by Victoria Vane
Virtue
Valor

Dry Bayou Brides Series by Lynn Winchester
The Shepherd's Daughter
The Seamstress
The Widow

Men of Blood Series by Rosamund Winchester
The Blood & The Bloom

Crispin Ashforth returns from battle the newly inherited Duke of Whitley with two sisters under his charge. Publicly lauded as a hero, he is haunted by the bitter mission that nearly saw him killed and cost the life of his best friend. He's desperate to drown out the demons tormenting him by any means, regardless of how depraved.

All he needs to do is find a proper governess for his hellion sisters so he can drink and wench himself into oblivion. Enter Miss Jacinda Turnbow, who is as lovely as she is prickly. It doesn't take Crispin long to realize he's found precisely the sort of distraction he needs in the prim governess.

But Jacinda has secrets of her own, and she's no ordinary governess. To save herself and her father from ruin, she has agreed to infiltrate the duke's home and search for evidence that he's a traitor.

Resisting his advances grows more difficult by the day, however, as she discovers there's more to Crispin than the careless life of sin he's cultivated. And the greatest danger she faces is losing her heart to the man she has no choice but to betray.

PROLOGUE

Spain, 1812

CRISPIN FACED THE most dangerous and feared Spaniard on the Peninsula, and despite the unease roiling through his gut, he did not flinch. A dark, embittered figure flanked by two large, armed guards, the man always dressed in simple peasant garb. But his speech, commanding presence, and almost flawless English marked him as something more than the picture he presented.

He was known as El Corazón Oscuro.

The Dark Heart.

To some, he was a fabled hero. Like an avenging knight of old, he fought against French tyranny and oppression, striking back against rampaging armies that decimated towns, pilfering and ravaging homes and families. He avenged innocent civilians who were left to bleed to death in the courtyards of their small towns.

To the French army, there were far more appropriate appellations for the man. *Le Diable*, they called him, or *Le Sans Couer*. Anything less would be a misnomer for a man responsible for killing over a thousand French troops in guerilla attacks all across the Peninsula. But he did not stop at enemy soldiers. Anyone suspected of harboring the enemy was fair game for death and violence. Even the innocent.

Unlike most meetings called by El Corazón Oscuro, this one was being conducted beneath the cover of an early spring moon in a home that had been commandeered and subsequently destroyed by the

French. Window panes and frames had been removed, and neither a stick of furniture, nor a jagged shard of crockery remained within. The place had been eviscerated as surely as if a howitzer had blasted it to hell.

The air was crisp and cool, the scent of impending rain looming as surely as the siege that would soon unfold upon Badajoz. The time to strike had imbued Crispin and his men, as it always did, with a reckless, pent-up energy that could not be settled upon one task. He felt it now as he and his best friend and fellow intelligence officer Morgan, Marquess of Searle, stood shoulder to shoulder and stared down El Corazón Oscuro.

Part of him wanted to charge the fortifications of the city now. Part of him wanted to withdraw his sidearm and aim it upon the Spaniard. He did not trust the man. Never had, never would, and something about the evening meeting, with its unusual stipulations and obscure location, chilled him to his marrow. He could not shake the feeling that he would either return to his post in the morning victorious, or he would die this night and rot into the earth the same way so many other soldiers before him had.

"More cannon," El Corazón Oscuro charged into the uneasy silence.

They had navigated this delicate dance many times before. Wellington supplied El Corazón Oscuro and his band of cutthroats and mercenaries with as many supplies, armaments, and funds as could be reasonably diverted. In return, the bloodthirsty men attacked vulnerabilities in the French line with a complete disregard for those they slaughtered. Last month, El Corazón Oscuro had attacked a French field hospital, the already wounded soldiers sheltering there nailed to trees to bleed to death.

Crispin and Morgan, who had been friends well before their days as war comrades, exchanged a communicative glance. The Spaniard always asked for more at each meeting. But his campaigns against the

French—limited, lightning-fast attacks—were too successful to resist. Inevitably, they would reach a compromise. Their commanding general had given them their utmost limits prior to their departure.

"How many more cannon?" Crispin asked.

"We have seven to spare," Morgan added.

El Corazón Oscuro's lip curled. "Seven? Do you jest, *Coroneles*? We require at least fifteen for the French blockhouses in this region alone."

The defensive blockhouses of the enemy dotted major arteries, providing garrisons for infantry that protected intelligence and supplies. Attacking the bastions led to disruption in communication and provisions the French could ill afford. Already, their messengers traveled with cavalry numbering in the hundreds. Crispin and Morgan had been sent on countless missions to ensure the loyalty and success of local guerilla bands in the last two years alone. El Corazón Oscuro and his men were no different.

Except for the stark evil of the man. War was hell, but murdering innocent women... Crispin's gut clenched at the recollection of the aftermath of El Corazón Oscuro's bitter campaigns of vengeance. Battle had a way of expunging all empathy from a man—he must either become impervious or succumb to death. But there remained some parts of his inner sensibility as a gentleman that he could not entirely dismiss.

"We have seven," Crispin repeated. Rumors regarding El Corazón Oscuro had begun to swirl, and Wellington had determined not to provide the leader and his forces more funds and armaments than any other band, in spite of his brutal successes. No one trusted the bastard.

It was said El Corazón Oscuro had a French mother, which clouded his intentions beneath a shroud of suspicion, and that the chief motivator in all his actions was greed. It was also said that he could be easily bought. Even so, they had never denied El Corazón Oscuro any of his wishes before, having been given *carte blanche* to appease his bloodthirstiness.

"Seven is insufficient," growled the ruffian.

"We feel confident that seven is adequate," Morgan offered smoothly in his bland, drawing-room accent.

Morgan's cool, unflappable air was the stuff of legend amongst their ranks. After taking a bullet to the tip of his pinkie at Talavera, he had lopped off what remained with his sword and continued to fight.

"Adequate, you say." El Corazón Oscuro grinned without mirth, the effect more like a snarl.

The man's barely leashed savagery, coupled with his rampant ire, sent a chill down Crispin's spine. He pitied those who had seen this vagabond's angry visage as their last sight before oblivion. Men buried alive to their shoulders so they could die a slow and painful death, unable to free themselves. And then there was the French captain who had met his end over the hearth of this very home, hung by his feet over the fire so that his head roasted.

"Adequate," Crispin affirmed, tamping down the bile that rose in his throat when he thought of the still smoking body of the captain. The vile scent of charred human flesh would never leave a man.

"Who are you to decide what is adequate, *bonito Inglés?*" he thundered, his gaze slicing to Morgan with dark, undeniable rage. "You with your fancy uniforms and your undying love from sweet-scented, pious *hermanas* and *madres* at home? You who have never had to watch your people be raped and killed. How the hell could you know what is *adequate*? We are tired of this cursed war, and we want it to end. It can only end with more cannon, more French *cerdo* blood. Give us the cannon, and the heavens will open to rain *escarlata*."

"French *cerdo* blood is it now?" Morgan raised a brow, challenging their reluctant ally for the first time. "How odd for you to react thus when I am given to understand you are half French yourself. With the rumors surrounding your… heritage, one cannot help but wonder at your true loyalty."

"My *heritage*," El Corazón Oscuro repeated, his tone taking on a deadly quality. A quiet, violent rage. "Elaborate, *bonito*."

Bloody hell. Both the Spaniard cutthroat and Morgan vibrated with aggression as they squared off, looking like two wild dogs about to fight to the death.

"Idle rumors often abound," Crispin intervened. "Some question your motives. I am afraid that such word has reached our superiors. You understand, surely, they cannot allow for a surfeit of armaments to be put into the hands of forces that cannot be trusted implicitly as allies.

El Corazón Oscuro spat. "Our ravens are hungry for their daily feast of Frenchmen, but perhaps they would like pretty Englishmen just as well."

"Do you dare to threaten us, vile son of a French whore?" Morgan gritted.

El Corazón Oscuro's eyes flashed. "You will regret your words, Searle. I will take great pleasure in making you eat them before I let the birds peck out your tongue." He gave a jerky nod.

A splitting pain crashed through Crispin's skull in the next moment, and his vision went black.

Chapter One

London, Six Months Later

"READ THEM ALOUD once more if you please, Jacinda. I think I may have inadvertently missed a number, for the sequence has no notable pattern."

Jacinda glanced up from the carefully transcribed document to her father. He was beloved in the lamp glow, his white hair askew from his familiar habit of running his fingers through the thinned strands whilst in thought. Their deciphering sessions grew increasingly tedious and fraught with blunders. At first, she had suspected his eyesight had grown worse than he wished to admit. Now, she could not help but wonder if something far worse was at work.

Worry lanced her stomach, curdling the modest breakfast she had consumed not an hour before. But, she nevertheless lowered her eyes to the copy of the enciphered dispatch that had been discovered on the body of a French aide-de-camp. "One hundred. Ten. Twenty. One-and-thirty. Three. One hundred and four. Fourteen…"

Painstakingly, she recited the numeric ciphers that had been transcribed for the eighth time. She had been reading aloud the documents that had arrived from the Peninsula, written in precise, small script, because Father could not read them. He recopied each number painstakingly in large scrawl his double spectacles rendered legible.

Father frowned. "I do believe I transposed this fourteen to one-and-forty," he murmured, bent over his task, nose frightfully near to the paper he scoured. "How many fourteens have you, Jacinda dearest? I have two-and-thirty at most recent count."

"I do as well," she said gently, wondering how she could broach the subject with him. How he hated to see his physician, for being the preeminent decipherer in London meant he could afford no weakness of body or mind. "According to my charts, fourteen is the most commonly appearing number in the dispatches written in the new method of enciphering."

"Yes." Father raked his wizened hands through his hair without glancing up. "If only we knew what fourteen substitutes. Is it a word or a letter?"

Jacinda's mind turned to the matter of cracking the new French cipher, one so complicated that Wellington's field officers could not unravel its mysteries. Like Father, who descended from a line of deciphers and remained one of a small, elite handful that worked for the Crown, she loved the sport of decoding. So much so that after James' death, aiding Father was all that kept her feeling alive.

"Dispatches number three, seven, eight, and ten all contain a combination of words," she pointed out, confident they could exploit the weakness in the cipher by using the slipshod methods of the harried soldier who had not bothered to encrypt the entire communication.

"Of course you are correct, as always, Jacinda." Pride underscored Father's words. "You are sharper than a rapier, my dear girl. Together, we shall unlock the keys to this and our army will have the advantage it requires against the enemy."

Tenderness rushed through her. Mama had died when she was quite young, and it had been just the two of them for so long now. She was grateful he had taught her everything he knew, that he prized her mind and encouraged her pursuit of knowledge. Not every gentleman possessed his heart of gold.

"Thank you for always believing in my capabilities," she said softly, tears pricking at her eyes.

She refused to allow them to fall. She had not wept since the day she learned of James' death. Nor would she cry now, for she had promised herself nothing could ever hurt worse than the certain knowledge that her soldier would never come home to her.

"You have been blessed with both the intelligence and beauty of your mother," Father said, smiling forlornly. "Nearly twenty years later, and the ache only grows stronger. How I miss her."

He had been speaking of her mother with a marked frequency, which added to the misgiving swirling through her. Father was her only family, the strength that carried her through each grim day. The thought of losing him made her chest tighten and her stomach curdle. But before she could respond, a knock sounded at the study door.

Their butler Graves appeared, a fellow who never failed to make an illustration of his surname. "Your guest has arrived, sir," he announced in his dour accent.

Guest? She and Father seldom entertained, for he was content to confine himself to his studies every bit as much as she. The outside world with its social calls and teas and drawing-room boredom held no appeal for her. Hers was a life that needed purpose, and she found it in the hopes her efforts with Father, in some small fraction of a way, could help to defeat the enemy that had slain her husband.

"Thank you, Graves. See him in, if you please," Father announced, further startling her with his lack of surprise.

Clearly, their visitor was an expected one.

"I shall excuse myself," she said, coming to her feet, for she was not dressed to receive company.

"No, Jacinda. You must remain."

Father's command, sharpened by an edge she could not define, stayed her. "But Father…"

He sighed, the sound weary, and passed a hand over his cheek. "Forgive me, my dear. I would have denied his request outright, but as it concerns a matter of great import, I could not do so. I have been meaning to speak to you about it ever since I received the missive yesterday, but we have been so consumed by this cipher, I forgot."

He had also forgotten his cravat yesterday. Two days ago, he had misplaced his most treasured possession, a text that had been passed down to him by his father before him outlining the methods of deciphering. She had located it in the library stuffed amongst the great philosophers with a pair of his spectacles haphazardly placed atop.

"Father," she began again, meaning to address, at last, the fact something was very much amiss with him.

Once more, she was interrupted, but this time it was by the reappearance of the butler with their mysterious guest.

"Lord Kilross," Graves announced before disappearing and closing the door smartly in his wake.

Her stomach clenched anew at the identity of their unexpected caller. Jacinda had met the Earl of Kilross on several occasions, and on this occasion, no less than those prior, he unsettled her. Something about the man was repellant. She tried to keep the distaste from her expression as he bowed, for he was the man responsible for Father's continued position of honor as lead decipherer. Kilross had made clear if he was displeased with Father's work or if Father showed any hint of frailty, he would be replaced without hesitation. And Father's work was his life.

She would do anything in her power to keep Father happy and to hide his poor eyesight and absentmindedness from the earl. Even if it meant smiling as if she found the blackguard charming.

But Kilross had no time for pretense anyway. He pinned Father with a pointed stare. "You have spoken with her, I trust, Sir Smythe?"

Color suffused her father's cheeks. He cleared his throat. "I am afraid I have not, my lord."

"Then I shall have to tell her." The earl clenched his jaw and swung his stare to Jacinda. "Your father assures me you are a proficient decipherer. And while I hesitate to believe the female mind capable of such complexity of thought, I am willing to witness a demonstration."

Jacinda bit down to keep from offering a retort. What a despicable creature the earl was. "What manner of demonstration do you require, my lord?"

How she hoped it was one in which her palm connected with his insufferable cheek.

"One of your ability to break a cipher, Mrs. Turnbow." His expression remained hard, as harsh as his voice.

She glanced to Father, who refused to meet her gaze, and knew a sudden, consuming flare of panic. Her hands tightened on the fall of her serviceable muslin gown. "Forgive me, but I do not see the necessity for such a thing. I am not a decipherer at all, as you must know."

The last thing she wished was for Kilross to somehow use her ability against Father. From the moment he had assumed his position at the Foreign Office, the earl had been loathsome in his endless displays of the power he wielded. Was that what this was? One more way for the earl to attempt to remove her father from service to the Crown? *Dear heavens*, she hoped not. If Father should lose his position...

"I do not require your protestations of false humility, Mrs. Turnbow," he snapped. "I require the demonstration for which I have asked. Have a seat, if you please."

Swallowing her resentment, she did as he ordered, resuming the seat opposite her father at his large, ornate desk. Kilross extracted a folded missive from his coat and opened it, laying it on the desk before her.

"You have precisely one-half hour to tell me what this says, madam."

"She will have it solved in less than ten minutes, my lord," Father said with calm, paternal faith.

Jacinda stared at the paper before her, a mass of jumbled letters that contained no outward meaning. She was confident in her abilities, but she had never before been observed or timed. Her palms went damp. It would seem she had no choice but to play her role in Kilross's despotic exercise.

"Your time begins now," he clipped, hovering over her shoulder.

Doing her best to blot out his odious presence, she took up her pen and put her mind to work. Alphabetic ciphers were often formed with the use of a cipher wheel. Testing her theory, she sketched out a square of the alphabet running in varied rows and columns. Observing the variance of the letters and the frequencies, in no time she was confident she knew the meaning of the simple cipher.

"*Full fathom five thy father lies,*" she read aloud. "*Of his bones are coral made; Those are pearls that were his eyes: Nothing of him that doth fade, but doth suffer a sea-change into something strange and rich.*"

The words were Shakespeare's, and their subject sent an ominous quaver through her. Even so, they were not quite right. She glanced up at Kilross. "The last line ought to be *into something rich and strange*. The rhyme is off, you see."

The earl's lip curled as he leaned over her to study the page. The sour scent of sweat and pipe smoke assailed her. "Clever, Mrs. Turnbow. But one must take care never to be considered too clever, for it hinders one's usefulness, I find."

An icy tendril of alarm licked through her. She kept her palms flattened to the desk, took a deep, calming breath. It would not do to betray her sense of disquiet to Kilross. The man was like a dogged fox who had scented the weakness in his prey. But she would not allow either herself or Father to be taken up in his jaws and made his sacrifice.

"What usefulness have you in mind, Lord Kilross?" she asked softly then, for there must surely be a reason for his appearance today and the demonstration he had forced her to make. Some motivation behind his use of the passage from *The Tempest* and his thinly veiled threat.

"Before we proceed, let me be clear to the both of you." Kilross straightened to his full height and slanted a narrow-eyed glare of warning at first Jacinda and then Father. "This is a matter of supreme import and confidence. If a word regarding what I am about to say should be breathed beyond this chamber, I shall find out. And when I do, your days as a decipherer for the Crown will be done. I will crush the both of you beneath my boot heel without the slightest qualm. Am I understood?"

Jacinda shot to her feet, outraged at the man's temerity. "Lord Kilross, my father has been an esteemed decipherer for the Crown all his life. Not only that, but he is the best decipherer in England, capable of assisting our army as no other. How do you propose to remove him after all his years of flawless service when he is currently engaged in deciphering Napoleon's greatest cipher?"

It was a gamble to take a stand against Kilross, she knew, but she could not countenance the odious man threatening her father in such hideous fashion.

"Jacinda," Father cautioned, sounding pained.

The earl's sneer deepened. "My dear, naïve Mrs. Turnbow. You cannot imagine I am unaware of Sir Smythe's ailing health. I am sorry to say the infirm and frail-minded cannot be entrusted with matters as profoundly impacting as that of unlocking the mysteries of enemy ciphers."

Dread settled upon her, heavy as a stone. "What do you want from us?"

Kilross smiled, the grooves bracketing his thin mouth deepening. "What a delightful question. I shall be succinct. Specifically, I require you, Mrs. Turnbow."

The stone became a boulder of Sisyphean proportions. "Me, my lord? What need can you possibly have of a widow who lives a quiet life with her father?"

The earl inclined his head. "Whilst I have no need of a widow, I do have need of a female who can decipher, one who will have easy access to correspondence and other private documents in the home in which she is employed."

Employed? She was a simple woman, but surely he did not intend for her to become a servant? She had lived a genteel life as the daughter of a knight, and whilst their staff was small and she aided with household tasks, neither was she suited to be a maid.

"It sounds to me as if you wish me act the spy," she said coldly. "I neither have the inclination nor the talent for subterfuge, nor will I engage in servitude to settle your whims, my lord. I am afraid you will have to seek someone else for the task you have in mind. Is that not right, Father?"

But when she looked to her father for reassurance, his milky gaze flitted away, like a bird scared by an encroaching feline that was about to pounce upon its dinner. "I am afraid I have already promised you will assist Lord Kilross," he admitted, his shoulders slumping. "There is a great deal at stake, and I am afraid no one else can be trusted but you."

Dear heavens. Father had already committed her to the earl's plot. She went cold. "Father?"

Father closed his eyes and pressed fingers to his temples. "Please, my dear daughter. Listen to what the earl has to say."

It would seem she had no choice. Her gaze swung back to Kilross. "Tell me what I must do, my lord."

His eyes gleamed with triumph. "For one month's time, you will become the governess for the Duke of Whitley's sisters. Your task will be to comb through his correspondence and private documents, seeking any that are written in French or in cipher. You will then decipher all such messages and transcribe them for me, taking care to return them to their original placement without detection."

Her heart took up a rapid beat. The new Duke of Whitley had a reputation as dark as the devil himself. "But I am a widow, and I know nothing of being a governess."

Never mind she would be expected to live beneath the roof of a man as wicked as the duke, that she would need to trespass against him by riffling through his private papers, and expected to report back to the loathsome Kilross.

"I will provide you with references, and you will present yourself as Miss Turnbow when you interview for the position. Whitley's sisters have run off three governesses already, and he is desperately seeking a replacement. It is the perfect opportunity." He paused. "You do have the knowledge necessary to teach the little viragos, do you not? Watercolor, French, and the like."

"Yes, of course." The earl was deadly serious, she realized as she studied his face, hoping somehow this was all a depraved jest. "What need can you possibly have for the private correspondence of the Duke of Whitley?"

"Simple, madam." Kilross's countenance darkened with undisguised hatred. "The man is a traitor, and with your help, I am going to be the one who unravels his deceptions."

CHAPTER TWO

THEY SAID HE was a war hero.

What rot.

Crispin swigged his whisky as he preferred, straight from the bottle, seated in the darkness of his study. The drapes were drawn, and he despised even the lone, wraithlike beam of light that crept past the window coverings through a tiny gap left by some harried parlor maid. He disliked the blazing orb that decided to rise in the eastern sky each morning with the ritualistic precision of a soldier.

It reminded him that he was alive when he did not deserve to be.

Give him darkness, drink, and warm, willing flesh over the bright lunacy of the sun any day. Give him night, everlasting distraction, mindless pleasure, any cursed means by which he could forget.

The lauds he received were not rightfully his to claim. The true hero was dead, tortured slowly to death by a Spanish butcher, what remained of his broken body never found. The true hero had possessed the daring of a thousand men, the fearlessness of an immortal, the fierce, bone-deep loyalty no other soldier could ever claim.

By contrast, Crispin was a pretender. A poor, faded imitation who had somehow survived the bludgeoning attack in that Spanish farmhouse and woke to the ghastly specter of the dead French captain's burned head looming over him. He would never forget the sight or the blood, dark and red and copious, the severed hand wearing Morgan's signet ring on the stone kitchen floor.

The sickening realization that he had been left for dead while his best friend had been taken to face unfathomable horrors still brought bile to his throat. He drank again, liquor burning its devil's path down his gullet, straight to his empty stomach. He was soused, and he knew it because he couldn't recall the last time he'd consumed a morsel of food. The inkiness of his study swirled about him, hazy and indistinct.

And though he did not recall summoning his butler or answering a knock at his door, suddenly, Nicholson stood at the threshold, clearing his throat in a long-suffering manner. "Your Grace."

Crispin shook his head as if it could clear his stupor. It could not, and so he lifted the bottle back to his lips for another generous draught.

"I beg your pardon, Your Grace."

Glowering in the direction of his butler because his eyes refused to sharpen, he slammed the half-empty bottle onto his escritoire. "What can it be, Nicholson? Can you not see I am otherwise occupied at the moment?"

He preferred to live his life in a fog of whisky-induced stupor and licentiousness. Presently, there were no whores about, but that could be rectified at any moment with but a note from the famed Duke of Whitley and the proper amount of coin.

Yes, a whore did sound like just the thing, now that he thought on it. Before his butler could respond, he raised an imperious finger into the air, jabbing the darkness. "Nicholson, have a carriage sent round for Mrs. Nulty, if you please. Send along a note making it clear she is to bring her friends Madame Laurier and Mrs. Reeves, as well."

The golden-haired Mrs. Nulty, the raven-tressed Madame Laurier, and the redhead Mrs. Reeves. His cock stirred in his breeches despite the substantial amount of whiskey he'd consumed. Ah, yes. The perfect trifecta. He'd had them before, but never all at once. Why not begin with Madame Laurier sucking his—

"Ahem, Your Grace." His butler had the temerity to interrupt the bawdy bent of Crispin's thoughts.

His gaze, having flitted into the ethers of his dismal study, the better to entertain his fantasies, now snapped back to the servant. Two Nicholsons stared at him with twin disapproval until his eyes at last began to function properly and the twain met as one. "Why the devil do you linger, Nicholson? Send for my companions at once."

"I would, Your Grace," began the servant he was about to sack for insubordination, "but earlier this morning, you advised you wished to interview Miss Turnbow yourself, and as she has arrived and has been awaiting you for the last half hour, I thought—"

"I do not pay you to think," he snapped, biting off the remainder of the servant's words. He wanted his distraction. Needed his distraction. Now. Already, his hands had begun to tremble, a weakness he despised. "And precisely who the hell is Miss Turnbow?"

"The gentlewoman who wishes to become Lady Constance and Lady Honora's governess, Your Grace."

Ah, hell.

His innocent sisters.

The burden left to him by his sainted brother Phillip, who had, of all things, choked on a beef ragout whilst disguised. According to Nicholson, his brother had consumed half a bottle of blue ruin in the better part of an hour and then commenced his final supper.

Crispin had seen years of duty on the Peninsula, had faced scores of enemy soldiers. Infantrymen, guerilla soldiers, cannonades. Musket fire and the hell of dead and wounded men. He had infiltrated enemy lines with the ease of a mosquito. But his brother, the heir, the duke, the-larger-than-life hero, had met his end with one bite of a dish that— judging from Crispin's experience with the chef's dubious capabilities—likely had not even been edible.

Yet another person who had died when he ought to have lived.

Whilst Crispin continued in his purgatory-of-a-life, with only cunny and liquor to soothe him. It all seemed so horridly unfair. Not a day passed where he didn't wish he had been slaughtered by El Corazón Oscuro in Spain instead of Morgan.

But he had defied the devil and all the odds against him, and here he was, cupshot, reasonably randy, with his bloody butler staring him down. Why the hell was Nicholson looming like a corpse risen from the dead, his expression frozen with haughty disapproval that not even a seasoned domestic like him could suppress?

"What is it again, Nicholson? I am, as you can plainly see, quite occupied at the moment. I wholeheartedly dislike disruption of any sort. It is grievously disquieting to the constitution, you understand. If you will not fetch me the quim I require, then leave." He sent the servant an evil grin, enjoying keeping the stodgy bastard at attention. His depravities shocked the stoic domestic, that much Crispin knew, but he also understood frankness disturbed him in an almost equal measure.

"Miss Turnbow," the much-aggrieved fellow intoned. "If Your Grace wishes to conduct the interview as planned, I shall have the green salon readied and you may join her there at your leisure."

Yes, that would all be very tidy and proper, wouldn't it? But Crispin was not proper. Decidedly not tidy. Indeed, he did not give a good damn about anything other than burying himself in pleasure so he could forget the past. Except for his sisters, devil take it.

He loved the minxes, and his duty to them took precedence over his need to quiet the monsters festering within his soul. Which meant he needed to interview the would-be governess. They had already run off... how many had it been? Three? Four?

But as much as he loved them, he still had no intention of curtailing his lifestyle. His lifestyle was unconventional, he knew. Shocking to some. Appalling to others. He had long ago ceased to care about small-minded genuflections to societal whims. Facing death each day and witnessing the barbarities he'd seen had a way of changing a man forever.

"Not the green salon," he decided, gainsaying his butler. "Bring her here, if you please."

Nicholson looked, for the briefest moment, as if he had swallowed a slug. He hastened to school his features back into a semblance of calm, politic imperturbability.

"Would you care for me to tie back the window dressings, Your Grace?" he asked with just enough pointed suggestion to make Crispin aware the darkness of the room was a thing to be remarked upon.

A thing which Crispin ought not to do.

A sign of his weakness.

A sign that, while he bore no scars from his years at war save the bullet nick on his upper left arm and the sabre slash on his thigh, he was nevertheless wounded on the inside. Less than whole. Scarred, cut up, bitter, and ugly.

"Leave the curtains as they are," he ordered curtly, irritated already.

Why did everyone insist upon gainsaying him? He was the duke, and though it was a hollow title he had never wanted, it was his. It bloody well ought to mean something.

"Do you require a lamp be lit, Your Grace?" Nicholson asked, his tone solicitous.

Crispin gritted his teeth. "I require nothing, sir. Fetch the girl. I have needs to attend this evening, and none of them can be satisfied until this interminable interview with Miss Torncrow is concluded."

"Of course, Your Grace." His butler bowed, sounding humble. "It is merely that I do believe the prospective governess's name is Miss Jacinda Turnbow and not, in fact Miss Torncrow. As you wish."

Torncrow, Tornbow, Turnbow. Who gave a bloody damn? The chit's name mattered not. All that did was completing this wretched audience so someone could take his hoyden sisters in hand and leave him more time to go about the business of drowning himself in blue ruin and quim, the order of these twin indulgences *pas nécessaire*. Some days, he hungered for the comfort of his flesh pounding into another's. Others, all he required was a bottle and his hand.

Today was a sousing and fucking sort of day. The nightmares had returned. He'd woken to earsplitting screams he realized were his own. Even now, he could feel the blood on his hands. Smell the foul reek of death. See Morgan's disembodied hand.

He took another drink of whisky, wondering what in Hades was taking the woman so bloody long to appear. Patience had never been one of his admittedly limited catalog of virtues.

"Miss Turnbow, Your Grace," intoned Nicholson then, splitting the silence.

His gaze flitted back to the threshold to find a short female form enshrouded in an unremarkable, altogether shapeless dress. He supposed he ought to stand, observe propriety and the polite nuisances society subjected upon its unwilling vassals, etcetera. And so, he rose, not with the grace he would have preferred, but with what he supposed was the proper amount of listing deference one ought to pay a prospective governess whilst in his cups.

Nicholson disappeared. The door closed, leaving Crispin in the mid-morning murk, the drapes still closed. The governess became hazy and indistinct. A vague shape, her form smothered in dour shades that seemed designed to disguise. Egad, was her dress brown? Even in the darkness, he clearly discerned the white cap atop her head.

Here was the sort of woman who fashioned herself into an inanimate object, something unworthy of notice. Unless one truly looked.

And he looked as she drew abreast of his desk. The darkness did not obscure her from him now in such proximity, for he had grown accustomed to the lack of light. He preferred it. Even so, there was something about this small woman that made him wish to illuminate the chamber. To draw back the window coverings and light a hundred tapers and oil lamps each, just the better to see her.

Ludicrous, that. But he was half sotted, and he had lost control of his baser impulses a long, bloody time ago. This woman woke his body in ways he had not experienced since… hell, since *ever*. It wasn't just his cock that stood at attention—which it most assuredly did—but his mind too was engaged. He was intrigued. All signs pointed to the conclusion this woman was lovely, with a ripe body, and yet she had hidden herself beneath a matron's cap and a travesty of fabric.

But she was looking upon him in expectation, which reminded him he was the host. And he was meant to be interviewing this luscious bit of skirts to be his sisters' governess. And if she was to become the governess, he must not consider the tempting notion of stripping her bare and kissing her everywhere until she was desperate for him.

He cleared his throat, banishing the wicked thought, delicious though it was.

"Miss…" he paused when he had once more forgotten her name. *Devil take it.*

The prospective governess took his forgetfulness in stride, however. Her lips—large, luscious, and with a delightfully delineated upper bow, tightened into a semi-frown. Hers was not the mouth of a governess, and it seemed a damn shame she ought to have found herself in such a plight. A woman with the allure of a courtesan ought to never be forced to conceal her charms and earn her bread schooling brats.

"Miss Turnbow," she supplied, her tone polite.

Distant.

This was no ordinary female. He could sense as much as he observed her, watched the way that lone beam of light betwixt the curtains found its way to her brilliant red hair, glimmering in the hint of her bound locks visible beneath the dreadful cap. If the sight of her potential employer rumpled and tippling straight from the bottle before midday disturbed her, she gave no indication of it.

"Miss Turnbow," he agreed, grateful when she did not seem to balk at his greeting, which meant he had recalled her surname correctly for the first time since hearing of her existence. Although she had just spoken it moments before, the whisky had begun to at last dull his senses so that he had fallen into a delicious state of inebriation, and he could not be entirely sure what he heard, recalled, or said.

He was here. Existing when he had no right to. Doing his damnedest to forget all the reasons why.

She dipped into a semblance of a curtsy then, grasping her skirts and lowering herself, keeping her eyes trained to the floor. He wished he could see her properly—could read her gaze. Were her eyes dark and soulful, or were they blue and bright? Perhaps even green and exotic. How he bloody well wished he could know and see all of her.

"Your Grace," she returned.

"Please do seat yourself." He stroked his jaw, watching, wondering what she would do next. Surely to her, this would seem odd, interviewing for her post in the darkness with an inebriated duke who had a bottle at his right hand? And yet, she seemed unmoved. It sure as hell left one wondering. He brought the bottle to his lips, taking a swig just to see if he could goad her.

Her brows rose, but she sat as prompted, primly arranging her voluminous skirts as she did so. "Thank you, Your Grace."

He had never seen such a horribly outfitted female. The waist of the colorless sack was not even properly fitted, and the skirts billowed about her like an unfortunate sail on a boat. Her breasts looked like handfuls even beneath the loose lines of the monstrosity. But a massive lace fichu that would have been more at home on a turbaned dowager than on a young, comely lady obstructed him from a proper view.

Despite her atrocious gown and unfortunate inability to show her womanly figure to full distraction, her face was arresting. Even garbed in the ugliest dress he'd ever seen, half covered by lace, the sight of her hit him like a fist to the gut.

"Your Grace?" Her voice, tentative, interrupted the wicked vein of his thoughts.

"Hmm?" Rudely, he wiped the back of his hand across his wet mouth, removing all traces of liquor before he lowered the bottle to the table and focused upon the governess once more, only to realize he had once again forgotten her bloody name. *Turncrow? Tornstow? Devil take it*, he didn't know.

But her eyes... Lord God, he could see them now at this proximity, and they were extraordinary. Warm, sherry-brown with golden flecks and framed by long, thick lashes. This woman looked more like a mistress than a governess.

She looked, in a word, beddable.

Would it be wrong to pin her to the desk, ravage her mouth until she was breathless, and then raise her skirts to her waist? Could he take the prospective governess? Was he that depraved? The longer he stared at her lush mouth—currently flattened into a peevish line that did nothing to distract from his desire to claim it—the more the idea of debauching her consumed him.

He stole another gulp of whisky from the bottle, watching her. A fierce, burning need flared to life within him. Revealing the delicious curves beneath her hideous costume would be more thrilling than swiving all three of his favorite whores at once.

Curse it, no. There were boundaries even he could not cross, and ruining an innocent governess in the morning darkness of his study was just such a boundary. *Think of Mrs. Nulty*, he ordered his mind. *Mrs. Reeves. Madame Laurier. The perfect trifecta.*

As though she had heard the bent of his thoughts, she spoke, cutting into the heavy silence he'd allowed to fall between them in his lust. "You wished to determine my ability to act as governess for your sisters, I understand?"

Erm, yes, that was rather the point of this wasn't it? He should feel like a beast for plotting her seduction, for not even bothering to recall he was meant to determine her suitability for Con and Nora. But that was rather the trouble, these days. He didn't feel a damn thing.

"How long have you been a governess, Miss…" *Hell and damnation*. He'd forgotten her name again. "And I assume you have letters to recommend you?" he continued, ignoring his pause as if it hadn't occurred.

She did not blink. "I have been honored to be a governess for four years, Your Grace. The Earl of Aylesbury vouches for me."

"Honored?" He could not stay the brow that winged up his forehead, could not tamp down the disbelief.

"Honored," she echoed, her chin tipping up a scant inch, the only sign of defiance. "I take great pride in my charges. When they flourish, I flourish through their successes."

Good God. Who would enjoy being relegated to servitude? For that was a governess's lot in life. She enjoyed a slight distinction above the rest of the domestics, but she was still a paid servant, ever aware of her station. Ever serving at her master's whim.

But he said none of those things aloud, for he was a drunkard but he was not a fool. "You find your role a rewarding one, then?"

"Of course, Your Grace." She folded her hands in her lap, almost as if in prayer.

He thought about binding her wrists together and tying them to his headboard. "You are fluent in French and Latin? Adept at playing the pianoforte? Can you teach watercolors, proper decorum, and whatever other bloody nonsense is required of females?"

She flushed. "I am well-versed in the feminine arts, and I am able to speak fluent French and Latin, with a smattering of Spanish. I am a fair hand at all musical instruments, watercolors are a particular joy of mine, and decorum shall be a foremost objective for Lady Constance and Lady Honora."

His eyes narrowed on her for a moment. The chit was well-prepared. Quick with her answers. Facile with her tongue. He had no objections to her suitability as governess, and his amenable nature was no doubt aided by both his inebriation and his desire to watch her riding his cock, those full breasts bouncing.

Lord God, now he found himself wondering about the precise shade of pink her nipples would be. Would she cry out when he suckled them? Would she prefer the nip of his teeth? *Beelzebub and hellfire*, this had to stop.

"Why did you leave your position with Aylesbury?" he forced himself to ask, willing his fierce arousal to abate.

"My charges had outgrown their need of me, and I was no longer required in the household."

Fair enough. He studied her for another moment. There was only one manner in which he could proceed. Con and Nora had been running wild in the absence of proper guidance. If the new governess proved too distracting or too much of a temptation, he could always sack her and find another. Or spend more time at The Duke's Bastard, buried in whisky and lightskirts.

"You may begin the position immediately," he decided, hoping it was not a mistake. "In the interest of disclosure, I must warn you I possess a certain *reputation*."

"Idle gossip does not concern me, Your Grace." Nothing seemed to shake her. She continued to assess him with those brilliant eyes. "I can begin today, should that suit you."

Today. Yes. The heavy weight of guilt and obligation lifted from his chest. Con and Nora could become someone else's headache. What a bloody relief.

"Today is agreeable, Miss..." *Damn it all*, he still couldn't recall her name.

"Turnbow," she supplied. "Thank you, Your Grace. I would be honored to accept the position, and I look forward to meeting Lady Constance and Lady Honora."

A great, clanging commotion reached his ears then, and Crispin was reminded of precisely why his sisters were in such desperate need of management. "Perhaps you can meet them now. I'm afraid the crashing and clanging you've just heard was caused by the both of them."

For the first time since she entered his study, the governess's eyes went wide. "Caused by them?"

He took another deep swallow of his liquor for good measure and then stood. "Come with me, Miss Governess, and you shall see."

CHAPTER THREE

THE DUKE OF Whitley was a lecherous drunkard, and his sisters were wayward hoydens who were currently delighting in the act of riding silver salvers down the carpeted staircase of Whitley House.

No.

Jacinda's eyes were not mistaken.

Two girls, awkward and willowy of figure with striking ebony hair like the duke's, were racing each other down the stairs, each on her own salver, laughing. The butler was huffing and demanding the nonsense cease. A pair of chamber maids hovered about, gawping.

And the duke simply turned his glittering gaze to Jacinda and smiled that wolfish, predatory smile of his that made her forget who he was and how she had come to be standing in his townhouse this morning. Made her forget what she was meant to do—nay what she *must* do—in order to help Father.

For one frantic beat of her heart.

But then she forced the unwanted blossom of heat in her belly to cool. *He is a hedonistic wastrel*, she reminded herself. And if what the Earl of Kilross had said was to be believed, he was also a traitor who assuaged any guilt he'd felt at being responsible for his friend's hideous death by drowning in drink and ladybirds. He could have been Beelzebub himself and she would not have been surprised as he had sat in the darkness of his study, quizzing her in an indolent voice that suggested he had not a care whether she would be a decent governess to his sisters or not.

She had foolishly thought herself well-prepared for this post, con-signed to her fate if it was what she needed to do to help Father. Kilross had given her a great deal of information concerning the duke and her would-be charges. He had arranged for her interview, provided her with the necessary references. Everything thus far had proceeded as planned, despite her sweaty palms and the unease clenching her gut.

But there was one thing she had not expected, and that was for the Duke of Whitley to gaze upon her as if she were a sweet he longed to devour. And then, her father's words echoed in her memory. *You are not to allow him to notice you. Though you must undertake this unwanted task, I will not have you defiled by that lecherous coward.*

Too late. He had already noticed, and the knowledge only served to heighten the foreboding rioting in her. She had taken great pains to bury herself in shapeless dresses and lace, to hide her vibrant hair beneath a cap, and to seem as unremarkable as possible.

He was still fixed upon her, that lazy grin curving his beautiful mouth, those alarming, gray eyes smoldering into hers, when one of his sisters reached the bottom of the stairs on her salver and went hurtling into him.

"Your Grace, behind you," Jacinda called out as the girl collided with him, sending him pitching forward. For reasons unknown to her—reasons she instantly regretted—she stepped forward, her arms outstretched, and steadied him against her.

She staggered a few steps in retreat, grappling with his large, heavy body, and somehow the duke's face wound up pressed into her bosom. Her face flamed with horror and humiliation as the man did nothing to remove himself. Instead, he rumbled a sigh of appreciation she felt between her thighs.

His arms traveled around her waist, anchoring her to him when she would have extricated herself. "Your Grace, are you injured?"

"Crispin," came the chiding tone of the sister who had nearly sent him sprawling to his knees. "You ought to know better than to stand beneath the stairs whilst Con and I are having our races."

Good heavens, she had entered Bedlam. The duke's face remained buried against her in the most inappropriate fashion, and he took a great inhalation. "Lovely catch, Tottlebrow," he muttered into her bodice.

He still could not recall her name, the drunken fool. She hesitated to touch him, but her patience was thinning, and there was something about being in the Duke of Whitley's embrace that a disturbing and most wholeheartedly unwanted part of her rather enjoyed. Jacinda flattened her palms on his shoulders and shoved, while settling a disapproving glower upon the intrepid young lady who had nearly laid her brother low.

"Lady Honora?" she guessed.

"Indeed... Tuttlebum, was it?" The girls' brows raised in feigned innocence as she gave an exaggerated blink. "Are you to be our new governess?"

"Turnbow," she corrected, thinking her covert duties would be the least of her worries while she remained at Whitley House. She would have two minxes to contend with and a duke who seemed to be acquainting himself with her bosom.

Until... *good Lord, was that a snore?*

The other sister approached their odd tableau, her cheeks rosy from her exertions, salver in hand. "I do think our brother has fallen asleep, Nora."

Saints preserve her. The man had fallen asleep with his face buried in her bosom. "How can a man sleep whilst standing?" she demanded before she could catch her tongue. Servants were meant to mind their manners, and above all, never question the peers who ruled their lives.

"He goes days without sleeping," Lady Honora confided in her, frowning. "Best call for some sturdy footmen, Towerbottom. When he finally falls into slumber, there is no waking him, and he will need to be carried to his chamber."

"He can sleep for an entire day," Lady Constance added. "When he finally does wake, he's an utter bear. Would you not agree, Nora?"

Lady Honora cocked her head, considering her sister's question. "Perhaps he is rather more like a vicious nest of bees that has just been disturbed and all are bent upon stinging anyone in their paths."

Jacinda controlled her features with great care. In truth, the notion of the duke sleeping for a whole day sounded quite promising. But his dead weight was beginning to become a problem, as was his heated breath, which permeated her dress and undergarments, landing right between her breasts. "Call for the footmen, if you please, my ladies," she said in a strangled voice. "I fear I alone cannot support His Grace's weight for long."

Two strapping footmen appeared before the girls could raise the alarm, and Jacinda was grateful indeed to the butler, who seemed a long-suffering sort. The footmen's expressions were blank canvases. This was not the first time they had dragged their sleeping master to bed. As they hauled him from her, his head lolled, eyes closed, lips moving.

He murmured something.

Jacinda stepped nearer and lowered her ear, which proved yet another mistake on her part.

"The most delicious bubbies in all Christendom," he mumbled.

If her face had been red before, it was fairly on fire now. She retreated from the dozing blackguard, hoping no one had heard him.

"I do think Crispin likes you, Tornbud," Lady Honora said brightly. "Do you not think so, Con?"

Lady Constance beamed. "Oh yes, Nora, I agree. Tornrow, Crispin especially likes your—"

"Lady Constance," Jacinda interrupted coolly, cutting off whatever her charge had been about to say. "That will be enough, thank you. Furthermore, my name is Turnbow. Please do endeavor to remember it, as it seems we shall be spending a great deal of time in each other's company in the future. His Grace has enlisted me to be your new governess, beginning today. Since His Grace is... otherwise occupied, perhaps we can begin with you showing me your schoolroom and explaining where your previous governess left off your studies."

It took all the control Jacinda possessed to refrain from grimacing as she said the last. She had thought she could handle what she must do with aplomb, but how wrong she'd been. Deception was not something that came easily to her. The knowledge she was lying to the duke and his sisters—regardless of the man's innocence or guilt—was a knife of unease lodged in her belly.

Lady Constance and Lady Honora exchanged a glance that gleamed with wicked amusement.

"How lovely," announced Lady Honora. "You shall be a great improvement upon old Miss Humphrey. She only lasted four days, and she smelled of spirits."

"How could we have known she was terrified of spiders when we caught one and hid it beneath her bedclothes?" Lady Constance added.

Jacinda coaxed a feigned smile to her lips. "Fortunately, I have no such fear of arachnids."

The sooner she could accomplish her abhorrent task, the better, she vowed inwardly. There was no earthly means by which she could survive an entire month at Whitley House. She would search the duke's correspondence at her first opportunity.

He walked through a field of bodies. A fortress loomed over him. Cannon thundered. Acrid gun smoke burned his lungs. In the distance, guns rang out. Above the tumult rose the moans of the dying, the cries of agony, and the screams of pain.

The sounds of war. The smells of war. The sights of war.

The bodies strewn over the earth were plentiful. He could not see dirt or the crops once grown there, planted by a hopeful farmer who never could have imagined the horrors to be visited upon his verdant fields. There was nowhere for him to walk but upon them.

The coppery scent of blood muddled with gun smoke, mingled with the unmistakable scent of death.

He walked over them. His own men. Enemy men. Faceless men. He could not even offer apology, for this was battle. He needed to find Morgan. Where the hell was he?

A hand caught his ankle in a manacle grip. He looked down to find the hand had been stripped of its flesh. White bones clenched him and no matter how hard he tried, he could not free himself.

Desperation rose in his chest. The hand jerked, bringing him facedown atop the bodies. Blood splashed on his hands and face. One of the dead men's eyes opened. And it was Morgan, his best friend and comrade, blood blossoming scarlet and horrible over his chest.

"Damn you, Crispin," the corpse growled. "You killed me."

"Morgan!" he called out. "No!"

The hand pulled him deeper into the pile of bodies, until he was drowning in a sea of death. He scrabbled and fought, but he could not free himself, and the darkness beckoned, ready to claim him…

With a jolt, Crispin woke, shooting into a sitting position, gasping for breath. Darkness surrounded him, and for a brief moment, he thought he was still trapped in the confines of the same nightmare that had been plaguing him ever since the day Morgan had gone missing. Awareness descended upon him in stages.

The ticking of a clock. The familiar scent of his room. The softness of the bedclothes, the comfort of the bed. His eyes adjusted, and he could see the outlines of the furniture in his chamber.

He pressed a hand to his heart, willing it to cease its rapid thumping, forcing his breath to slow and calm. His head ached and his stomach threatened to revolt. A fine sheen of sweat coated his skin. Crispin knew the signs all too well. He needed a damned whisky, and he needed one now, but the stores in his chamber needed replenishing.

Fortunately, he had an ample supply of panacea in his study.

Rising from his bed, he scrambled for his dressing gown, left precisely where he preferred by his valet. Curse it, he was getting worse. Self-loathing washed over him as he donned the robe and knotted the belt at his waist. This was what his life had become—an endless cycle of drinking, swiving, and sleeping until the nightmares roused him enough to begin again.

He didn't know how many hours had passed since the moment he had fallen into his stupor and now. The last time, he had been unconscious for a day and a half. Judging by the darkness, it was the blackest hour of night. But he preferred it to the cursed light of day, when he could see his bleak reflection in the looking glass and hate himself all the more for being alive.

He should be dead. Every dream, every bitter, sober moment reminded him of the day he had woken in that damned Spanish farmhouse. When he had seen Morgan's spilled blood, his severed hand, all that remained of him. When Crispin had been as helpless and as stupid as he was now, shuffling down the hall of his townhouse in search of the only thing that would numb him.

But the whisky wasn't working as well as it once had.

He didn't need a taper to find his way to his study. That was how accustomed he'd grown to remaining in the dark. But as he crossed the threshold, he knew at once he was not alone.

At first, he sensed the presence, his old instincts flaring to life. Gooseflesh pebbled his skin. Then, a hint of jasmine reached his nose. Taking care to move as silently as possible, he stalked toward the vicinity of the interloper. A soft exhalation reached him, almost a gasp. Closer he went, determined in his pursuit, until he could discern a shadowy figure near his desk.

With a growl, he launched himself at the intruder, his hands meeting with the unmistakable curves of soft, womanly flesh. Whoever she was, she was trespassing where she was most unwelcome, but that didn't stop his cock from asserting a twitch of approval as he gripped the lush curve of her waist and hauled her against him so her bountiful breasts crushed into his chest.

His opponent began trying with all her might to remove herself from his grasp. She twisted, pulled, stomped on his instep, and clawed at him. He remained immovable. Whoever she was, she did not know the part of him that knew the capacity to feel pain had died a long bloody time ago.

"Who the hell are you and what are you doing in my study?" he demanded, fury surging through him.

How dare anyone have the gall to invade his territory? To so trespass against him?

If it was a chamber maid, he would see her dismissed. If it was a whore, he would never tup her again. She did not belong in the last place where he could find some semblance of peace. He wanted to know why she was there, and then he wanted her gone, damn it.

But all she gave him was her silence and her desperate fight. Whoever she was, she was a bloody hellcat. When her hand escaped his grasp and her nails raked his cheek, the last thread of his patience snapped.

"Cease, damn you." He caught her wrist in a punishing grip. She refused to heed him, continuing her struggle.

His head pounded, reminding him of his need for that whisky. Reminding him this banshee was keeping him from the only thing that kept him sane. And he had endured quite enough. He wanted an answer, and he wanted it now.

When she refused to concede defeat, the beast within him roared to life. The lines between the man he had once been and the man he was now, between reality and nightmare, life and death, all blurred into one indistinct mass. He forgot any reason why he ought to treat his opponent with care. He forgot she was female. That he was a duke and ought to behave with at least a modicum of caution and reason.

They fell to the carpet as one, she on her back and he atop her. His thighs straddled hers, trapping her against the floor as he gripped her wrists and pinned them above her head.

He leaned forward so his weight kept her immobile. "Say something."

She writhed beneath him, continuing her ridiculous attempts at escape. But her actions only served to brush her breasts over his chest and to grind her pelvis into his. With only the thin barrier of his dressing gown and the accommodating bit of muslin she wore separating his cock from the undeniable heat of her mound, he went rigid.

"Christ Jesus."

She felt bloody good. Bloody right.

"Please, Your Grace. You are hurting me."

The voice, hushed yet familiar, sliced through the fog of rage and lust clouding his mind. He knew that mellifluous tone, the sweet huskiness. Knew the lush temptation of the breasts swelling beneath his chest.

For he had fallen into them headfirst before the darkness had claimed him.

Memories returned. He recalled conducting an interview with a flame-haired siren while soused. His cock remembered as well, for if possible, it went even harder than it already was, his ballocks tightening as lustful reveries assailed him. All too vividly, he could imagine her riding his cock, her heavy breasts begging to be sucked...

But he could not tup the new governess on the floor of his study in the depths of night. Nor could he tup her at all, curse it. She was not his to defile, no matter how much he longed to debauch her. And oh, how he longed with her beneath him, her sweet, womanly body curved into his. Temptation had ever been his weakness.

No. He must not.

He banished the unwanted thoughts from his mind, willed his cock to wilt, and asked the looming question.

"Tumblebow," he growled. "What in the devil are you doing in my study?"

CHAPTER FOUR

T HE DUKE OF Whitley was atop her. And scantily clad. And—good, sweet heavens—*aroused*. Though she had not long been a wife before being made a widow by war, she was certainly not ignorant about the male anatomy.

One thing was certain, she was even less prepared for the magnitude of Kilross's request than she had supposed. For nothing could have primed her for this moment in the dark with an irate duke settled between her thighs as if it was where he belonged.

What a miserable thief she made. She had been caught before she had even left the chamber with the documents she'd pilfered from his desk.

Think, Jacinda. How can you extract yourself from this predicament?

Moreover, how could she quell the disturbing reaction his large, lean body pressing into hers caused? The Duke of Whitley was a reprobate and a drunkard, and according to Kilross, a despicable coward who had betrayed his best friend and caused his death. If he had no qualms about orchestrating the death of the Marquess of Searle, what would he do to her should he discover the reason for her presence in his study?

She forced the chill of a frigid winter's day into her voice as she spoke, taking care to hold herself very still lest further movement incite him. Rumors of his dalliances and bedchamber prowess were abundant. He did not strike her as the sort who enjoyed ravishment, but one could never exercise too much caution.

"My surname is Turnbow, Your Grace," she informed him. "And as for your query, I was under the impression that I was in the library." With great effort, she kept the breathlessness from her voice.

To her dismay, he neither removed his person from her nor released her wrists, which remained pinned to the Aubusson above her head, thrusting her breasts into his chest in a most disconcerting fashion. How she wished she were more prepared to do battle. She had nothing save her wits with which to defend herself.

"This is not the library, Miss Governess," he hissed. "Why the hell are you wandering about in the dark?"

"Forgive me for the intrusion, Your Grace." She paused, attempting to gather her wits. "Would you be so kind as to release me so that I may return to the sanctity of my chamber? This is most improper."

"Improper is you wandering about my study in the dead of night dressed in nothing more than a diaphanous bit of muslin," he growled, his face so near to hers, his hot breath fell over her mouth like a kiss. "Was it your intention for me to find you here?"

"I can assure you it was not my intention to be dragged to the floor and pinned down by a man." She tried to free her hands from his grip, exasperation and desperation mingling with a fierce, molten want. "I demand you release me at once."

"You demand, do you?" He chuckled without mirth.

A trill of fear at being discovered unfurled within her, but it was fear mingled with desire, and somehow the combination was a heady, forceful pressure that washed over her body like a warm, shameful caress.

In that moment, fear and desire were not so far removed from one another.

What if he suspected her? What if he knew she had been rummaging through the papers in his study, searching for evidence of his correspondence with France?

The bitter reminder of the gravity of her position and what she was meant to do cut into her with the sharp precision of a blade. She shivered, and it was not because she longed for him to do more than lay atop her—which she was ashamed to realize she did—but because she was at this man's mercy. Nothing lay between her life and his ability to deal her a death blow. Nothing but her ability to avoid detection. Nothing but her fluency for deception.

"Please," she said. "Your Grace."

"I will release you when you answer my bloody question, Miss Governess. What in the name of all that is holy were you doing in my study?"

His guttural demand was perhaps what she should have expected. "Forgive me for my ignorance, Your Grace, but in the darkness, I thought I had entered the library."

His face lowered, his beard-roughened cheek abrading hers. His nose and mouth pressed against her throat. "I do not care for your excuses, Governess."

Frustration boiled to the surface within her. "Respectfully, the truth is not an excuse, Your Grace."

His body stiffened. "You dare to gainsay me, Miss Turnbellow?"

Why could no one in his cursed family seem to be capable of recalling her surname? She ground her teeth. "Turnbow, Your Grace."

"What of a bow, now, Miss Governess?" He dragged his nose over the cord of her throat, inhaling deeply.

Jacinda swallowed. Something about this beast-of-a-man, so jaded and wounded, so thoroughly depraved he was not above tackling his new governess and taking liberties with her in the dark, this beautiful man—he affected her in a way she could not like. In a way she could not allow.

She gritted her teeth and writhed against him. "*Miss. Turnbow.*"

"Miss Turnbow?" he asked, his voice thick, low, and intimate as her movements achieved the opposite of her intended effect. His body settled more firmly atop hers, her thighs opening wider to cradle him through the thin muslin of her gown. Her breasts brushed against his chest with each movement, eliciting a spark of sensation.

His lips grazed her neck, banishing all thoughts. She could not suppress her shiver. Being beneath him thus, at his mercy, did not concern her as much as it ought. Rather, it intrigued her. Brought her to life in a most sinful and unwanted fashion. No fear coursed through her. Only reckless, heady need, the likes of which she had not felt in years.

Wanting him was wrong, Jacinda reminded herself. Impossible.

"Miss Turnbow is my name, Your Grace. I was merely reminding you," she said softly, hating the breathlessness that had leaked into her voice.

"Ah, how helpful of you, Governess." His mouth found a particularly vulnerable swath of skin. His lips opened, his tongue darting against her for a brief, mesmerizing moment. "Thank you."

He dragged his lips lower, to the space where her neck and shoulder met.

Despite herself, she arched her back, thrust her head into the carpet, and opened herself for his feasting. What was wrong with her? He was a reprobate. A rake. More than likely—for she had no way of knowing whether or not the Earl of Kilross's evidence against him was accurate—a traitor.

She should be protesting, demanding her release. She lodged her knee between his strong, horseman's thighs so that he could no longer press the hard prod of his staff into her. Above all, she should not be enjoying the forbidden sensation of him against her center.

"You are most welcome, Your Grace," she forced herself to say with as little emotion as possible. "Now, if you please, would you be so kind as to allow me to stand so I may return to my chamber?"

He made a humming sound in his throat, and whether it was enjoyment or contemplation, she could not say. But his lips did not leave her flesh except for a beat. "No."

Here was where fright should begin. Where duty to Father and protecting his position at all costs ought to take over.

He found the curve of her breast above her modest décolletage. He sucked her skin. Open-mouthed, hot, and wet. It was unlike anything she had ever known. It was also the weight that tipped her internal scale. If she allowed herself to remain beneath him, if she encouraged one more liberty, her foray into his study to extract information would instead end in her thorough debauchment.

She could not afford such a risk. Could not tarnish the memory of James and the love they had shared by engaging in a loveless romp with a man she dared not trust. Could not risk costing Father everything he had worked all his life to build.

She sucked in a breath, forced the ardor crashing through her veins to cool, and made her body go stiff. "Do you intend to force yourself upon me for the crime of entering the wrong chamber in the dark, Your Grace?"

With a bitter curse, he rolled away from her, the weight of his body leaving hers as swiftly as it had descended. Cool night air rushed over her heated body and she felt oddly bereft at his disappearance. She lay on the carpet, eyes straining into the inky night, attempting to gauge where he had gone.

"Do not enter my study again," he bit out curtly, his voice ringing out from somewhere to her left and above her. "Consider this your warning, Turnbellows."

An icy prick of shame speared through her. What had she been thinking to enjoy the attentions of the Duke of Whitley? He was everything her father had warned a hundredfold over. He would have taken her on the floor of his study, a man who could not even be bothered to recall her name.

And she would have let him.

Worse, she would have enjoyed it.

Swallowing down the bile that rose in her throat, she scrambled to her feet, smoothing out her skirts. Her hands shook as she reached into the concealed pocket of her gown. The tips of her fingers grazed the small packet of papers she had liberated before his arrival. Her foolishness knew no bounds, but at least her prize remained intact.

She turned to flee, but halted in the act. He was somewhere in the room. She could feel his presence more than she could see or hear him. He lurked in the shadows like any predator, watching her. Waiting.

"Governess," she announced to the chamber at large, gathering what remained of her dignity and honor both.

"Pardon, Tornpill?"

She glared into the night, wishing she could see him. "If you cannot recall my name due to your advanced age, you may refer to me as Governess."

"Mmm. And why would I do that, depriving myself of the enjoyment of goading you, Turnblossom?"

Denying him her response, she stalked from the room, followed by the mocking dissonance of his disembodied chuckles.

"LADY HONORA AND Lady Constance," Jacinda addressed the empty chamber where she was meant to be teaching her pupils French. They had breakfasted early, all the better to begin the day and their studies. And yet when she had arrived at their schoolroom following their morning meal, her pupils were nowhere to be found.

The drapes at the floor-to-ceiling, eastward-facing windows of the chamber twitched, first on the right side and then the left.

"You are in the window dressings," she announced. "I see them moving. There is no point in further subterfuge, my ladies."

A low, thunderous sound reached her ears then, emerging from somewhere within the cavernous elegance of Whitley's townhouse. It sounded like a roar at first. She stilled, listening. How odd.

The din took shape.

"Miss Governess!"

Dear heavens. Surely it could not be... no, it would not be... dissolute as he was, surely the Duke of Whitley was not hollering from somewhere within his stately edifice as if he were a farm laborer calling across a pasture.

"Miss Go-*ver*-ness!"

She pressed her lips together, staring at the drapes that had begun to twitch wildly, accompanied by the sound of stifled girlish giggles. Jacinda glared in the direction of her concealed charges. "What have you done to distress His Grace, my ladies?"

No answer was forthcoming from the drapes.

The only response she did receive was yet another bellow, this time even louder than before. "Miss Go-*verness!*"

Jacinda heaved a sigh. "I will address this with the two of you directly," she warned before spinning on her heel and exiting the chamber.

There was really no other word to aptly describe it. The Duke of Whitley was hollering for her like a madman. And perhaps he was. Mayhap she had allowed her body's traitorous reaction to a handsome man to blind her to the truth. Pray God she would never again need to conduct a covert operation involving lunatic dukes with more looks than wits and a brace of naughty minxes as her charges.

By the time she reached the breakfast room, she was breathless and irate, prepared to deliver His Grace a dressing down of the first order. She stopped still at the sight of him, elegant in a blue coat and snowy white cravat, his dark hair carefully combed. By the bright light of day, with some rest and sobriety in his favor, the Duke of Whitley was a sight to behold.

But it wasn't the duke himself that commanded her ultimate attention.

Rather, it was the creature dangling from his fingers.

"Your Grace?" she asked breathlessly. Needlessly.

"Governess," he clipped, his voice dripping with ice, his gaze equally dismissive as it raked her head to foot and presumably found her serviceable brown gown as lacking as her person. "Would you care to explain how it is your charges placed a dead rodent alongside my breakfast plate this morning without your notice?"

Drat those girls.

But most importantly, damn the Duke of Whitley. Last night, with his fiery body atop hers and his hands and mouth on her skin, he had made her feel—for one wicked moment—as if she were the only woman in the world. By the bleak light of morning, he pinned her with a supercilious sneer that he likely reserved for pickpockets and swindlers. He was treating her as a servant. As *his* servant. Which was what she was, for now.

Recalling herself, she offered him a curtsy. "Forgive me, Your Grace. Please accept my apology. How may I rectify the matter?"

His lip curled with further disgust. "You may begin by disposing of this outrage, and then you may proceed with maintaining control over your charges. I did hire you to manage them, did I not Miss Governess?"

Manage them. She suppressed a shudder. Not one blessed thing about the wild young ladies who had been riding down the stairs on silver salvers yesterday suggested they were the least bit manageable.

The duke snapped his fingers. "Miss Governess? Take this away at once."

Jacinda forced her feet to move toward the odious man, schooling her features into an expression of contrition. "Yes, of course I shall do away with it forthwith, Your Grace, and once more, please accept my sincere apologies on behalf of myself and my charges."

Nicholson, who had danced attendance upon His Grace's breakfast with an admirable stoicism until that moment, stepped forward. "If I may, Your Grace, I shall remove the offense at once. There is no need for Miss Turnbow to handle the carcass."

"Yes," insisted the duke, his voice ringing through the room with enough command to stop the butler in his tracks. "There is *every* need. Miss Governess, do what you have been hired to do. Nicholson, do not ever gainsay me again, or you will find yourself on the street without reference. Am I understood?"

"Yes, Your Grace. I pray you forgive me for the affront, Your Grace," Nicholson said, and melted back into his position standing sentry.

Jacinda was certain she had not, in fact, been hired to dispose of dead rodents. But she had not taken on this unwanted position to displease the Duke of Whitley or give him cause to dismiss her, or for that matter, to take notice of her in any fashion.

She was here to gain the proximity necessary to comb through his correspondence and to translate any enciphered messages in his possession. She was here to help Kilross discover what had truly occurred on the day the Marquess of Searle was murdered, and in so doing, keep Father's position secure.

She could not allow herself to forget the man responsible for the death of Searle, their great national hero, was none other than the man bellowing at her to cart off the mouse he still held dangling from his long fingers.

Reminded of the magnitude of her position, she hastened forward, calmly taking a linen napkin from the beautifully dressed table and wrapping it about the mouse. Though she meant to tug it from Whitley's grasp and spin to take her leave, the duke had other ideas. He held firm to the tail of the thing, refusing to relinquish it.

"Look at me, Miss Governess," he ordered in a quieter tone that nevertheless demanded obedience.

She did not wish to look directly upon his face. Or to meet his eyes. She had been focused solely upon the dead mouse. She caught her lip between her teeth and made her gaze slip past the napkin-enshrouded rodent to the duke's arresting form.

How was it possible that a man so darkly beautiful could also be a traitor who was the heartless architect of his best friend's painful demise? Her eyes dipped to his mouth, the sculpted bow of his upper lip. That mouth had been upon her skin, and all the secret places it had touched in the night burned now as if scalded. The reminder of the liberties she had allowed him stole her breath.

Little wonder there had been so many whispers about his conquests. He was the male Helen of Troy, the face that launched a thousand ships. Also, the face of madness and avarice, the face of cruelty and despair, of betrayal and treason, she reminded herself firmly. A man who was not to be trusted. One to whom she must never succumb.

Her chin rose. "Yes, Your Grace? How may I be of service to you?"

Her cheeks flushed immediately after the last question fell from her lips, for she had not intended to impart them with any hint of suggestion. She was doing her utmost to remain unnoticed. To be as uninteresting as a wall covering. To do as she was asked, feign humility, and obtain the documents Kilross required. His mouth quirked, as if acknowledging the double entendre she had not intended. His eyes, gray-flecked with blue she could discern now that she stood so near, burned into hers. "First, I expect you to remove this abomination. Secondly, you shall bring my sisters to me for their reckoning. Thirdly, and I do insist upon this, Miss Governess, both you and Lady Constance and Lady Honora will dine with me each evening, at which time I shall be regaled by the progress they have made. Last but most assuredly not least, each morning, you will report to me in my study. I require a daily summary of the previous day's lessons, along with your assessment of the progress my sisters are making."

Beneath the folded linen square, the body of the mouse was a repulsive lump that her fingers curled about. She tugged again, hoping he would release the tail and allow her to retreat to the safety of the schoolroom. He held firm.

"Yes, Your Grace," she said, tamping down her inner defiance, for it had no place there.

His eyes raked her form, lingering on first her lips and then her breasts. "If another event such as this occurs, you will be sacked without reference. There will be no future dead mice alongside my plate. Am I perfectly clear?"

She bowed her head so he could not see the fire sparking in her eyes. So she could hide the stubborn clench of her jaw. "You have my promise, no more such indignities shall be perpetrated upon you by my charges, Your Grace."

"You will meet my gaze when you address me, Miss Governess." His curt, clipped baritone struck her like a lash.

Jacinda closed her eyes and exhaled a calming breath before raising her head, careful to erase any evidence of her true feelings from both her gaze and expression. "As you wish, Your Grace."

He flashed her a smile that could only be described as feral. "Yes, everything that happens within these walls is precisely as I wish. Endeavor to remember that, Miss Governess."

Without warning, he released his grip upon the rodent's tail, leaving her with a fistful of dead mouse that slapped into the modest fall of her gown. The weight of the thing, lifeless and lumpy like a small sausage, was enough to make her suppress a gag. "I will recall that, Your Grace. Thank you, sir."

When she would have left, he stopped her. "I have not yet dismissed you, Miss Governess. Do not think to flee now that you have the mouse in hand."

Jacinda ground her molars together and forced a polite smile to her lips at the same time. She would not allow him to see how much he affected her. How much his arrogance enraged her. "I do beg your pardon, Duke."

"You are forgiven your haste this once, but be advised, I do not tolerate disrespect from any of my servants. From this moment forward, you will not depart from my presence unless you have asked and I have given you leave to do so. Am I understood?"

"Perfectly, Your Grace," she answered through gritted teeth. Just barely, she stifled the urge to ask him if it was permissible for her to breathe without his approval.

"Excellent. You are dismissed now." He sent her another savage smile. "I shall see you and my sisters at dinner."

She offered a one-handed curtsy, still clutching the mouse in her right hand. "Thank you, Your Grace."

As she carried her unwanted burden away and escaped from the room and his arrogant presence, she could not help but be grateful for the icy detachment Whitley had treated her with this morning. She must never again allow him such familiarity or liberties with her person. To do so would only invite ruin and shame. Last night had been an aberration that would never be repeated, one she ascribed to the darkness and her shock at being discovered.

Far too much was at stake. She could not—nay, she would not—let Father down.

Frowning, she marched back to the schoolroom, holding the mouse carcass outstretched as she went. Lady Constance and Lady Honora were devils in skirts, but she was anything if not determined. Once given a task, it was her nature to not only complete it but to see it accomplished to the very best of her ability. A true governess she may not be, but she did have her own share of backbone.

The pair of minxes in her charge were not going to avoid repercussions for their little prank. Up the stairs and down the hall she went, her mind formulating her battle strategy. She, too, could be positively Machiavellian when the need arose.

Apparently, the hoydens had believed they had managed to scare her off for the rest of the morning, for when she threw open the schoolroom door, they were giggling, each bearing a salver tucked beneath her arm.

"My ladies," she snapped, lifting the napkin-enshrouded creature in her hand and shaking it in their direction. "I do believe you left something behind in the breakfast room this morning."

Their giggles died in unison, eyes going wide. They had the same unique gray eyes as the duke, and it truly was disconcerting staring at that gaze in female form. Jacinda shook herself from the thought and gave the dead mouse another shake. "Well? Have neither of you anything to say for yourselves?"

The girls shared a wide-eyed glance, almost as if to express their mutual disbelief they had been caught. It was apparent to Jacinda that Lady Constance and Lady Honora had been running wild and running the household both. Belowstairs was rife with talk of the previous duke if one was clever and knew when and where to listen. Whitley's brother had been a drunkard with little time to spare for his sisters, who in the absence of parents, entertained themselves by making mischief.

But their past did not excuse their abominable behavior, and here was her line to draw. They could either reach an understanding, or she would begin to retaliate.

She assessed them with a calm she did not feel. "If neither of you shall tell me who placed this dead mouse at His Grace's chair, I shall cut it in two and place one half upon each of your pillows."

Lady Constance's brows shot upward. "You would not dare to do such a thing."

"Maintain your silence and your defiance and we shall see." Jacinda gave the girls her most menacing frown. "You have until the count of five to unburden yourselves. One. Two. Three. F—"

"We both did it," Lady Honora admitted, her expression turning sheepish. "Con stole the mouse from Cook's trap in the kitchens and then she distracted the footmen and Nicholson whilst I left it upon the table."

"Excellent." A triumphant smile chased away her frown. "Come along with me, then, both of you."

Lady Constance's expression grew wary. "Where are we going?"

She quirked a brow. "We are holding a mouse funeral, and the two of you shall be doing the honors. I do hope you know where to find a spade. Now who wishes to carry the unfortunate thing? I believe I have had quite enough of carrying him about."

"You are the youngest," Lady Honora told her sister. "You carry it."

Naturally, Lady Constance protested. "But I already carried it through the kitchens and all the way through the house to Crispin's seat at the table."

"My ladies," she interrupted. "Time is wasting, and soon this wretch will begin to stink."

"Oh, very well," Lady Constance grumbled, flouncing forward to accept Jacinda's offering.

Jacinda's smile grew, a feeling of immense satisfaction blossoming inside her. Now this, at least, was progress.

CHAPTER FIVE

W HY HAD HE insisted upon his sisters and the flame-haired
governess joining him for dinner? It was the fifth consecutive
evening of foregoing his club in favor of dining at home with the
hellions that were his sisters and the woman charged with correcting
their ways. The fifth day of excruciating torture wherein the minxes
chattered, acted inappropriately, the governess hid her fiery locks
beneath an ungodly mobcap, and he pretended not to recall the silky
smoothness of Miss Governess's creamy skin upon his tongue.

Crispin stabbed at the unfortunate slab of Westphalian ham on his
plate.

"Lady Honora," the governess's soft, husky voice rose above the
gentle din of cutlery on Sèvres porcelain, "would you care to inform
His Grace about the lessons you received today?"

He issued an unnecessary, fierce cut to his already eviscerated
ham. Damnation, why did even the sound of her voice make his cock
twitch in his breeches? Somehow, he had imagined, lost in the depths
of his own arrogance, that spending time in the woman's presence,
flanked by his sisters, would lessen the effect she had upon him. But
having her at hand and treating her coolly did not force his inconvenient attraction to her to abate. But gentleman was not a role he played
well, and he had been wrong. Thoroughly, stupidly, utterly wrong.

That night in his study when he had almost lost his bloody wits
and lifted her skirts had left him enraged. Determined to prove he

could inure himself to whatever hold it was she had upon him. But even the efforts she had undertaken to make herself as unnoticeable as possible were wasted upon him. Beneath her drab brown muslin, he knew the seductive flare of her hips, the softness of her thighs parting to welcome him. Hidden behind her matronly fichu and far too much lace, he knew her bosom swelled high and lush and full. He knew her nipples would harden, beg for more.

"The dancing master arrived," Honora said sullenly. "He is an evil, beady-eyed little French weasel, and I do not like him."

Miss Governess gasped in outrage, her rosebud-pink mouth opening in such fashion that Crispin could not help but envision his cock sliding home within it. He stuffed a bite of ham into his mouth, feeling every bit of the animal that he had become. It was wrong to lust after a female in his household he had hired as the governess for his innocent—though admittedly wild—sisters. But he could not summon even a pinch of outrage as he made Miss Governess his sole concentration. Those lips quivered. He longed to lick them.

"Lady Honora, your conduct is not becoming of a lady. Please apologize to His Grace and the table at once."

Damn, but she took his breath. *Miss Turnbow.* He didn't like the name and he refused to use it on principle. Her Christian name was what he wanted. That and so much more. He also wanted her beneath him again. Willingly this time, and not because he had stumbled upon her inadvertently in the darkness.

But he could not have her.

Honora huffed. He hated to tell Miss Governess, but 'ladylike' and his sisters did not belong in the same sentence. They were cut from the same, wicked cloth as he. No one could tame them.

"Lady Honora," she pressed, her tone sharp, unrelenting. No one could deny Miss Governess possessed backbone. "We are all awaiting your apology."

Another inelegant snort issued from his sister, this one smaller than the last. "Very well. I am sorry, Crispin, for my unfortunate choice of words. I apologize to you as well, Miss Tornblossom, and Con of course."

Miss Governess pursed her lips, drawing his attention once more back to her lush mouth. Damnation, why had he not found some dog-faced chit to tend to these spawns of Satan instead of a vixen disguised as a spinster? Nothing had ever tantalized him more than the notion of peeling away her endless lace fichu to bare the creamy swells of her breasts.

"In my experience, Lady Honora, your memory is faultless," said Miss Governess then, "which is perhaps why I find it so perplexing that you cannot recall my correct surname. Lady Constance, will you aid your sister in remembering it?"

Con grinned, because of course, she was as much of a minx as her sister, merely two years her junior. "Of course I shall aid her, Miss Towerbottom. It is Towerbottom, is it not?"

Bloody hell. Did the little miscreant not know she could not go about mentioning *bottom* and the governess in the same sentence? Now his palms ached to be filled with the supple curves of her arse. There was no chance of him withstanding a fifth evening of such torture.

He needed to visit The Duke's Bastard, his favorite hell, forthwith. To find a willing whore to warm his bed and distract him. The inconvenient fascination he had for Miss Governess was becoming a distraction that could only be remedied in one fashion. But sinking his cock into the governess upon the dinner table as his impressionable sisters watched on seemed depraved, even by his nonexistent standards.

Miss Governess was saying something now in her most scolding tone, but he was too preoccupied to pay her much mind. This simply would not do.

"... But I would not presume to... disrespectful... apology at once..."

Curse it, the female was more long-winded than a parson being paid by the minute.

"Forgive me for the interruption," he said, his sense of ducal and brotherly obligation weighing upon him in a manner it had not in as long as he could recall. "Lady Constance and Lady Honora, apologize to your governess at once."

"But Crispin—"

"We have not said a word that—"

"Silence," he bellowed, eliminating the twin dissension that was his sisters' voices. "You are being disrespectful, just as you have been every moment since Miss Turnbow came into this household. If you cannot admit your wrongdoing and apologize, you may both spend the next sennight in your chambers, penning apologies since none will spill forth from your lips."

His sisters stared at him in wide-eyed fascination.

He instantly regretted his interruption, for it revealed too much. Crispin was acutely aware he had not taken an interest in a domestic. Ever. Certainly, he had never championed a prior governess or invited one to sit at the table with him. Hell, he ordinarily did not even sup these days, unless it was upon cunny or whisky or both at once.

Supping upon Miss Governess certainly held its appeal.

Damn it to hell.

He glared at the feral young ladies it had fallen upon his black soul to look after, following the death of their brother. Why could not the Lord have blessed him with brothers? He would have known what to do with lads. Females were another matter altogether. "I do not hear apologies, my ladies."

"Pray forgive us," they chirped in unison.

"You are both forgiven," Miss Governess said in that august air she possessed that made her sound more like a queen than a lowly governess.

"I expect you to treat her with the respect she is due from this moment forward," he added, not entirely certain why he was coming to the defense of Miss Governess. Boredom? A desire to fuck her? Both?

She turned her attention to him, meeting his gaze for the first time since their unfortunate interlude several days past involving the dead mouse. He was aware he had been an ass. But the woman nettled him. He had not been able to return to sleep or even drink whisky the night after she had suggested he would force himself upon her, for he did not like to think his depravity had sunk so low.

The shock in her eyes—those orbs like dark, molten honey had a way of cutting straight to the marrow of his bones—made his cock twitch once more. He gritted his teeth and turned his attention back to his ham, pretending he had not noticed her or the gratitude shining in the luminous depths of those eyes. Christ on the cross, she had been looking at him as if he were someone worthy of her adulation.

No one in Christendom was less worthy of her admiration.

He clenched his jaw. "Lady Constance and Lady Honora, I expect a response when I speak to you."

"Yes, Crispin," Con muttered, her inner sense of rebellion already peeking through her feigned contrition.

"Of course, Crispin," Nora added, not even making an effort to excise the sarcasm from her tone.

Why should his sisters be saints when he was the greatest sinner of all? It stood to reason that, since they had all fallen from the same rotten tree, they would be horridly imperfect regardless of their sex. And yet, he resented his sisters for their wildness. For being creatures who required his guardianship and effort when all he wanted was to bury himself in the darkness and numb his mind and soul.

Responsibility was the devil.

And he had suffered enough of it. He wasn't hungry for ham. He was hungry for Miss Cursed Governess, who he could not bed regardless of how much he wanted her. For even if he could persuade her to become his mistress, he would be left finding another governess to reign in his intractable sisters and he would have the black mark against his soul of having debauched an innocent. Though he already had enough black marks against his soul to send him to hell where he belonged, he did not wish to make Miss Governess the cause of one more.

He would find another, far more suitable substitute for his inconvenient lust. A lovely one, with generous bubbies and an accommodating mouth eager to suck every last drop of...

He stood, not caring for propriety or manners or anything in that moment other than his need to remove himself from the ruinous presence of the bloody governess. When in the deuce had a brown gown ever been so alluring?

"I bid you ladies a good evening," he managed, bowing. "I fear I have other obligations for the evening. Please do continue in my absence, and sisters, I shall meet with Miss Governess in the morning. Should she have anything negative to report to me, you shall be facing the consequences."

With that, he turned and fled from the room. Con's voice traveled after him.

"Miss Governess? Forgive me for the confusion, but I could have sworn your name was Miss Turnbow."

At least the cheeky minx had gotten the surname right this time, when he intentionally had not.

Crispin left the unwanted tableau behind him, eager in the pursuit of distraction. Anything to escape the darkness that was never far from his heels.

THE PAPERS SHE had liberated from the duke's study had proved worthless, nothing more than mundane correspondence between him and others. She had not been able to discover any enciphered passages for all the hours she had spent poring over them into the night.

Which meant another visit to his study was necessary.

Jacinda waited until her charges had gone to bed and she was certain Whitley had left before venturing once more to his study. The benefit of her ruse was she had access to belowstairs, which afforded her an endless supply of useful information. It had not taken long to discover the weaknesses of the domestics, or to discern who would be a valuable ally and who she ought to avoid.

Confident in His Grace's absence, she closed the door and extracted a rolled strip of linen from the hidden pocket in her gown. She sank to the plush carpet on her knees and wadded the fabric beneath the crack between the carved mahogany door and the floor to impede light from being seen from the hall. Not wasting time, she rose and lit a candle.

Jacinda softly padded to the duke's large, intimidating desk and placed her candle upon it, memorizing the order and positioning of his papers before she began sifting through them. She had been far more cautious with this evening's foray into the duke's territory. Fortunately, he'd been willing to dismiss the last occasion as an innocent error. He would not be so understanding should there be another such discovery of her in his study.

She had gleaned, both from listening to chatter belowstairs and from Lady Constance and Lady Honora, that the Duke of Whitley was a creature of habit. He did nothing in small measure, and his black moods defined him. When he left for evening entertainment, he was not expected to return, oftentimes for days. She shuddered as she imagined how much depravity he could undertake in the span of several days.

At least his debauchery meant Jacinda was once again free to riffle through the duke's correspondence and private papers without fear of being discovered or—worse—finding herself beneath him. Yes, he could wield his formidable member upon a female who would appreciate his ardor and attentions. The sharp stab in her middle at the notion was not jealousy. Nor was the ache between her thighs caused by the remembered intimacies she'd shared with him.

She felt nothing for Whitley except disdain.

Her first impression of him, a man surrounded by darkness, trapped in a hell of his own making, returned. He had not seemed capable of treachery. He had seemed a man in desperate need of change. Dissipated and troubled, unable to sleep, tasked with a pair of sisters who were undeniably minxes, burdened by a duchy he'd never intended to claim…

No. She must not think of him in such a manner. He did not deserve her sympathy or her desire. He was a traitor. A means to an end. She could not lose sight of who he was, who she was, and why she was there.

Biting her lip, she focused on the papers before her, her eyes traveling over his words. His penmanship was bold and slanted, surprisingly well-formed for a man who seemed determined to drown himself in drink and other excesses. She extracted a cipher wheel from her skirts, examining the content of the letters.

The bulk of the letters seemed to be innocent communication concerning his various estates. With a practiced eye, she searched the nuances of his words and found nothing to suggest he was sending hidden messages to his correspondents.

She checked the time every quarter hour without fail, via a man's timepiece in her hidden pocket, staying attuned to her surroundings. The drawers on Whitley's desk were all unlocked, save one. The only evidence she unearthed in the drawers was proof the duke did not possess as black a heart as she had supposed.

A packet of envelopes bound together by a neatly tied ribbon revealed that Whitley was corresponding with the Marquess of Searle's dowager mother. And as much as Jacinda would have been pleased to discover otherwise, the letters suggested the duke was a caring and concerned friend. A man who, in spite of his eccentricities and undeniable darkness and licentiousness, nevertheless cared enough about his dead comrade to contact Searle's mother.

Five letters in, she realized not only was Whitley communicating with the dowager Marchioness of Searle, but he was also sending her funds.

It was an interesting and somewhat sobering development.

One she wouldn't have expected, for it was far easier to imagine the duke as a cold, calculated despoiler of innocents and avaricious murderer of a national hero. Far easier to imagine him as a villain than a man who oversaw the comfort of his dead friend's mother.

Jacinda read each letter thrice before returning them to their original envelopes and binding them with the ribbon once more. A cursory examination of the remainder of his papers yielded nothing but his efforts to raise his sisters, settle his brother's debts, and look after those most important to him.

She made certain she set Whitley's study back to rights before dousing her candle and slipping back into the darkness of the hall. Clearly, she would need to do some more searching if she wished to unearth the Duke of Whitley's guilt.

CHAPTER SIX

ORTUNATELY, THE DUKE of Whitley's absence from his town-home, coupled with his somewhat disorganized, lackadaisical household, allowed for Jacinda to escape at dawn the next day. By early morning light, she had arrived as promised at her father's home, half expecting the earl to be in attendance and yet still hoping he would not be.

Naturally, the earl was there, sharpening his talons, eager for the scent of blood. But she could not help him on that score.

"I have found nothing to implicate the Duke of Whitley," she reported. "Not a single letter is out of place, and there is not a thing to indicate he is guilty of anything."

Aside from being an arrogant reprobate, that was, she added silently.

"Nothing?" Kilross repeated, his tone as harsh as his countenance. He stood by the fireplace in Father's study, hands clasped behind his back, the picture of outrage. "Do you mean to suggest you have been ensconced in Whitley House for an entire week and have yet to read any of the duke's papers, Mrs. Turnbow?"

Jacinda blinked, taking a moment to recover from both the earl's raw, unabated ire and the newness of being referred to as Mrs. Turnbow once more. Just a fortnight ago, she had stood in this same study, terrified that the man before her would take Father's position from him and rob him of the one thing that brought him joy. Now, she wondered what the earl would do if the proof he sought against the duke never emerged. Each foray she made into Whitley's study rendered that notion more and more likely.

"What I am telling you, Lord Kilross," she explained coolly, "is that I have been acting as governess at your behest. I have also scoured the duke's correspondence, ledgers, and any scrap of paper I could find that is not kept behind lock and key. Not one letter is enciphered or written in French."

"That is absurd." The earl slammed his fist into the mantelpiece, giving Jacinda a start. "Not only absurd but impossible. The man has been consorting with the French. I have it on good authority he continues to receive and send ciphers."

"I invite you to weed through His Grace's correspondence in my place," she said before she could still her tongue. She knew to be on her best behavior. Kilross was unpredictable and cruel at best and Machiavellian at worst. "I have done everything asked of me, and the evidence you seek is simply not there. Short of inventing it, I have nothing to give you."

Kilross made a rude sound of displeasure in his throat. "You are a woman who does not know her place, Mrs. Turnbow. Clearly, you are not looking hard enough, else you would have something to show for your efforts."

Her own anger soared then, and she could not contain it. She had done everything asked of her. She had played the governess for a week. She lied to everyone about who and what she was. She deceived the duke and sifted through his correspondence. She betrayed his sisters by abetting Kilross in taking the one family member they had left. A persistent ache struck her heart each time she wondered how Lady Constance and Lady Honora would survive should the duke be taken from them as well.

And yet, the earl would dare to tell her she did not know her place. The thin strand of her patience snapped like a worn thread on an overly laundered chemise.

"My place is here with my father, Lord Kilross," she hissed, "and you have taken me from where I belong to perpetuate some misguided notion of justice. What manner of man forces a lady to do his bidding, my lord? Pray, tell me, because I cannot help but think the only villain in this tragedy is you."

Kilross sneered. "Mayhap you would be better served to lay that question to dearest Papa, who has been only too content to allow you to do work better left to a man."

She turned to her father, who had been watching her exchange with the earl in grim silence. His was pale. He raked his fingers through his thinned white hair, leaving it standing on end, and removed his double spectacles to polish them with a cloth.

Jacinda recognized avoidance when she saw it. She knew him too well. "What is Lord Kilross speaking of, Father?"

"You still have not revealed the truth to your beloved daughter, have you?" Kilross's voice was snide. "Or have you forgotten, since your mind is so frail that it cannot even comprehend the notion of wagering more than you possess?"

Wagering? Father had been spending many nights at his club in recent months, but she had thought it a boon. An excellent means for him to socialize with his peers. For much of her life, he had worked all hours of the day and night, candles burning until the early morning, solving ciphers and creating new ones that could be used by the government, armies, and navies. That he had finally slowed his pace and allowed her to shoulder some of the burden of his work had pleased her greatly on two counts, for it had given him some much-needed rest and it also meant he had deemed her work proficient enough to rival his.

As Father continued to avoid her gaze, icy tendrils of fear clutched at her. What if the nights at his club had not been harmless suppers and reminiscences with old friends? What if instead he had been gambling?

Once, she would not have believed him capable of such a vice. But given the changes in him she had witnessed over the last year, she could not discount the possibility.

"Father," she said again, her voice tense and shrill even to her own ears, "what does Lord Kilross speak of?"

"Will you tell her," the earl added, "or shall I?"

Father settled his spectacles back upon the bridge of his nose, meeting her gaze at last, and the profound sorrow she read there was more disheartening than his studious avoidance. "I am afraid I made a grave blunder, dearest girl. I owe Lord Kilross a great deal of funds."

"You owe me more funds than you own," Kilross interjected.

Good God, it was even worse than she supposed. Naively, she had imagined Father's eagerness to carry out the earl's plan was because he did not wish to lose his position. Now, it would seem his eagerness was caused by his desire not to lose everything.

"I... Jacinda, I am indebted to Lord Kilross." Her father's pallor grew. "I was caught up in the thrill of the game, and I am afraid I lost my prudence. He requested I infiltrate Whitley's home in search of documents proving the duke's guilt in return for forgiving a number of my vowels. That was when I had to admit I cannot decipher as I once was capable. That you have been carrying the weight for me for some time now, and that if anyone should be sent, it had to be you."

The breath slowly left her lungs, a searing sense of betrayal following in its wake. Father, who she depended upon, Father, who she loved, had lost everything to the Earl of Kilross. Worse, he had admitted his frailty to a wolf in sheep's clothing, a man who would not hesitate to use that knowledge against him at the slightest provocation.

She had thought she was saving Father from discovery. But instead, she was saving them both from utter ruin. They were at the mercy of the Earl of Kilross in every sense.

"So, you see," Kilross said smoothly, a triumphant smile creasing his face, "you have no choice, Mrs. Turnbow. You will return to Whitley House, and you will find evidence against the Duke of Whitley. Break every blessed lock you must. Do you truly imagine the man would leave evidence of his guilt strewn about for anyone to see?"

She flushed. "No, my lord, though I confess I do not possess the sort of mind that thrives upon duplicity."

His countenance darkened. "You have three weeks remaining to find the documents I need. If you fail to do so in that time, not only will your father lose his position with the Foreign Office, but you will both lose this home and all of your possessions. You will be cast into the streets where you both belong, and I shall not feel a moment's pity for either of you."

She looked back to her father, heart sinking. "Father?"

He heaved a mournful sigh, closing his eyes. "It is true, Jacinda. Every word of it. You must find what Lord Kilross seeks. The very roof over our heads depends upon it."

Sick, she excused herself from the room and fled back to Whitley House before her absence went noticed. Now, more than ever, she needed to uncover the evidence Kilross sought. For she knew without a doubt the heartless scoundrel would have no compunction about taking everything and leaving her and Father in the streets as he'd promised.

One thing was certain. She needed to find her way into the locked drawer of Whitley's desk, no matter the means.

CRISPIN STARED AT the indecent mural painted on the ceiling above him. A lush, naked pair of nymphs were kissing open-mouthed and pleasuring each other's cunnies. His prick didn't even stir. Cursed organ. Did it not know its use?

Obviously not.

He had been awake for a day. Or perhaps it was three.

Who the bloody hell knew?

He'd been indulging in drink and gambling at The Duke's Bastard and distracting himself from thoughts of a red-haired siren governess as best as he knew how. Which meant playing the tables, losing himself in whisky and gin, and retreating to a private chamber where he could pretend to sleep or reluctantly dismiss the lightskirts that Duncan sent him in what seemed to be an endless procession.

For although it had been his intention to find a bit of quim and satisfy the hungers raging through him, something dashed odd had happened to his cock. Something—he had no doubt—caused by Miss Governess herself. His ample opportunities for release had been met with an utter dearth of enthusiasm on the part of the necessary appendage.

And never let it be said that Duncan Kirkwood, proprietor of The Duke's Bastard, did not do everything within his significant power to see his patrons had entertainment aplenty by any manner of vice they chose. Wagers, faro, hazard, liquor, or cunny, Duncan had it all at the ready.

There had been blondes, brunettes, an exotic raven-haired beauty, another whose tresses were clearly blackened by her own hand, and a redhead who had almost suited him but not as well as the original flame-haired witch beleaguering his thoughts.

There had been full breasts, small breasts, hard nipples, lush hips, and eager mouths. They had come in pairs and even trios, touching and caressing and kissing each other in a bid to arouse him. One had fallen to her knees, burying her face between the thighs of another. The wet sounds of her tongue and suction should have aroused him.

But he had been left feeling distant, unmoved. Vaguely disgusted by the depths to which he had sunk. Utterly unappreciative of the show they'd offered him.

He couldn't recall the names of any of the whores. Didn't remember what they had been wearing. He could not even call to mind the image of the lightskirt who had been so intent upon licking her comrade to submission. At the very least, he ought to have been able to free his cock from his breeches and stroke himself to oblivion as he watched the two women pleasure each other.

But the notion held no appeal. Not while they appeared before him half naked and hungry for each other and certainly not now when he looked back upon it, an hour or so after their abrupt dismissal.

The only thing that hardened his cock was thoughts of Miss Governess.

Which was why he was laid out on the bed in his private chamber, fully clothed, half drunk, and hollow.

A rap sounded at the door.

It was likely a fresh round of harlots. And he didn't want any more painted faces and bare bubbies. He was tired to his bloody bones, sick to death of everything and everyone. Weary in a way he could not convey with words. His friend was dead. Nothing could ameliorate his guilt. He had wards to protect and a governess he should not want and no direction in his life or desire to live it.

"Be gone," he growled, gazing up into the mural.

"I come bearing whisky, Whitley," came the familiar voice on the other side of the portal.

Duncan.

He heaved a sigh. Kirkwood had become a trusted friend to Crispin. His only friend, in truth, now that Morgan was gone. Largely because Crispin spent a great deal of time and coin within the man's walls. But, also, because he and Duncan understood the ugly underbelly of life. They'd taken stock of each other and possessed a hearty amount of mutual respect. Though they came from disparate backgrounds, they had much in common in their mutual bitterness and cynical views of the world.

And with his vast connections to both the lowest rabble and the highest nobility, Duncan ruled the underworld like a king while quietly keeping the polite echelons under his thumb. It was said half the peerage was indebted to him, and Crispin did not doubt the veracity of the claim. If there was one person a man needed to know and have by his side in London, it was Duncan Kirkwood.

Another knock sounded. "Have you gone deaf? I do believe I said your favorite word just now, and nary a response."

"Haven't you a hell to run?" Crispin called out grimly.

"The beast runs itself these days," his friend responded, sounding irritatingly cheerful. "Do you want the whisky or not, Cris? It is an excellent year. Perhaps we can give the bottle a black eye together."

Crispin folded his arms beneath his head and grinned. "Am I expected to pay for the privilege or are you about the nasty business of getting me soused so that I lose a king's ransom at your *tapis vert*?"

"The whisky is my pleasure." An edge of irritation hardened his friend's voice. "Damn it, may I enter or are you *en déshabillé*? The last thing I wish to see is your hairy arse. I shan't be able to sleep for at least a week if I am forced to witness such a travesty."

He grinned, not bothering to rise from the bed. Born in the stews of London, Kirkwood could nevertheless ape the upper crust of society that would forever remain above his touch with unprecedented perfection. Duncan had been born to a Covent Garden doxy but his father was the Duke of Amberly. Though the miserable old sod refused to acknowledge him, Duncan had taken his revenge by building the most sought-after hell in all London, with an apt name that his sire could not help but be aware of.

"Do you intend to play valet if I am?" he called, darkly amused.

"Fair warning, Your Grace." Duncan's tone was grim. The door opened, and he swept inside, dressed in his customary black, down to his shirt and cravat. Even the man's ring was a skull. He was a dark, formidable presence on the best of days and a hulking menace on the worst.

Crispin sat up with great reluctance, and only because consuming whisky whilst resting supine was devilishly untidy. The chamber spun for a moment before settling. He noted the full bottle of spirits in Duncan's grip and smiled. Here was an offering he would gladly accept this evening. Or morning. Afternoon? Of all the delights the establishment boasted, heavily curtained windows that rendered daylight immaterial was by far one of Crispin's favorite.

"This bloody ceiling mural is appalling," he offered by way of greeting.

"A gift from my predecessor," Duncan acknowledged with a grim smile, retrieving two glasses and pouring three fingers into each.

Crispin eyed the whisky and debated whether or not he was motivated enough to rise and retrieve his glass. "Why are you here, aside from the obvious?"

Duncan took a sip of his own whisky, quirking a raven brow. "You declined the companionship of all my ladies."

He snorted and rose, deciding he wanted that whiskey after all, if this was to be the nature of their interview. "I fail to comprehend your insistence upon referring to your lightskirts as ladies."

Duncan scowled, offering him his glass. "They *are* ladies, Whitley."

Crispin had seen very little to suggest the veracity of Duncan's claim, though it was true the occasional Cyprian ball overtook The Duke's Bastard. On such occasions, the *ladies* turned themselves out with aplomb. Before long, however, the libidinous nature of the parties gathered always won out.

The last such soiree had been a blur of flipping skirts, wandering hands, bare breasts, and flushed cheeks, followed by the disappearance of most said *ladies* to private quarters. Others had been content to perform in the ballroom with an audience.

"I regret to say your *ladies* are the furthest one can reasonably get from the definition of a proper lady." He took a healthy gulp of whisky, relishing its fiery race to his gut.

The need to numb his body and mind had never been stronger. Miss Governess's face could not be shaken. How was it her lush form had burned into him as if a brand? A conflagration threatened to begin deep within him, and he could not countenance it. Would not.

He drank more.

"Ladies whose company you decline," Duncan persisted, observing him in that uncanny fashion he possessed. His light-blue gaze seemed to dissect a man.

Bloody hell, his cheekbones had gone ruddy. He blamed it on the spirits and took another healthy gulp, finishing the contents of his glass. "Your whores are tired," he snapped. "Would it be too much trouble to rotate them? Think of it thus, Kirkwood. A man does not always wish for the same horseflesh to pull his phaeton or his curricle."

Duncan finished his whisky and replenished both their glasses before meeting Crispin's gaze. "Each girl I sent you tonight was new."

"They were more interested in each other's cunnies than in ought else," he said coldly. "It would behoove you to find *ladies* who take pleasure in cock rather than quim, old friend."

"Forgive me." Duncan handed him his glass, solemn-faced. "You never took exception to multiple ladies entertaining you at one time in the past."

He accepted his glass and tossed back the entire content, swallowing with a complete disregard for the burn or the fact he had likely already consumed more than enough. Miss Governess and her mobcap and her ridiculous fichu mocked him. "Go to hell, Duncan."

He extended his glass.

His friend refilled it.

"Is something amiss, Whitley?" Duncan asked.

"Yes. Everything is bloody well amiss." He sneered. All the words he wished to say clamored for his tongue, but he would not forget that despite their friendship, he and Duncan came from vastly disparate circumstances. And though Kirkwood had never shown an inclination toward either vice or treachery, Crispin had learned to trust no one. "War devils."

As explanations went, it would have to suffice. Nor was it a lie, for the demons of his past haunted him each day. His days as a soldier were why he could not sleep unaided by drink or exhaustion. Memories of the last time he'd seen his best friend, about to face a more horrific fate than Crispin could fathom, made his hands shake and his gut clench.

He had seen what horrors the guerillas could visit upon a body.

"Not woman troubles, then?"

Was the man a soothsayer now as well as a peddler of vice? Duncan's query, too close to the truth, jolted him from the darkness that threatened to consume him. "Why the devil do you ask?"

And why did Miss Turnbow's lush skin taste like every sin he longed to commit? Here he sat, half-disguised, drinking whisky and declining willing wenches, taunted by the sweet scent of jasmine and the fanciful notion of flaming tendrils of hair unfurled on his pillow. Pathetic, really. It was just as well his prick was broken for everyone but *her*.

"I sent you ten of my loveliest new additions, and you refused to bed even one of them," Duncan observed, sipping his whisky with both greater aplomb and prudence than Crispin.

Damn. The governess was rendering him maudlin. Perhaps he ought to bed one of Duncan's bloody *ladies* just to remove the poison of lust from his blood and empty his ballocks. But the thought made his prick wilt faster than a plucked daisy in the July sun.

He tossed back the dregs of his second glass and stalked away from Duncan's keen eyes. "Damnation."

"More whisky?" came the wry query.

Crispin spun on his heel and paced back, holding his glass out like an offering. "*Preposterous Enquiries and Other Gems* by Duncan Kirkwood."

Grinning, Duncan offered his refill with a flourish. "I never fancied myself a scribbler, but I would not mind seeing my name on a spine, particularly if it would rankle dearest Papa."

Crispin took another hearty sip. *Yes, this was just the thing.* In no time at all, he'd be feeling right as rain, ready to collapse upon the bed and sink himself into oblivion, where he could no longer be troubled by the governess and her luscious body and curious predilection for wandering about in his study under the cover of darkness.

"Has the old bastard threatened you with legal action again?" he asked, spurred as much by curiosity as he was the need to divert attention from himself.

"Who is she?" Duncan evaded, his grin fading. He did not often speak of the duke who had sired him. The enmity he possessed for Amberly was obvious, but aside from the occasional reference and the name of his hell, he revealed little.

The whisky glasses had begun to do their work, bathing Crispin's mind in a comforting glow. "The new governess," he admitted, his grip on his glass and his jaw both tightening simultaneously.

His friend raised a brow. "Much as I hate to say this Whitley, if the governess is the woman you wish to bed, why do you tarry here?"

Why indeed? It was easier, for one thing. Safer, too. Here, he could not be interrupted by duty or importuned by sisters he had never wished to be responsible for. He had not wanted the title, damn it. Had not even wished to return to England. Or to live, for that matter. Guilt was a festering internal wound to rival that caused by any bullet or saber.

"It is a valid question, Kirkwood," he admitted. "Would you believe the answer is honor?"

Duncan cocked his head. "Have you any left?"

"Precious little," he grumbled, taking one more sip of whisky. "The feeble remnants of which dwindle with each passing moment."

His friend gave him a half-smile, approaching him and taking the glass from his hands with ease. "Get some rest, Whitley. Then go home on the morrow. Tup the governess if you must. Above all, *sleep*. You look like something Beelzebub raked up from the coals."

Tup the governess.

If only he could.

He inclined his head, knowing that like it or not, egregious lapse of judgment or no, he was returning to Whitley House this evening. Or morning. Or whatever the bloody hell time of godforsaken day it was. "How long have I been here, Kirkwood?"

The proprietor's brow furrowed. "I do believe this is the fourth day. Pray do yourself a kindness before you depart in the morning and avail yourself of the bathing chamber. With all respect, Your Grace, you stink."

He'd lost four whole days. He had no doubt Duncan was correct and he did look like some festering soul that had been sent to the bowels of Hades.

Hell. He *was* a festering soul. He would never understand the unfair whims of a God that had taken Morgan's life and left him behind to the agony of life after war. Of having to spend each waking moment drowning all memories of the atrocities he had witnessed and committed by pouring spirits down his throat.

He did not even take umbrage at Duncan's words. In another time, another place, and when he had been a different man—a gentleman who had never known the evils of the world, who had never met the horrors of war or the bitter fear of staring death in the face in the throes of battle—he would have been affronted and horrified. He would have issued a crushing setdown and put Kirkwood in his place.

But he was the man who had watched the lifeblood seep from his enemy, the man who had held his comrades in his arms as they breathed their last. He had faced cannonades and swords and hails of musket fire. He had ridden into battle knowing he may not return alive.

That man felt as if he was unraveling in the fashion of a tapestry, one thread at a time until all at once, half of him was gone. He was empty and hollow and bitter and numb to his core.

And soused.

Thoroughly bosky.

In his cups.

"I cannot tup the governess," was all he said. He could not, could he? Conscience and honor proved fiendishly elusive when one was drunk on Duncan Kirkwood's fine whisky. "But perhaps there would be no harm in returning to Whitley House in the morn since I have no further business here. Do consider reevaluating the quality of your whores, Kirkwood. None of them are up to snuff. If you had half an eye for excellence, I would not be leaving your premises unsatisfied."

Duncan snorted. "My eye for quality is unsurpassed, and that is why every lord in London worth his salt spends each night within my establishment. If anyone ought to consider evaluating anything, it is you. Swive the governess out of your system. But by all means, avail yourself of the bath first. I'll have a fresh change of clothes sent round for you."

Hell and damnation. He could not swive Miss Governess. Should not. It wouldn't be proper, not with his sisters beneath his roof. His rogue prick stiffened against his breeches at the mere thought of stripping her out of her dowdy gowns and ridiculous caps. Baring her to his eyes and lips and tongue. Curse it, he had to stop that errant vein of thought lest he embarrass himself before Duncan.

"Do not send more quim this evening," he growled.

His friend stifled a smile of amusement. "But of course." He deposited their glasses on a nearby, ornately carved table before bowing.

Being embroiled in war had stripped Crispin of the heartily ingrained notions of hierarchy with which he had been raised. Moments such as these reminded him that, for all their familiarity and camaraderie, he was nevertheless Duncan's better. Duncan catered to him, served him. The realization struck him in a raw place, and he did not like it.

He stepped forward, the chamber swirling around him, intent upon... bloody hell, he knew not what. "Thank you, friend," was all he said. "I will accept your offer of a bath this evening, I think. Lord knows I probably need one by now."

Duncan sniffed, then clapped him on the back. "There is no question of it, Cris. I offer irrefutable, olfactory evidence."

"Go to hell," he said without heat.

His friend offered him a sad smile. "We are already there, are we not?"

Crispin allowed the breath to flow from his lungs in a slow, steady exhalation. "Yes," he acknowledged at last. "We are."

CHAPTER SEVEN

THE DUKE OF Whitley was in attendance at the breakfast table, a shock to the senses, dressed for riding and unfairly handsome. His presence, solemn and arrogant and quiet and yet so very commanding, was all Jacinda could see when she arrived with her recalcitrant charges in tow.

For several mornings following his abrupt departure at dinner, he had been gone. Despite his demand she report to him twice daily on the progress of Lady Honora and Lady Constance, he had disappeared with no word to suggest when he might once again be expected.

The household had been unaware of his return. She could only assume he'd gone to his club or to his favorite hell, where he drowned himself in distraction and dissipation.

He stood and sketched a bow so elegant that it belonged more in a ballroom than here before his sisters and a mere governess. To her relief, Lady Constance and Lady Honora both performed passable curtsies.

Their lessons had progressed uneventfully for the last few days, and she was grateful for the reprieve. The mouse funeral had been a turning point, it seemed. Though she supposed the Portugal cakes she had whipped up for them—much to the horror of Cook—had aided in her storming of their battlements. Sternness and sweets worked wonders upon the two imps.

She dipped into a curtsy as well, knowing she must but careful to keep her gaze averted so the duke could not read the disapproval that was not her place to feel. It ought not to bother her that he was a dissolute rakehell and utter wastrel, but somehow it did. The false smile stretching her lips as she greeted him nearly broke.

Truly, why should she mind he had gone? His absence proved a boon, as it had enabled her to search his study, his library, and even his bedchamber. She had made a number of surprising discoveries during her quests. None perhaps more edifying than the dearth of evidence of his guilt.

But in addition to that, his chamber smelled like him long after he had gone, he preferred poetry over prose, and he had a heart after all. For in addition to his charitable endeavors regarding the dowager Marchioness of Searle, he also contributed handsome sums to several London orphanages.

Even so, although she appreciated his generosity, she was not about to christen him a saint just yet. The man was far too wicked and jaded for redemption. Had he not just spent four whole days in a den of iniquity?

"Good morning, Con, Nora." The duke paused. "Miss Governess?"

She had no choice but to look up from her hem where she had forced her gaze. His striking gray eyes seemed to sear her, to steal her breath, to see past all her trappings and lies, her lace and cap and linen and carefully crafted deceptions.

His nostrils flared and his sensual lips tightened, twin signs of his wrath. "You will speak to me when I address you, madam."

Did he wish her to dispose of a mouse carcass today? Or perhaps to fall to her knees and lick his gleaming riding boots? The seducer who had tempted her in the darkness days before was nowhere to be found. In his place was the cold, arrogant duke once more. Everything in her longed to spill his coffee and breakfast plate both in his lap.

She tamped down her inner rebellion with great effort and gritting of teeth. "Yes, Your Grace?"

"Your curtsy was abbreviated," he snapped, his lip curling. "I cannot countenance my sisters being taught by a governess who cannot even manage proper deference for her master."

Her master.

She stiffened. His words swirled through her, settling in her mind like a hundred tiny pinpricks. Irritating. Infuriating. But she was not at Whitley House to allow her temper to make her falter. She needed to maintain her position as governess. To act as a proper servant should. She had made a promise to her father, and she owed him the duty of seeing this to its fruition.

"Forgive me, Your Grace," she forced herself to say, though it did not sound sincere even to her own ears.

"Another."

His clipped demand rang through the chamber with the force of a whip.

She stifled a frown. "I beg your pardon, Your Grace?"

"Another curtsy, if you please, Miss Governess." A small, smug smile curved his lips.

His brow raised in challenge. Was he intent upon humiliation, or was it his power over her that he relished wielding? She could not be sure. Everything in her protested. Her fingers itched to flip his cup once more. To send the steaming liquid into his lap.

Instead, she bit her lip, kept her mutiny to herself, and dipped into the most elegant and prolonged curtsy she could manage, holding his gaze all the while. Cool gray eyes glittered into hers, dipping to her mouth as she raised to her full height.

"Will that suffice, Your Grace?" she asked when he remained silent, considering her in a regard that was far too warm for her liking.

For it sent a most unwanted frisson of something she refused to acknowledge straight to her core.

Irritation was all it was.

Loathing, perhaps.

"For now. Do join me for breakfast, my ladies, Miss Governess." His lips twitched.

She wished she had not looked at those lips, for she could not help but recall how his mouth had felt upon her skin. Warm and delicious and so very enticing, even if he was the last man in the world for whom she ought to develop a weakness.

Especially when she had never before—not in all her five-and-twenty years—allowed herself to feel something for a man other than James. But she would not think of James now, not in this moment of dangerous deception with the Duke of Whitley presiding over her like a sinful king. The two men could not be more disparate, and the shameful feelings Whitley elicited could not dare taint the pure love she'd shared with James before his untimely death.

He, too, had been a soldier. One who had met his end at the hands of the French cowards when he'd fallen behind on a winter's march through the Spanish mountains. Avenging him by helping her father had been her life's purpose ever since that day. She had never forgotten, would *never*, ever forget.

"Thank you." Jacinda turned her attention to her charges, busying herself with seeing them settled and acting as befitted their station rather than as lady pirates.

With filled plates, steaming cups of tea, and planted bottoms, Ladies Honora and Constance began breaking their fast. Jacinda almost heaved a sigh of relief at the ease of it. They had yet to issue a cheeky retort or plant a dead rodent anywhere. Or use the salvers as sleds.

She brought her tea to her lips and inhaled its rich scent, sipping delicately. It did need more sugar, but she was willing to accept it as it was, for she loved nothing better than a well-steeped cup of tea...

Until Lady Honora disrupted the silence.

"Were you visiting your mistress, Crispin?"

She swallowed her tea to avoid choking upon it.

"Mrs. Nulty?" Lady Constance added.

Jacinda's ears went hot. "My ladies, you must never mention such private, delicate topics of conversation. It is not your place, and neither are the duke's whereabouts your concern."

Never mind the twist of something rude and unpleasant in her belly at the name. Mrs. Nulty. Of course Whitley would have a mistress. Why should she imagine otherwise? Just because he had been so disconcertingly familiar with her person did not mean a man of the duke's considerable looks and licentious reputation would not have a dozen other women at his disposal. Keeping lightskirts was common enough among men of his station.

The reference to this mysterious female did not affect Jacinda one jot. The Duke of Whitley was a conscienceless rakehell. Her sole concern was obtaining the enciphered messages Kilross required and ensuring she and Father did not lose everything they possessed.

"Apologize to His Grace at once, my ladies," she added to the duke's impish sisters.

"Pray forgive us, Crispin," they chimed in unison.

Jacinda wondered if Mrs. Nulty was beautiful. Undoubtedly, amongst the demimonde, she would be a diamond of the first water. She poked at the pound cake on her plate.

"You are forgiven for the lapse in good sense and good comportment, sisters." His tone was low, almost a growl. "Miss Governess?"

She jerked her gaze up from her plate, finding herself the recipient of that flinty gray gaze once more. "Yes, Your Grace?"

"I wish to have a word with you in my study following breakfast." His jaw hardened, his beautifully sculpted lips tightening with what she could only surmise was either disgust or disapproval for her.

Perhaps both.

Mayhap he only liked to grope his servants in the dark of night, when he could not see them clearly. Of course she could not compare to a Mrs. Nulty, some lush creature who groomed herself to be the object of every man's desire so she might wheedle her living out of his purse whilst on her back.

Oh, bother. That was deucedly small of her. And perhaps shrewish. She was not in a position to cast judgment.

"Miss Governess?"

At his sharp voice, her back stiffened. Surely it was wrong for a despicable knave to also be so handsome. A little quiver happened in her belly each time she saw him.

"Your Grace?" she asked, expunging the ire from her tone so it was only sweet and biddable as befitted a lady of her station. Above all else, a governess must not berate her employer before her charges. She must never allow him to see she possessed pride or the base human emotion of anger.

With great effort, she schooled her features into a mask of poise and calm.

His gaze raked over her, pausing on her mouth. He took his time speaking, making certain, it seemed, that she knew he assessed her, making sure the servants and even his sisters noticed.

Her lips tingled.

His attention dipped to her bosom.

Her traitorous nipples hardened, her breasts feeling achy and full. Why did he have the power to reawaken old hungers she had thought long dead?

"I fear I did not hear your response," he said, forcing her to realize her gaze strayed back to his lips.

What had he asked of her? Mortification unfurled, her cheeks going as hot as her ears. Stupidly, she stared back at him, wondering how she—a lady of reasonable intellect and practicality—could be so undone by one tyrant duke she neither liked nor trusted.

Oh, but part of her liked him far, far too much.

She tamped down the troublesome thought.

"I beg your pardon, Your Grace." She paused, licking lips that had suddenly gone dry. "What was it you required of me?"

"Your presence." His lip curled. "In my study. Following breakfast. It was not a request, Miss Governess, but I do expect an answer just the same."

How had she forgotten? Why did he rattle her so?

A potted plant. She would be unremarkable. Unnoticeable. Unaffected.

She bowed her head, feigning humility and penitence both even as her lip longed to curl right back at him, the hateful oaf. When he had been in his cups, he had not been so cruel. The sober Duke of Whitley was a fiend.

Jacinda composed herself and forced her response. "Forgive me. Of course I shall join you following breakfast, Your Grace. I shall see Lady Constance and Lady Honora settled with their watercolors, and then I will report to you directly."

"Look at me when you speak to me, Miss Templebottom," he demanded.

"Turnbow," Lady Constance shocked her by correcting the duke.

Jacinda's wide, startled gaze flew to her youngest charge. Bless that Portugal cake. Perhaps later today, she would make them plum cakes. One of the advantages of living a frugal existence with Father meant she had learned how to perform a great many tasks for herself. As it happened, she enjoyed baking sweets every bit as much as Father liked to consume them.

"Her name is Miss Turnbow, Crispin," added Lady Honora. "You really ought to know that by now. She has been our governess for almost a fortnight."

The entire room stilled. The clinking of cutlery halted. The footmen presiding over the meal seemed to freeze. The duke's expression darkened. He glowered.

"Lady Constance, Lady Honora," Jacinda said, quick to fill the silence echoing in the chamber with her words. "You must not correct His Grace." *Regardless of how wrong he is or how well-deserved that correction is.*

"You have lasted longer than all the others," Lady Constance grumbled. "He should know your bloody name."

"Mind your language if you please, Lady Constance," she hastened to correct her charge. Jacinda was playing a role, but maintaining her cover necessitated her ability to convincingly portray herself as a governess. She could not shake the impression she was failing miserably. A fresh stab of guilt at her lies pricked her. For all that, Lady Constance and Lady Honora were trying. She had nevertheless begun to develop a fondness for them.

At least her charges seemed to have suddenly developed a hint of loyalty toward her. But she did not trust their abrupt allegiance any more than she trusted their brother.

"Forgive me, Miss Turnbow," Lady Constance said sweetly.

"Lady Constance, Lady Honora, you may take your breakfast in your chambers," Whitley growled. "*Miss Turnbow,* I will meet with you in my study. Now."

His voice suggested that opposition would be expressed at a great cost.

At least he had gotten her name correct.

Casting the luscious golden cubes of pineapple on her own plate a longing glance, she rose. "Yes of course, Your Grace."

Somehow, despite his arrogance, the thought of bringing the Duke of Whitley low did not fill her with the glow of satisfaction. Nor did the notion of him betraying Searle seem as certain as Kilross claimed. The duke was a condescending cad, but would the same man who had orchestrated the murder of his comrade also look after that man's widowed mother and younger brother? And what of the orphans?

She wanted to loathe Whitley. Wanted to believe him guilty, for it would make her task that much easier. Lessen her guilt. Force her to be tireless in her pursuit of the evidence Kilross wanted against him.

But nothing made sense.

And she had never been more hopelessly conflicted.

MISS GOVERNESS NETTLED him.

The aftereffects of the whisky he'd consumed during his stint at The Duke's Bastard still coursed through Crispin, but he had done his best to combat it with another hot bath that morning, an immense breakfast, and a hideous amount of coffee. As he stood behind the desk in his study and watched the siren he had foolishly tasked with corralling his hoyden sisters, he clenched his jaw.

This morning, she had dressed in yet another bloody sack the color of mud. Shapeless, inelegant, and hideous, the gown had not a stitch to recommend it. The abundant lace fichu tucked into her décolletage obstructed his view of her luscious breasts. Yet another large, unsightly cap concealed her vibrant hair.

Everything about what she had donned today was meant to detract from her innate beauty. She could drown herself in drab colors and yards of unnecessary muslin, could hide herself beneath caps and lace and averted gazes. But he saw her.

Miss Turnbow was not what she seemed. Something about her had pricked at his soldier's senses on the day she had first appeared in his darkened study, and it continued to prod him now.

He did not like his reaction to her.

It was inconvenient.

Perplexing.

Infuriating.

Also, wild and invigorating. The mere memory of her soft body beneath his had made him as randy as a sailor just returned to land after a year at sea. Lust was not a problem. Crispin adored fucking. His cock was large and he knew how to use it. His tongue was long and he knew how to use it. His mouth was wicked, and he... damnation. Best to stay further thoughts in that inappropriate direction, for it made his prick go rigid, and there wasn't a cursed thing he could do to assuage his hunger.

He wished for another glass of whisky—it had been nearly twelve hours since his last sip of poison—and made a dismissive gesture. "Sit, Miss Governess."

Her lips tightened, as if in censure. She did not do as he ordered. "Your Grace, I am heartily glad you requested this audience, for we have much to discuss. If I may be so bold, I cannot help but think your actions have a direct impact upon the behavior of your sisters."

Bold? She was bloody beyond the pale. Did the woman think to chastise him? He had requested her presence so he could give her the setdown she so richly deserved. His sisters were still hellions, and he could see no improvement in their comportment, save from the fact they had not ridden to breakfast down the staircase on salvers or hidden rodent carcasses by his breakfast plate.

He gave her a ducal sneer, the sort that usually made unwanted interlopers disappear from his path. "*Sit,* madam."

Color blossomed in her cheeks. She sat slowly and primly, as if she were reluctantly seating herself upon a garden bench encrusted in bird offal. "Lady Constance and Lady Honora should not be aware of your... your..."

Her fluster was adorable, and it somehow deflated his ire. Still, he could not resist the opportunity to further her discomposure. He sat, for he could not politely stand in her presence, and even soulless bastards like him could recall their manners now and again.

"I beg your pardon?" A wolfish grin curved his lips. "My what, Miss Governess? I confess I had not previously realized you possessed a stutter. Though it grieves me to say this, I am not certain my sisters ought to be instructed by a female who cannot speak her mind without needless repetition."

"I do not have a stutter, Your Grace," she snapped, the flush overtaking her entire face until her creamy skin was tinged a delectable shade of pink. Not even her ears were exempt. "I am simply searching for a polite means of relaying what I wish to say."

He frowned at her, recalling his reason for requiring this private audience. "Miss Governess, I did not require your presence in my study so you could berate me. Let us consider it best that you cannot find your errant tongue."

"Mrs. Notley," she said on a rush, full lips still pressed into a fine line of condemnation. "Surely you cannot think it proper for your impressionable, innocent sisters to know of such a woman's existence, never mind her name."

"Mrs. Nulty," he corrected smoothly, wondering if she had intentionally gotten the demimondaine's name confused. Miss Turnbow was as sharp as a bayonet. He could see it in her eyes, read it in her every interaction. Her intelligence did not escape him. It intrigued him. *She* intrigued him.

"Precisely." She busied herself with settling the fall of her dreadful skirt, avoiding his gaze. "The female in question ought not to be known to your sisters. I hope they have never made her acquaintance."

Of course he had not introduced his sisters to the woman. Did Miss Governess think him a complete blackguard? His outrage dimmed when the conscience he had believed long dead reminded him he had entertained Mrs. Nulty—and some of her fellow actresses—in his townhome whilst his sisters were in residence. The woman was as beautiful as she was proficient at—

No. He stifled that vein of thought. The only pertinent fact was he did not dabble in mistresses. He had never offered Mrs. Nulty or any other female *carte blanche*. Given his notoriety and reputation, scandal sheets and town gossips tended to run rampant with falsehoods.

Falsehoods that had somehow reached the eager ears and eyes of Con and Nora. By God, he knew not how the little minxes managed to find such nonsense. They were more effective at getting what they wished than a phalanx of enemy soldiers.

Even so, the tone Miss Governess had taken, coupled with her attempt to control their dialogue, peeved him. He planted his hands upon the polished surface of his desk and leaned forward, forcing her to meet his gaze. "I must wonder at your fretfulness, Miss Governess. Why should Mrs. Nulty concern you? I would hate to think your remonstration is grounded in envy."

Sherry eyes flashed at him, the only sign of her pique. "Rest assured I do not envy such a creature. My sole interest is the wellbeing and reputations of my charges, Lady Constance and Lady Honora."

"As is mine." Irritation surged. "That is the reason I required this audience, Miss Governess."

She straightened in her seat. "Perhaps you would care to enlighten me, Your Grace?"

Even now, her daring aroused him as much as it irritated him. Who did she think she was to speak thus to the Duke of Whitley, the man who paid her wages and provided the bed in which she slept? "You have been in my employ for twelve days."

"Eleven," she corrected.

He snorted. "Do you wish for this to be the last day, Miss Governess? I could dismiss you without reference."

Her chin went up in defiance. Ah, there it was, her true self. The one she could not hide behind her mud-brown gowns and yards of lace. "Do you want to sack me, Your Grace?"

Yes, for then he would never need to see her again. He could forget about her and remove the lust that threatened to consume him like a diseased appendage. And perhaps *his* particular appendage would once more be capable of functioning as it ought.

Also, no, because it would mean he would never get to feel her beneath him once more or to strip her of all that ugly cloth and her godawful cap. Or to kiss a path straight from her rose-pink lips to her cunny.

What would she taste like? Would she whimper beneath him or moan and cry out, bold and unashamed in her passion?

Hell.

He skewered her with a narrow-eyed glare. "I wish for a governess to demonstrate humility. One who forces my wayward sisters to act with a care for comportment and a regard for manners. One who does not castigate me for imagined indiscretions which are of no concern to her regardless of their dubious veracity."

"Dubious veracity?" She shot to her feet, her eyes blazing. "Why would your sisters be aware of that woman's existence or her name if not because you brought her here to this very house? Do not think for a moment that belowstairs is not rife with information. I am aware you entertained that... female here on numerous occasions whilst your innocent sisters were in residence."

By God, she was beautiful when enraged. All the brightness and boldness she sought to hide came to life in her anger. His body took control of his mind. He had intended to remonstrate her, to inform her he had hired her to bring a modicum of order to his restless household, to rein in his hoyden sisters. He had hired her, damn her lovely hide, so he would no longer need to think or worry or fear for their futures. So he could be free to live his life as he wished.

He had not hired her so she would haunt his bloody cock to the point that he could not seek pleasure with another woman. When had he ever gone to The Duke's Bastard and turned down the company of whores? When had he ever been unable or unwilling to bed a lightskirt? Or two at one time?

He stood, slammed his fist into the desk with so much force it made his knuckles ache. "Do you dare to question me, Miss Governess?"

She stared at him as if he were repugnant, and how he longed for the oblivion of drink. For the darkness of the night. For mindlessness and weightlessness and the freedom from all the guilt and demons that dogged him.

"I do not question you, Your Grace," she said at length, her voice tight with her irritation and condemnation both. "But I do question your judgment. Lady Constance and Lady Honora should not have access to scandal. Nor should they have any knowledge of your... improper associations. They should remain innocent and blissfully unware of all licentiousness. Indeed, if your actions should besmirch their characters due to their association with you, no suitable gentleman will take either of them as his wife, regardless of the fact they are the daughters and sisters of a duke. Your pedigree, estimable though it may be, cannot save them from you."

Save them from him? Damn and blast, the female had gall.

The irritation and lust raging within him met in that moment. Blackness and anger and desperate need collided. There were at least a dozen different reasons why he ought to dismiss Miss Turnbow from his study—hell, from his damned employ as well—and return to the simplistic comfort of gloom and drink. Equally, as many reasons why he should eviscerate the inconvenient, wild attraction continued to spark to life and draw him to the infernal woman opposite him.

She thought herself a worthy opponent, did she? Well, she thought wrong. For if she wanted to battle him, she ought to acquaint herself with one fact.

She would never emerge the victor.

A growl sounded deep in his throat. "You have gone too damned far, Miss Governess."

Her gaze grew wary. "Your Grace?"

Perhaps she was asking if she needed to fear him.

The answer was yes.

It had always been yes.

Would forever be, simply, *yes*.

He had demons in his soul, and they wanted to consume her. To make little Miss Governess his delectable sacrifice. Perhaps she could assuage the ache. The blinding need. The all-consuming hunger.

He skirted the desk. Before he could control himself or ponder the wisdom of his reaction, his hands found the supple curve of her waist. The vile, filthy creature he had become screamed to be unleashed.

Crispin tread a dangerous line between control and rampaging lust. It seemed the more she enraged him, the more he wanted Miss Governess. Beneath him. Atop him. On her knees before him. That tart mouth of hers filled with his cock.

Curse it, the lust was winning his inner battle. He wanted her to sit on his face so he could thrash her with his tongue until the only word that left her beautiful lips was his name.

"Apologize to me, Miss Governess," he demanded. "At once."

Her chin tipped up, and she threw her shoulders back, the image of foolish, beautiful defiance. "I will not apologize for uttering the truth, Your Grace. Nor will I express contrition for advising you to act in a fashion befitting a gentleman with two sisters he shall need to see married in the next few years. You do them a great disservice in your lechery, and someone must alert you to the error of your ways."

Haughty and condescending to the last.

The frenzy inside him grew. It doubled and tripled and quadrupled.

He should release her. Should have never touched her.

But now that he had done so, he could not deny the rightness of it. Her waist was far smaller than her shapeless gown suggested. And soft as it had been that night in his study. He would hazard an experienced guess that beneath her gown, a chemise and stays were all she wore. A surge of hunger so violent it almost took his breath shot through him. What was it about this woman, with her ridiculous penchant to cloak herself in linen and lace and hideous colorlessness that drew him to her?

It could not be beauty alone, for while her features themselves were undeniably fine when considered apart from her appalling toilette, he had known and bedded more than his fair share of attractive women. Bored wives, happy wives, sad wives, widows, actresses, countesses, duchesses, ladies, and lightskirts… the appellation mattered not. A beautiful woman was a beautiful woman.

He studied Miss Turnbow with hardened concentration, determined to see what part of her drew him to her. Surely she possessed no quality that was peculiarly remarkable. Her high cheekbones? The slender nose kissed with copper freckles? Her pink, wide lips? Those luscious sherry eyes? Her full bosom and well-curved waist?

Bloody hell. As he stared down at her, he could see nothing more than a comely woman striving to hide her looks however she might, but nevertheless one who ought not to affect him in a way no other before her had. Was it that she should be forbidden to him since she was his servant and responsible for his sisters? Perhaps he had grown bored with the crop of willing women ever ready to spread their milky white thighs for him. Or was it she was the opposite of every other female he'd fucked in his desperate bid for distraction since his return from the hells he'd faced on the Continent?

Crispin could not think. Could not force his mind to circle round the matter one more time. Not when the heat of Miss Governess's body and the distinct, feminine feel of it both burned into him like a wicked, inescapable flame.

He lowered his head so his nose almost brushed hers. So her heady scent washed over him. Floral, feminine, and delicious. He stared into her wide eyes. "Do you think me licentious, Miss Governess?"

Her hands were on his biceps, fingers squeezing with a gentle pressure. "I think you a very dangerous man, Your Grace."

The attraction between them was mutual. He sensed it in the way her body subconsciously relaxed against him, so that her curves filled the hard planes and angles of his. In the way she clutched him rather than pushing him away. Damn her. If she had been aloof, if she had attempted to escape, he would have let her go. But she had not, and he could not let her go now.

Because he wanted more, and so did she.

"You are correct in your assessment," he bit out angrily, for she tempted him beyond reason and he resented her for the weakness she created, a weakness that had never previously existed. "I am very dangerous to you." He stepped closer, until they were nose to nose. His forehead touched hers. "Dangerous to your virtue, Miss Governess."

Her pupils were obsidian, large and beckoning, giving her away. Her glittering eyes, honey and sherry, gold and warm, were wide and clear and unblinking. He could lose himself in their depths, in the sweet scent of her. Jasmine and woman and... Holy God, his cock pressed the fall of his breeches like a madman determined to be released from forced incarceration.

"You would force yourself upon a helpless female dependent upon your largesse for her supper, Your Grace?" she asked softly.

Ah, here they were at the crux of the matter.

He inched nearer, allowing his lower lip to brush against hers from left to right. Once. Twice. Thrice. "Would it be force then, Miss Governess, if I kissed you now? Would you kiss me back, or would you slap me? I confess, I cannot help but wonder."

Her eyes remained wide, the shallowness of her breathing and tightening of her grip on him the only indication that she was affected. He waited for her to respond. For her to deny she wanted him.

Their push and pull was inexorable. Undeniable. He had never wanted to strip a woman of her trappings more. The cap, the lace, the muslin. He would divest her of every tool she used to diminish her beauty until she was all he could see.

Silence fell heavy between them. For a few beats, neither of them said a word. His already limited patience snapped like a twig. He gave her waist a gentle, coaxing squeeze. "Answer me, damn you."

She sighed on a humid exhalation that feathered over his mouth like a caress. He was so desperate for her, even the air she expelled from her lungs seemed precious, and he longed to somehow take it into his body, claim ownership of her in this small, mad sense. As if breathing her air could make her his. A sudden, stark jolt of possessiveness seized him. Damnation, but he wanted to claim her in a way he had never experienced.

"Answer me," he repeated, needing to hear the admission from her lips. Needing to know the wild want he felt for her was reciprocated, that she could not deny it any more than he could. His mind began to form solutions. It was his nature, what had made him an excellent soldier. "Do you want me to kiss you?"

Her hands slid to his shoulders and then twined about his neck. Her lips parted. Another sultry gust of tea-scented air hit him. He bit his lip, reining in his need with Herculean effort. Still, she said nothing.

Not yes.

Not no.

Not. A. Bloody. Word.

He was about to set her from him when her fingers sank into his hair. Her nails raked over his scalp in a delicious abrasion. She swallowed, seemingly to prepare herself, almost as if she was about to face a wall of enemy soldiers with bayonets drawn. Which was ridiculous. He was not her enemy. They were not at war. He was a dark and demented bastard, it was true, but he would not hurt her. Would never take anything more than what she would willingly offer.

"Yes," she whispered.

Her fingers guided him. She rolled to her tiptoes. Their mouths met, hungry, hot, and open. On a groan, he sank his tongue past her lips, and he knew for certain in that moment of feverish capitulation he would not rest until he was inside her. Until she was his. The instincts that had infallibly guided him through years of war—instincts he had ignored on the godawful day he'd lost his best friend—had never betrayed him.

He could make her his mistress, grant her *carte blanche*. Although he had never offered his protection to anyone before her, he knew having her once or even a handful of furtive times would never satisfy him. Her tongue tangled with his. *God, yes.* He could find another damned governess. This woman was his and his alone. His sisters could not possibly require her as much as he did.

He hummed his satisfaction into her mouth, knowing he had found the perfect solution, and deepened the kiss.

CHAPTER EIGHT

THE DUKE OF Whitley kissed the way he did everything. Full-force. Blistering. Unpredictable and wild. His mouth upon hers was passionate and demanding, a conflagration of the unwanted pull between them from the moment she had first entered his study. His kiss owned her. It savaged her. Left her reeling.

Heat blossomed low in her belly, mingling with desire and a raw, frenzied need. The restless sensations he sparked within her were real and insistent though she did not want to acknowledge them. The barbarous molding of his lips to hers both shocked and enthralled her. He kissed as if he claimed her, hot and hungry, and such a disparity from his cold, harsh mien.

Caution and warning attempted to intrude. But she had plainly taken leave of her senses. That was the only explanation for the grave mistake she had made in kissing the Duke of Whitley.

In continuing to kiss him now.

In running her tongue along his, tasting him—bitter coffee with a hint of ruthlessness—in plunging her fingers into his hair. Merciful heavens, the strands were soft and thick and lustrous. She gripped handfuls and held him in place, angling his head so he would apply the pressure of his lips to hers in the fashion she preferred.

But Whitley was not a man who could be controlled, and just as quickly, his large hand cupped the base of her skull, holding her still so he could ravage her lips to his satisfaction. He took command.

Groaned into her mouth. His free hand clamped to her waist. He spun them about as one, moving her backward without once breaking the drugging kiss she could not resist.

The hard edge of his desk pressed into her bottom. He lifted her effortlessly, his arm tightening like a band, and deposited her on the hard, polished expanse of intimidating mahogany. When she had first been seated opposite the exquisitely carved piece of furniture, she had never imagined she might one day be settled upon it as the Duke of Whitley kissed her more thoroughly than she had ever been kissed in her life.

She met him with an ardor she could not explain, with a fervor that shamed her. Some wicked part of her, the part that wanted more of the sin the Duke of Whitley offered, longed for this wild moment of abandon to never end. How she wished they were different people, in a different time and place, free to pursue the madness flaring to life between them.

Somehow, without taking his mouth from hers, he settled between her thighs. The voluminous draping of her skirt accommodated his intrusion. Her legs parted naturally, and her body was traitorously eager for the invasion. Her core ached and pulsed. The need spiraling through her was frightening. She had never wanted another man as she wanted the Duke of Whitley.

Not even James.

It stood against all reason. Against all logic, for Whitley was the enigma she was bound to deceive. If the accusations hurled against him were to be believed, he had betrayed his best friend. He was a traitor. And if rumor was to be trusted, he was also a depraved rakehell, returned from war with an insatiable hunger for thirst and ladies of ill repute.

But another possibility had been niggling at her with increasing certainty. What if Kilross was wrong about Whitley? The papers she had found thus far certainly did nothing to indicate his guilt. He did not feel like a monster in her arms.

No indeed. Quite the opposite.

She scooted forward on the desk, seeking more of him. His groin came into contact with hers. Even with the barrier of her skirts and his breeches, she could feel the hard, thick length of him. His arousal spurred an answering pulse of want within her.

Jacinda told herself she could allow one more kiss before putting an end to her ill-advised lack of inhibition. She could not afford to make herself vulnerable to him in this fashion, and even if she were not charged with uncovering his darkest, most damning secrets, she could never in good conscience carry on with such a lack of respect for her charges. She had not come to Whitley House to be seduced by the Duke of Whitley. Kissing him, allowing his hands to freely roam her body, had never been part of her task here.

He bit her lower lip. She could not suppress a moan as he kissed a path over her flesh. His wicked mouth found her ear. He nibbled the lobe. Licked a particularly sensitive patch of skin. Buried his nose in her hair and inhaled.

"I want you."

His guttural admission settled in her belly like molten honey. Her nipples tightened. The part of her pressing against his manhood ached. It had been so long since she had been touched intimately. Since she had been desired. Since she'd been kissed. Needs she had buried along with her husband's memory woke from years of dormancy.

That was why she didn't protest when he snagged her lace fichu and removed it. Why she didn't even notice his hand had moved from her nape to the buttons on the back of her serviceable gown until she felt them sliding from their moorings one by one.

She did not move to stop him or to escape.

Mindless longing had taken control of her faculties.

"Do you want me, Jacinda?"

Jacinda.

It was the first time he had used her given name, and the intimacy of it slid over her like a caress. His wicked mouth did not stop its decadent exploration, trailing down her throat. His tongue flitted to the hollow where her heart thumped madly.

"Tell me," he urged, kissing his way across her collarbone. "Do you want me?"

Yes, and desperately.

No, because she ought not to want him. Ought not to allow him to affect her at all.

She had promised Kilross she would obtain the information he needed. She had a duty to uphold to Father. So very much depended upon the outcome of her month at Whitley House.

Everything, it would seem.

But when the duke dragged those sinful lips across her breast, and when her gown, chemise, and stays lowered in one swift tug, she could do nothing but arch her back. Her fingers tightened in his thick, dark brown hair.

Still, she would not capitulate. Nor would he give her what she wanted without her affirmation. He stilled, glanced up at her with his unnatural gray gaze that cut straight through her. Now was the time to put an end to this. To brace her palms on his shoulders and shove him away.

He blew a long, hot breath over her nipple, never taking his eyes from hers. "One word. Say it. Your body already speaks for you."

Her breasts had stiffened into taut peaks over breakfast, and they craved his mouth. *She* craved it. Merciful heavens, what had he done to her? Perhaps the Duke of Whitley truly was the devil Kilross would have her believe.

"Yes."

The whisper fled her lips before she could contain it. The duke flicked his tongue over her. "Louder."

He was such a demanding man. She should not be surprised his arrogance extended to lovemaking. And though her marriage bed with James had been soft and gentle, tentative and sweet, something in the savage dominance of the Duke of Whitley made her weak. She wanted to battle him. She wanted to let him have his wicked way with her. She wanted to have her wicked way with him.

Lord, how she wanted.

"Yes," she repeated.

"I could not hear you." His tongue swirled over her areola. "When you are settled, I want you to be as loud as you bloody please. I won't stop until you're screaming the roof off the damned place."

When you are settled.

The words lanced the haze of lust fogging her mind. Conscience and guilt returned to her, and in a moment of blinding clarity, she felt nothing but disgust for herself. How had she allowed the Duke of Whitley, a man she did not like, a man she was meant to condemn, to remove half her gown and undergarments, to bare her breasts to his gaze, to use his tongue upon her flesh?

"No," she said with as much vehemence as she could muster. She gripped her bodice and assorted layers and hauled them back into place. He thought to make her his mistress, and the shame of her actions, of the assumptions he had made about her, stung. He thought she could be bought. That her honor and her body could be claimed with a house and some pretty baubles.

He straightened, a thunderous frown forming between his brows. "I beg your pardon?"

She supposed the almighty Duke of Whitley was not accustomed to being denied. Jacinda raised her chin. "I will not be your mistress."

He sneered. "I do not recall asking, Miss Governess."

His cruelty should not surprise her, but it stung all the same. The heat fled from her, leaving her only cold and shocked at her lack of care for her honor, her loyalty to Father and James, her own body. How had she even countenanced the duke's touch? How could she have betrayed the memory of the beautiful love she had shared with her husband by engaging in such despicable lechery?

She felt ill.

Would she have lain with him?

Allowed him to couple with her upon his desk?

What had she been thinking? This man was her enemy. He had never even exhibited a capacity for kindness or compassion. He was depraved. He drowned himself in drink, brought women of loose morals to his very home. He had betrayed his best friend.

Jacinda shoved at the great wall of Whitley's chest. "Your words suggested an assumption. An assumption I cannot allow."

His lip curled even more, his features hardening. "Your actions suggested otherwise."

Her cheeks flamed. She leapt from his desk, reached behind her to tug the parted sides of her bodice upward so she could reach the buttons he had undone. "You coerced me. I was held in your thrall for a brief moment, but it is over now and the mistake shan't be repeated."

The duke clenched his jaw, raking her form with a dismissive gaze. "Yes, a mistake. I see that now. I suppose this is how I am repaid for attempting to show a dowdy spinster in shapeless sacks that there is more to life than being a pinch-lipped harpy."

A dowdy spinster? A pinch-lipped harpy?

Her mouth fell open. She struggled with her buttons, not caring what a ridiculous sight she must make. She would not ask for his assistance. "How dare you?"

"Oh, I dare quite a bit, Miss Governess." He took a step forward, crowding her with his big, powerful form once more. "Unlike some who are afraid to dare anything."

If only he knew how much she dared.

But if he did, he would likely wrap his hands around her throat and choke the life from her.

She tipped up her chin in a show of defiance she little felt. "That is where you are wrong about me, Your Grace, for I can assure you, I fear nothing."

Having nothing left to lose tended to render one foolishly brave, and Jacinda was no exception. Still, how she wished she could remove herself from his employ and his household. No one in her life had ever been so disrupting. So upsetting. So enraging. So bitterly tempting.

Blast. She would not dwell upon the last, disconcerting fact. Not whilst the grim Duke of Whitley scowled at her as she attempted to hook her buttons. And after he had dismissed her with such calculating viciousness. It was true, she dressed to be ignored. But she was neither a spinster nor a harpy.

She was...

The truth walloped her as she stood there in ignominy in the Duke of Whitley's study. She didn't know who she was any longer. She didn't even recognize herself. Once, she had been a wife with an open heart and a future. Now, she was a bitter, broken-hearted widow consigned to a quiet life with her father.

This wicked interlude had been an aberration. One that would not be repeated. One she could not dare to repeat. She struggled with the last of her buttons, mortified she could not sink them within their moorings. Perhaps it was his intense regard that flustered her. Perhaps it was the unwanted thoughts unraveling in her mind.

Either way, she needed his aid.

He moved nearer still, bringing with him his heat and the muscled distraction of his masculine form, the scent of him. *Good God*, she would never again be able to look upon him without recalling the sensation of his tongue upon her breast.

"Turn about," he directed in clipped tones still redolent with his combined disapproval and dismissal.

Surely he could not think to seduce her once more? "Your Grace, I have already made amply apparent to you I do not wish for a...

dalliance."

"Your buttons, Miss Governess," came his sibilant explanation, curt as ever. "As I am the one who undid them, it seems the responsibility to fasten them falls upon me as well."

"No." Her lips firmed into a forbidding line as she frowned at him. She did not want him to get any closer. To touch her again. Something about this man made her weak. "I shall fasten them on my own."

He muttered something beneath his breath that sounded suspiciously like *stubborn bloody wench*, but she hadn't the time to reflect upon it for his hands clamped on her waist. He spun her to face the wall opposite him, and then his fingers—nimble and long and tapered as she had not failed to notice—skipped along the line of buttons as if he were a lady's maid born and bred. In a trice, he had her refastened.

Strong hands clasped her waist once more. He spun her to face him. His countenance was hard, harsh, and expressionless. She swallowed, wishing she had never lost her wits. That she had never fallen so precariously into his arms and kisses.

"Have we reached an understanding then, Your Grace?" she queried softly, because it was necessary. Perhaps her foolishness would land her on the street, and she would need to beg Kilross for mercy. She would shoulder the blame for her own injudiciousness. No one had forced her to give into her wicked longings. She would face Father and confess all if need be. And she would make amends.

Whitley raised an imperious brow, looking as majestic and forbidding as any king in that moment. "We have not. As I distinctly recall, I required this dialogue so I could reprimand you for the lack of progress I see in Lady Honora and Lady Constance."

If anything, there had been a wealth of progress, and she was willing to wager he knew it just as well as she did. Her frown sharpened. "Forgive me, but I fail to see the lack of progress you allude to."

A second brow joined the first. "Either you are foolishly comfortable in your position here or you are mad, Miss Governess. Do you dare to gainsay me?"

She supposed she was being unaccountably forward for a servant in his employ and at his mercy. But they had already crossed firm boundaries, and she could not stymy her self-defense now that it had emerged, glorious and bold in a way the real Jacinda was not. Or at least the Jacinda she ordinarily was. She had almost become a different person, it seemed since her arrival at Whitley House, so that she no longer knew where one Jacinda ended and the other began.

The duke continued to stare her down, awaiting her response. Her gaze flicked to his mouth of its own accord, watching as the finely molded lips quirked into a knowing grin.

Shame stole over her cheeks in a heated flush as she snapped her eyes back to his, unflinching. "Do not forget, Your Grace, you were gone for nearly half the time I have been in your employ. I hardly think the limited amount of time you have spent in Lady Constance and Lady Honora's presences can imbue you with the necessary judgment."

He caught her chin in his grip, not hard enough to hurt but firm enough that he reminded her of his larger size, his well-muscled frame. He could easily overpower her. Force her to do his bidding. "Enlighten me, Miss Governess. Prove to me you are deserving of maintaining your position."

How dare he? Anyone could see his sisters had been hellions absent of even a modicum of direction. Their parents had been dead for years, their previous guardian had been a drunkard who choked to death on his supper, and their closest living family member and guardian was a degenerate rakehell who spent his time alternately drinking and wenching for days. Until he passed out and began the cycle anew, that was. How were young ladies meant to thrive when everything in their world was arranged to their severe disadvantage?

Fury soared through her, replacing the witless lust he had inspired. Fury for her charges. Fury at herself for her damnable weakness for this man. Fury at his arrogance and condemnation. Fury she had allowed him such shocking liberties.

Regret that she had stopped him.

No. She scrubbed that rogue feeling from her being at once and plowed forward with what must be done. She clenched her muslin skirt to blunt the sting of her aggression and took a deep breath before responding with a poise and calm that shocked even her. "If you truly wish for me to prove myself to you, then I challenge you to put forth an effort. Cease disappearing and drowning yourself in spirits. Be present for your sisters. Observe how far they have come since the day I arrived to find them sledding down the staircase upon silver salvers whilst your horrified domestics looked helplessly on."

He ground his jaw, glaring. "Hiring them a bloody governess is putting forth an effort. As is tolerating their hoydenish ways."

How little he knew about the human heart if he believed his cold, limited interaction with his sisters was sufficient. A sadness she was not meant to feel cut through her. In that moment of utter clarity, she saw him in a way she had not before. He and Lady Honora and Lady Constance had lost everyone but each other. And yet he kept himself apart, buried himself in whisky and demons. Beneath his icy aloofness and arrogant cruelty lay a man who carried his scars on the inside. He was hurting, and it seemed the Duke of Whitley either did not know how to heal himself or had not the desire to try.

Another emotion mingled with the sadness, unfurling within her like a spring bud, and she recognized it for what it was: compassion.

Was it his kiss that had unlocked this unwanted reaction? She could not be sure. All she knew was her time at Whitley House was not a stark matter of right versus wrong. Good heavens, it would seem she had begun to form an attachment to not only her charges but to their older brother as well.

She couldn't stay the understanding beating in her heart. She considered him, gentling her voice as she spoke. "Your sisters need you now, Your Grace. You are all they have just as they are all you have. They need more than your occasional presence. They need more than a governess's direction and care can provide them. Above all, they need your love."

"Love." He gave a short, bitter bark of laughter. "If you believe such rot, I have answered my own question and you are as queer in the attic as I suspected."

She frowned at his crude dismissal of her suggestion. Of course it came as no surprise, but part of her wished he would let her past his grim defenses just once. Jacinda told herself the inclination sprang from her need to carry out her task. Uncovering his guilt was a burden she could not shed, and the knowledge she would one day betray him weighed heavily upon her.

She touched his coat sleeve, willing him to soften. To show her a sign he was not the depraved traitor he was suspected of being. "Think upon what I have said, Your Grace."

Reacting with lightning quickness, he removed his coat from her touch and clasped her hand in his, holding her captive when she would have departed the room. His gaze was fierce upon her, his expression unreadable. "Do not forget your role here, Miss Turnbow."

He released her just as abruptly. The man had a way of using his words and frigid mien as effectively as the lash of a riding crop. How thoroughly he had undone her. How wicked and wrong she was to weaken for him.

She had been right when she told him he was dangerous.

From this moment forward, she could not allow herself to be alone with him. She must hold true to her course and remain impervious to him in every way.

"I would not dream of forgetting my role here," she assured him, meaning it more than he could possibly know.

Offering him an abbreviated curtsy, she fled.

It was only when the door clicked safely closed behind her and she heaved a sigh of relief that she realized she had left her lace fichu behind. She hesitated for a beat before deciding—wisely, she was sure—that entering the Duke of Whitley's den of iniquity once more would only lead her further into ruin.

He could keep the fichu, for now. She would rescue it later. All that remained for her to do was to return her mind and focus to the twin tasks at hand: play governess to his sisters and prove his guilt.

Or his innocence.

As she walked away, heart galloping and palms damp, she could not honestly say which of the two outcomes would prove worse.

CHAPTER NINE

THE PROFICIENT NOTES of Pleyel on the pianoforte that evening were not as much of a chore as Crispin would have expected. He listened and watched as Nora played with skill he had not imagined she possessed because he had never asked. Nor had he remained following dinner if he dined with his hoyden sisters at all. The sight of them—not to mention their bloody antics—generally gave him a headache, and he strove to eschew their company altogether in favor of the immeasurably more pleasant presence of whisky and strumpets.

His gaze flitted over the occupants of the chamber. Nora was dressed in pink and looking far too much like a young lady as her fingers deftly navigated her instrument. Con's wide-eyed expression as she surreptitiously glanced his way—as if to ascertain he had not disappeared from his chair—struck him.

And there *she* was, dressed like a blind beggar woman in her latest dun-colored sack, hiding her glorious hair beneath yet another hideous cap, and presiding over the tableau with a smile of satisfaction she did not bother to hide. There was something oddly comforting in the scene. In the place where his dark, vicious heart beat within his chest, something odd happened.

He felt, in a way he had not for as long as he could recall, *content*. What a singular emotion. How perplexing and confounding. He could scarcely countenance it himself, but here he sat with his minx sisters and their governess, and he was not bored or restless or angry. He did not even long for a drink. And wonder of wonders, he was not incapable of feeling as he had supposed.

Here, in this moment, a wealth of other assorted emotions he had not fancied himself capable of washed over him, reviving him, demonstrating he was more than the shriveled husk that remained in the wake of that cursed day in Spain. It was mystifying, this unexpected capacity to feel. He did not like it, and all the same, with it having been unleashed, he was not certain he could stifle or contain all such natural human inclinations.

The blame for his current predicament could only be placed upon one sunset-haired witch. He stared at the vexing woman he could not help but want more with each passing breath. Those stolen kisses had undone him. Even now, he could recall the precise shade of her nipples.

Their gazes clashed for a beat before she frowned and looked away.

Damn and blast.

Perhaps Miss Governess was not wrong.

Perhaps he had not given any part of himself to the very ladies who needed it the most: his sisters. For although Con and Nora had not been on the battlefield and would never know the hells of war, they, too, had suffered loss and upheaval and bitter disappointment.

He did not wish to think her right about anything. Indeed, he would prefer not to think of her at all now that she had so thoroughly rejected his suit. But there she sat, mere feet from him. She slept beneath the same roof. They walked the same halls. This morning, he had been so very close to making her his. He longed for her so much his teeth ached.

Tup the governess, Duncan had urged. What a strange creature she was, for it almost seemed to him she would have sooner allowed him to take her right there on his desk than to accept his protection and become his mistress.

As his mistress, she would want for nothing. He would set her up in a fine house, buy her whatever fripperies and gowns she wished, and see her settled with a proper household. But as a governess, she had no freedom. She was at the whims of his sisters most days, little better than a servant, and bloody hell, he had been an unabashed bastard to her as often as possible.

Because she nettled him.

She burrowed beneath his skin.

She bloody well unsettled him. And he did not like it. Not one whit.

The haunting strains of the piece Nora had chosen to play reached their crescendo before lulling back to a fulfilling finale. He clapped loudly as the last note settled, perhaps with more force than necessary, but he wished to distract himself from the unwanted spring of his erection against his breeches.

Whilst he was relieved that his cock was not broken, he did not wish for the damned appendage to be asserting itself in the presence of his sisters. Unfortunately, he had somehow abdicated control of his body and mind both, however. He could neither force his arousal to abate nor banish maudlin sentiment. For it was surely nothing more than that which made him recall days in his youth when he would listen to his mother play pianoforte.

"Well done, Nora," he said with a throat that had gone suddenly thick at the reminiscence. "It is apparent that you inherited Mother's gift for playing."

Nora's cheeks flushed pink enough to rival her gown, a smile quirking her lips. "Thank you, Brother, but Con plays just as well as I."

He turned to his youngest sister. "Con, is this true?"

She grinned, looking a trifle embarrassed at their sister's words of praise. "Nora is far more skilled than I, I am afraid."

"That is not true, Lady Honora," came the dulcet voice of Miss Governess. "You are equally talented. Would you not like to show His

Grace your proficiency as well? I am certain the duke would adore hearing your command of the pianoforte. Would you not, Your Grace?"

She snagged his gaze once more, and he felt the connection of their stares like a physical jolt. He could not keep himself from glancing at her lips and recalling them against his that morning. He would not rest until that mouth was wrapped around his cock. *Yes, that was precisely what he needed. Miss Governess on her knees before him.* He would pluck the cap from her hair, sink his fingers into the lush skeins of red-gold, and guide her to his prick. Debauching her would be his greatest pleasure. Spending down her throat his paradise on earth. Second only to spending between her luscious thighs...

"Your Grace?"

Her tone held a slight edge, and he forced his mind and gaze from his fiery imaginings. Belatedly, he realized he must have been mooning over her like a green lad whilst she and his sisters looked on.

He clenched his jaw, sensing he was agreeing to something but having no notion what after his mind's wicked tangent. "Of course."

"It is all settled." Nora sounded like the proverbial cat who had got into the cream. "Con, come and play a Scottish reel with me. The one we have been practicing with Miss Turnbow, I should think."

"That will be just the thing, Nora. *Mrs. McLeod of Eyre* is the song," Con added to Crispin. "You must dance with Miss Turnbow. She has taught us a modified version of the reel with only two partners, and it is great fun."

Dance with Miss Governess? The notion held appeal, and he could not deny it.

He swung his eyes back to her in askance. From the flush that had settled upon her cheeks, he could readily discern dancing with him had not been a part of her scheme. He grinned. All the better, then. "I would be more than happy to dance with Miss Turnbow if she will have me."

He would be more than happy to do anything with the woman.

Any day.

Any hour.

Any bloody thing. Especially if it involved the both of them nude and in proximity to an accommodating bed. Or floor. Or divan. Carriage. Table. Desk.

Lord, the list went on, and he'd better stifle his depraved mind before it made his cock so hard he couldn't dance after all.

"I do not think it proper," she said stiffly into the expectant silence of the room, averting her gaze.

Oh, no. Miss Governess was not going to dodge him. After all, his presence this evening was her fault. He had lingered on account of her soliloquy because, although she had enraged him, her words had made more sense than he'd cared to admit.

"We have chaperones," he said smoothly.

She frowned at his sisters, still avoiding looking in his direction. "Lady Constance, Lady Honora, your enthusiasm is commendable. However, a duke does not dance with the governess. It is simply not done."

He supposed there may be some merit to her objection, but he was the Duke of Whitley, and he had cut his teeth on the battlefield rather than in the ballroom. He didn't give a damn about manners and etiquette or the rarefied world into which he had been born. The sole reason he existed in London was thanks to the crown of thorns that was his coronet and the necessity of seeing to his sisters' welfare.

"Miss Turnbow," he said her name in his most authoritative tone, "I hardly think we will find ourselves mired in scandal broth if we dance a reel in the presence of my eleven and twelve-year-old sisters."

She frowned, her gaze snapping back to his at last. "I suppose I should not be surprised to discover you are not even aware of the number of years they have spent upon this earth."

The disdain she did not bother to hide from her voice needled him.

He frowned right back at the vexing creature. "Of course I am aware. They are *my* flesh and blood, after all."

"I turned fourteen last month," Nora supplied helpfully, the minx.

"I am almost thirteen," Con added.

He ground his teeth, wondering why they could not have exhibited loyalty just the once and pretended to be the ages he'd mistakenly guessed them to be. Apparently, time did not cease to move forward whilst one spent years caught up in the grim machine of war. "It would seem I stand corrected. In this matter, as in so many others, the lady is infallibly correct."

"Many matters?" Nora's eyes twinkled with a devious glint of glee he recognized. "Would you care to provide us with a list so we may remind you of them whenever the occasion warrants?"

Hellfire and eternal damnation, this evening had suddenly taken a turn for the gallows. "There will be no bloody list." He glared at the imp.

She grinned back. Con chortled. A suspicious sound even emerged from the direction of Miss Governess. His eyes swung back to settle upon her, drinking in the sight of her small, gloved hand raised to her lips. Those sherry eyes were crinkled at the corners. Incredibly, he was not mistaken. Miss Governess possessed the capacity for mirth.

"Astounding," he marveled aloud.

Her eyebrows shot upward, almost disappearing beneath her dowdy cap. "What is, Your Grace?"

"You know how to laugh." He could not contain his grin, for he was enjoying every bit of this little vignette. He had not been so at ease in years. "I confess I did wonder."

Her lips pursed. The need to claim that sultry, tart mouth once more was a driving force inside him that would not be denied. He wanted the infernal cap gone. He wanted to see the rich beauty of her hair. To lead her from this room and the watchful gazes of his sisters, to gather her in his arms and not stop until he had deposited her precisely where she belonged. Upon his bed.

"The same could be said for you, Your Grace," she countered then, and he could not help but admire her pluck, for his laughter or lack thereof was beyond the realm of her concern.

At least until he made her his mistress, after which point, her concern would be pleasing him and being pleasured by him in equal measure.

But matching wits with her before an audience was not nearly as thrilling as being alone with her. And he did not wish for his sisters to make assumptions or unwittingly carry gossip to the servants. Sensing they were about to sail into dangerous waters, he stood, walked to Miss Governess, and offered the finest bow he could muster.

He extended his hand with a chivalrous air he did not feel. He had not attended a ball in ages. Unless one counted Cyprian balls, that was, and one should definitely not count Cyprian balls. Even he, black-hearted scoundrel that he was, knew that much.

"Will you do me the honor of dancing with me, Miss Turnbow?" he asked with aching formality.

No one would ever guess only that morning his tongue had been in her mouth and his cock had been wedged against the welcoming heat of her cunny. It would be there again in short measure. All in good time, however. First, the dance. He told himself it was to please his sisters, but that was not entirely true. Any excuse to touch Jacinda Turnbow would do.

Her frown deepened. She opened her mouth to once more deny him, he was sure.

"Please, Miss Turnbow?" his sisters asked in unison before she could respond.

"We play well together," added Nora. "You said so yourself. But a reel is not nearly as lively without dancers."

He cast an approving glance back at his sisters. Here was the loyalty he'd been seeking.

"Our brother will not trounce your feet if that is what your fear." Con dimpled. "The scandal sheets say he is an excellent dancer."

Perhaps not. Tightening his jaw, he turned back to Miss Governess, whose expression had gone sour.

"If he were not, I daresay Mrs. Nulty should not be nearly as fond of him as she is," said Nora.

Most decidedly fucking not.

Crispin almost choked. The color drained from Miss Governess's cheeks, her lips thinning back into the line of disapproval he had come to know and lust after so well. Blast, one would not think a woman's condemnation and dreary dress could be so damned arousing, but she set his blood on fire. Still, his sister needed to be reminded of her insolence.

He singed Nora with a glare. "Lady Honora."

She raised a brow, blinking and beatific. "I beg your pardon, Crispin. Is not Mrs. Nulty exceedingly fond of you? Why else should she visit you so often? Penny said that—"

"Who the dickens is Penny?" he growled. *My God*, they were making a fine muck of things.

"My lady's maid."

He would sack her for gossiping at the first possible opportunity. With a suffering sigh, he returned his attentions once more to Miss Governess, whose color had returned to her cheeks but whose sour mien had not sweetened. Blast.

"Let us have the dance then." He wiggled the fingers of his outstretched hand. "Come, Miss Turnbow. Surely one lively Scottish reel cannot harm you."

"One with you could," she said so only the duke could hear.

She would find him a persistent man. He would not stop until he had what he wanted, and he wanted her. Whether it be a reel or in his bed until he had his fill of her, he would have it, by God.

"Or you could enjoy yourself and please your charges," he countered.

"They can be pleased in other ways."

"You could please me," he murmured. And he did not just mean the bloody dance, but it was a point on the map upon which they could begin.

She stilled, her eyes flaring wide. "Why should I wish to do such a thing?"

He gave her a feral grin. "Because I am your employer, and you are subject to my whims. Now no more tarrying, if you please. Con and Nora are prepared to demonstrate their talent for 'Mrs. McSomething of Somewhere'."

At last, and with a suffering look cast his way, Miss Governess deigned to rise, settling her hand in his. He would have rejoiced over his victory had she not trampled it beneath her slipper by pursing her lips and murmuring in a tone steeped in condemnation, "You do not even know how to perform the dance, do you?"

Of course he didn't. Dancing and idle ballroom chatter and tepid ratafia was for virgins and desperate, matchmaking mamas and preening dandies. But improvisation was one of his many skills, and he would turn Miss Governess about any ballroom any day. In fact, he could not think of anything else he would like to do more in the moment, aside from acts that could not be committed in the presence of his sisters.

"I know how to dance, Miss Turnbow," he assured her, winking at Nora and Con, who looked on with an undisguised combination of astonishment and delight. "Moreover, your capitulation has pleased your charges immensely."

"Hmm," came the noncommittal sound of her lovely voice. And then she gave his sisters a beaming, brilliant smile that rendered her positively radiant and could not help but elicit a response in his eager prick. *Devil take it*, she was a lovely bit of baggage, her governess weeds be damned.

"I knew you could not resist your inner desire to please me," he murmured, wanting to nettle her.

Her color rose, but she kept her gold-brown gaze settled across the room. "Lady Honora, Lady Constance, I would dearly love to hear the two of you play together at once. If it pleased you for us to dance, I suppose I shall be willing to eschew propriety on this solitary occasion."

Con clapped, and Nora gave an excited bounce. Their enthusiasm was infectious. And, if he was honest, endearing. Miss Governess had been more than correct in her assessment of the situation. He had never seen his sisters this happy. Nor had he ever felt as light as he did in this moment of freeing, uninhibited pleasure.

It was deuced odd. Never would he have supposed that something as trivial and commonplace as dancing a reel with a governess could imbue him with such a sense of innate gratification. But then again, it could not be denied that Miss Turnbow was not just a governess. She was not *just* anything. She was somehow... different. And she made him feel alive.

Since his ignominious return to England for Phillip's funeral, which had occurred not long after Morgan's death, his existence had been steeped in misery and the attempt to escape it by any means possible. Particularly by drowning his demons in whisky and numbing himself as best as he knew how. The deaths of his brother and best friend still shook him to his core even now, six months later.

But now was not the time for mourning, or grief, or dwelling in the pain of his past. It was instead about seizing the moment. About remembering how to enjoy life. About twirling Miss Governess until she grew so dizzy and fell so far beneath his seductive spell, she could not help but acquiesce and become his mistress.

He smiled down at her as they faced each other and waited for the music to begin.

She stared up at him solemnly, and the height difference between them struck him for the first time. She was petite in stature, the top of her head only reaching to his chin. He extended his hand, and she placed hers in his. Con and Nora began to play the lively tune.

Because he did not know how to dance Mrs. McWhatnot's reel, and because he certainly did not know Miss Governess's special two-person version of the bloody thing, he found himself in the unusual position of allowing the female to lead. Of allowing his sunset-haired, stubborn, vexing, con-bloody-founding siren to lead. It took only a note or two of the music for her to realize he was waiting to follow her. And then she took charge.

Predictably.

Maddeningly.

As they danced, his hand slid to her trim waist—hidden beneath the shapeless lines of her drab gown—for a turn before she wordlessly rebuffed him. He bit back a grin and spun about her, copying her footwork. Odd, but he didn't mind allowing her to lead. She took the reins and went with abandon. They twirled and circled each other, they did their paces up and down the chamber. Con and Nora picked up time, playing the reel faster and forcing them to speed up their steps.

By the time the song ended, he was as breathless as Miss Governess. They stood opposite each other, hands still linked, and when she would have extricated herself from his grasp, he held firm for one moment longer. Wild color bloomed on her cheeks from her exertion, and a genuine smile curved her pink lips. Small, curled tendrils of her lustrous hair had escaped her hideous cap, making her look even younger and softer and lush.

How he wished he could kiss her. How he wished they did not have an audience.

But he could not, so he sketched a bow and brought her hand to his lips instead. "Thank you, Miss Turnbow."

She stared at him, a stricken expression on her face before she schooled her features back into her prim and proper governess mask. She dipped into a smooth curtsy. "Thank you for the honor, Your Grace."

Her soft words and sweet voice moved over him like a caress. His gut tightened, and only partially because he wondered at the reason for the emotion he had seen glittering in her eyes before she dashed them away. She was a mystery wrapped inside an enigma, cloaked in intrigue. What was it about her that burrowed beneath his skin in a way no other female had? Why could he not shake the instinct that there was a great deal more to Miss Jacinda Turnbow than she pretended?

He forced himself to release her hand and turn back to his sisters, who were both looking on with avid interest. Curious little articles. "Thank you as well, Con and Nora. It was a lovely way to spend the evening, and you are both quite skilled."

"Miss Turnbow has been busy teaching us all manner of new dances," Con said, exhibiting an enthusiasm he had never seen in her before. "She knows so many lively ones."

Well, he supposed he could not say Miss Governess did not perform her duty. It seemed she was quite industrious. "Excellent, though you cannot have learned to play with such *finesse* in a mere week."

He could not resist alluding to their intentional increase in the tempo so he and Miss Turnbow were skipping about like Bedlamites by the time the last note rang out. He was more than aware of their every attempt to make mischief.

"Mother taught us to play," Nora said softly then, shaking him with her sudden candor. "She liked to entertain us in the evenings. The sad ones were always her favorite, but we could persuade her to play reels if we promised to read her the letters you wrote us."

Mother. He stiffened as a fresh rush of sadness flooded him. She had been the kindest, gentlest soul. Nothing but sweet and good, with the compassion of an angel and a faultless ability to see the best in everyone around her, she had been the heart of the family. She had been many years younger than Crispin's father, whose first wife had died birthing a stillborn daughter. Where the old duke had been aloof and cool, Mother had been the opposite. When she had died unexpectedly while he was on the Continent at war, it had eaten him alive.

It touched his black heart to think his mother had longed to hear the silly epistles he'd written his young sisters. His words had always been careless and light, never alluding to the horrors of battle. Even the letters he had sent to Mother had been carefully expunged of anything that would cause her undue worry from afar. All the time he had been gone, he had imagined no one had truly missed him. That his family had simply carried on in his absence, as if he were a wound that had healed over to form a scar. A memory and nothing more. Had he been wrong?

"Brother?"

Nora's voice, questioning and tinged with confusion, jolted his wandering mind from its reminiscences. He blinked, focusing on her, but his vision was suddenly blurred. He blinked more furiously, frowning. Why were his cursed eyes wet?

"Are you crying?" Con asked in hushed tones.

No, he damn well was not. Gritting his teeth, he reached into his coat and extracted a monogrammed handkerchief, dabbing at his infernal eyes that refused to cooperate. "Of course not," he dismissed. "I am merely..."

Brimstone and Beelzebub.

He was *crying* like a babe. The liquid in his eyes was *tears*.

What in the bloody hell? Such a revolting show of weakness had not emerged from him since the day he had killed his first soldier on the field of battle, and even then, the liquid in his eyes had been more a product of his violent retching of bile than anything else.

He scrubbed at his eyes with more force than necessary before hastily stuffing the scrap of fabric back into his coat. "Miss Turnbow trounced on my toe," he announced, daring anyone to contradict him.

Bad enough he had been assailed by such a lowering, unacceptable emotion as melancholy. But to have been witnessed turning into a watering pot by three females, two of whom were his minx sisters and one of whom was the woman he wanted to tup until his cock went raw... it was the outside of enough.

"You are weeping," Nora said in the same tones she might use to announce he had sprouted cloven hooves.

"That was a lovely rendition of 'Mrs. McCleod'," came the firm, dulcet voice of Miss Governess as she swished past him. "Thank you for playing, Lady Honora and Lady Constance, but I do fear the hour grows late, and it is already half past eight."

The heady fragrance of jasmine trailed in her wake, and for the first time it occurred to him it was rather odd for a woman of her reduced circumstances to wear a scent. Then again, the only females he dallied with these days were strumpets, and even they perfumed themselves equally above and below.

He cleared his throat, pretending he had not just made a fool of himself, for what else was he to do? "If you will excuse me, sisters and Miss Turnbow, I have some urgent correspondence to which I must attend. Thank you again for the evening's entertainment."

"Pray forgive me for my misstep," Miss Governess could not resist calling after him as he gave them his back and made a hasty retreat like the coward he was.

"You are forgiven, Miss Governess," he clipped, not bothering to turn about. Not wishing to face her knowing gaze or the wonderment of his sisters. Not even certain how such a thing as his unrefined, unfettered feelings had come to be. He had thought himself impervious to that rot.

Tears. Crying like a bloody maudlin female.

He slammed the door at his back. It was not to be borne. There was only one swift solution he could countenance. One reliable means of dulling the unwanted intrusion of old ghosts and grief.

The time was half past eight, Miss Governess had said, and he had not had a drop of whisky since yesterday at The Duke's Bastard. That injustice was about to be rectified, posthaste.

CHAPTER TEN

S OMEONE HAD BEEN in his study.

Crispin made the realization the moment he sat down at his desk, glass of whisky in hand. His correspondence was not stacked in the neat order in which he had left it, bound by a ribbon and ordered according to the date of receipt. Several envelopes were scattered in a paper waterfall, and the ribbon was nowhere to be seen. His quill and ink had been moved. The letter he had been in the process of writing to the dowager Marchioness of Searle had been smudged.

Suspecting Con and Nora of yet another prank involving a creature or a carcass, he lowered his glass to the polished surface of his desk and began a cursory inventory. Aside from the misplacement of his papers and the missing ribbon, everything appeared to be in order.

He opened each drawer, taking care to rummage about lest the minxes had hidden something prone to rot and stink. About a month ago, they had left a decaying potato beneath his bed, and his chamber had been befouled and uninhabitable for an entire evening before a chamber maid discovered the source of the stench and removed the malodorous thing. The carpet had required a thorough scouring, and he had been ready to tan their hides.

When he reached the drawer where he kept the journals he had written during his years at war, a scratch upon the lock gave him pause. He had not known his sisters to attempt to pick locks, but the effort had clearly been made. Anger unfurled in his gut. His journals were private, damn it. Did the hoydens know no bounds?

Retrieving the key from his pocket, he unlocked the drawer. What he found within was more troubling than a rotting potato or a dead mouse, however. His journals seemed to be in their proper order, the small leather-bound volume he'd kept during his first year of war atop the tidy pile.

Just to be certain, he extracted it, flipping through the pages of his familiar scrawl. Tucked almost imperceptibly between the pages of battle observations, he discovered not one but two folded notes.

Frowning, he removed them, unfolding the first and scanning the contents. Not only did he not recognize the handwriting, but he could not make sense of the gibberish scribbled upon the page. A series of letters that failed to make words, the note rather called to mind the enciphered dispatches of French soldiers that had repeatedly fallen into the hands of the Spanish guerilla fighters.

This did not seem like the work of his sisters. Con and Nora had yet to learn the finer art of subtlety. When they made mischief, the results were obvious, whether it be a shrieking governess or an unpardonable stench.

The second note contained more of the same nonsensical alphabetic lines. Retrieving the other two journals from his drawer, he searched them as well, until he had unearthed a total of seven letters altogether, all penned in the same neat hand, all a sequence of letters that appeared to bear no obvious pattern. An icy chill he could not shake settled deep in his bones. These were no ordinary letters, and though he had not an inkling as to their contents, he was willing to wager everything he owned that they were not the product of hoydenish tomfoolery.

But why would someone pick the lock on his drawer and hide ciphered letters within it? More to the point, who would do such a thing? Whoever it was, he had done an abysmal job at covering his tracks, for he had left quite an easy trail for Crispin to follow. Indeed, the fellow was likely a novice to make so many errors.

Briefly, his mind flitted to his run-in with Miss Turnbow on her first night as governess. She had been in his study, trespassing where she did not belong, had she not? But a governess who went about stashing ciphered letters in his desk drawer seemed as farfetched as a Gothic novel.

The person responsible had placed the letters where he had for a reason, and if Crispin wished to catch the villain at his game, there was only one manner in which he could conceive of doing it. Allowing his whisky to go untouched, he painstakingly copied each letter before placing the originals back in his journals, stacking them in their place within the drawer, and locking it once more.

There was only one man in all London he trusted. One man upon whom he knew he could rely for anything he required. Crispin hastily scrawled a note to accompany the copies, tucked the lot into an envelope, and sent the missive on its way before going in search of the one quarry he longed to corner more than the scoundrel who had planted the worrying letters in his desk.

Miss Jacinda Turnbow.

A glance at his pocket watch revealed that she would be completing her daily duties at any moment. His timing was perfect.

The mystery of the bloody ciphers could wait until tomorrow morning. For now, he had far more pressing matters to concern him.

JACINDA WAS STILL puzzling over the Duke of Whitley's inexplicable behavior when she left Lady Constance and Lady Honora behind for the evening. They had said their prayers, washed their hands and faces, and settled into bed for the night. One fortnight into her tenure as governess, and she could not help but feel she had made wondrous progress with the girls. They had come a long way from the hellions of her first day. And while she had never before acted as governess, delighted in her accomplishment. Challenges had ever thrilled her, and Lady Honora and Lady Constance were no exception.

Nor was their brother.

Thoughts of the handsome, wicked duke brought the inevitable frown and accompanying amalgam of guilt and anger. She stepped into the hallway, headed in the direction of her comfortable apartments, so mired in her thoughts, she did not realize she wasn't alone until it was too late to flee.

She stopped, her skirts swirling around her ankles with the force of her cessation of motion. Her hand went to her wildly slamming heart, willing it to calm. She swallowed and licked lips that had gone dry.

The Duke of Whitley leaned his hip against the papered wall, the flickering light of the candle sconces bathing him in a golden glow. She was not certain if he had given her a fright with his unexpected presence or simply by being a man she did not dare trust herself to be alone with.

This morning had been a revelation. So, too, had the evening. He had attempted to seduce her and make her his mistress. And then, shockingly, he had listened to her impassioned speech. Most stupefying of all, he had been on his best behavior following dinner, conversing with his sisters, humoring them by dancing to their reel.

And crying at the mentioning of his dead mother.

Her heart still hurt to recall the grief in his expression, the vulnerability, the confusion. He had been perplexed by his own emotion, and a fierce urge to protect him had risen within her. One she could not quite tamp down as she knew she must.

Feelings.

How very vexing.

She was susceptible to the Duke of Whitley, and not just physically as she had supposed that morning following her utter folly. But emotionally as well. He was dark and wounded, and something in him called to something primitive in her. She could not shake the impression there was a great deal more to the man behind the façade he presented to the world. That he was suffering and jaded and bitter, desperate for redemption.

And she was the one who would snatch it from his grasp.

She went cold.

"Your Grace," Jacinda whispered, mindful of the fact that voices could carry in the hall at this quiet time of night, when the servants had dwindled in ranks and most of the day's tasks had been done. "Is something amiss?"

"Something is amiss," he said. "Yes."

And still he did not move. Did not elaborate.

She drank in the sight of him in a way that ought to shame her. Heat settled between her thighs, chasing the cold. She told herself it was a base physical need. Somehow, he had unleashed an old urge in her that she had thought long gone. Her flesh was not yet dead, apparently. But her honor and duty both precluded her from seeking solace in the bed of the man before her.

"Is there something you require of me?" she asked, her cheeks going hot when she realized the unintentional implications of her query. "In regard to my charges, that is?"

He grinned. "How good of you to clarify the nature of your question, for I was about to respond in a manner most unbecoming of the gentleman I am."

She snorted, the lateness of the evening and the intimacies they had shared making her bold. "I was not aware you are a gentleman at all."

"By birth, though not by nature," he agreed, a devastating grin on his lips.

Still, he did not move. Did not go away as she hoped he would. Her ability to resist him waned by the moment. If he had been arrogant and cruel, if he had been clipped and demanding, hiding himself behind his disdain and his superiority and his power over her, she would have continued on her way. But this Whitley was far more dangerous even than the man who had kissed her and stripped half her gown away in his study.

"Perhaps you are more of a gentleman by nature than you suppose," she suggested softly.

He inclined his head, his sudden proximity to her disturbing. "I am a soldier, madam, and a soldier must be adept at playing any role given him even when it does not suit."

To her dismay, she realized he had not moved. It had been she who had drawn closer to him, like a blossom growing toward the sun. She stopped, pressed damp palms to her gown, willed her galloping heart to calm its pace.

"Do you mean to suggest being a gentleman does not suit you?" she dared to ask, the need to prolong their interaction unassailable. She told herself it was for the good of her task that she encouraged candid speech between them. Perhaps in this fashion, she might discover truths about the Duke of Whitley that might have otherwise evaded her.

"Not any more than being a soldier did," he said somberly.

"You did not enjoy being a soldier?" If surprise tinged her voice, it could not be helped. Aside from the secret suspicion cast upon him by the Earl of Kilross, public consensus of the Duke of Whitley was he was a celebrated hero who had exhibited fearlessness and unmitigated bravery on the field of battle.

His gaze shuttered. "No."

She stared at him, wishing she could read him better, but he was far more complex than any cipher whose secrets she had ever attempted to unlock. If he was truly guilty of conspiring with the French, why could she not find evidence of his sins? How could Kilross be so very certain of the veracity of his claims when Jacinda had spent the better part of half a month attempting to unearth a modicum of proof without success?

Perhaps, whispered her heart, *he is innocent after all.*

That notion frightened her the most, for she realized now she wanted more than anything for it to be true. She wanted to pry open every lock at Whitley House, search each scrap of paper, and return to Kilross with not one shred of evidence against the duke.

She searched for something else to say into the heavy silence that had fallen betwixt them, some means by which she might continue their dialogue, before settling upon the grief he had displayed earlier that evening. "I suppose you missed your family."

Of course it was a soldier's fate that he spent his days, months, and even years from his home and hearth and all who were dear to him. Jacinda had known it on the day she had bid James farewell and sent him on his way with a kiss and her heart. But that did not mean that every day she'd spent without him had not hurt like a festering wound.

Nor did it mean she had not agonized over the knowledge he had spent his final living moments alone, bleeding to death in the snow of a strange land as if he were no better than a slaughtered hog. The old pain, the flooding, intense surge of grief so fierce it threatened to consume her, rose like a tide.

"Of course I missed them," he shocked her by admitting. "I did not realize how much, perhaps, until today."

She frowned, a fresh assault of guilt mingling with her other unsteady emotions. She felt raw all over, like skin that had been abraded to the quick. "Lady Constance and Lady Honora were pleased to share their keen talents with you. Thank you for humoring them."

"I should have given them more of my time and attentions long ago." His voice was low and rough. "It would seem you are not as inadequate in your role as governess as I would have initially believed."

The duke's words were far from praise, but somehow coming

from his unforgiving mien, she recognized they were as close as he could manage to an apology for his ire of that morning. A heated warmth pervaded, chasing away the icy chill caused by the strains of the present and the pain of her past.

"Thank you, Your Grace," she managed. "If you will excuse me, I must seek my chamber as well. My charges require me to be well-rested in the morning."

But something in his expression made her linger when she should have curtsied and skirted around him, hastening her stride on her way to safety. His frank regard was warm upon her, and it glittered with an intensity that had not been present before. She wanted to look away. To treat him as the Gorgon she knew and flee.

She could not stop staring. He was so very handsome in his buff breeches, navy superfine coat, and snowy cravat. His dark hair had a slight curl to the ends, and she longed to run her fingers through it just once more. It had been softer than the sleekest of furs.

"Would you care to join me in the library instead, Miss Turnbow?" he invited, his deep voice sliding over her like a naughty caress.

If only she could, but if anything, this evening had served to remind her of the disparities between them. Not only was she the governess, and he the master of the house, she, his subordinate in every way, but she was also deceiving him with each moment that passed.

She had been mad to entertain, even for the spate of a few wild moments in his arms, the pull she felt toward him. Even if he had not committed the sins he was suspected of, he remained beyond her touch. She was a simple soldier's widow. He was a duke, a man who would make her his mistress rather than his duchess. Jacinda must not forget.

She shook her head. "It would not be proper, Your Grace."

His expression hardened, the angle of his jaw going tense. "We are beyond proper, Miss Governess. Surely you recognize that by now."

Back to *Miss Governess* again. They had skirted each other as if in wary battle formations, and now they had returned to the place where they had begun. Nothing had changed. Or had it?

"We are not beyond propriety," she denied, at last calling to mind the futility and danger of remaining in his presence a moment more. She made to swish past him on her way to her private apartments.

Whitley stepped into her path, blocking her dismissal of him. "I had you half-naked on my desk this morning."

Much to her shame.

And wicked enjoyment.

No.

She banished the rogue thought from her mind, knowing she must stay the course. She had a duty to carry out. Kilross was not a patient or benevolent man, and he held all the power. She was but his puppet.

I had you half-naked on my desk this morning.

Lord in heaven. Those sinful words should not make her weak. Should not make her ache.

"I bid you good evening, Your Grace," she forced past lips that did not wish to oblige, stepping around him and continuing on her way as though he had not just set her aflame with his velvet reminder of the liberties she had allowed him. The liberties she had so freely and wantonly given.

"I had not taken you for a coward, Miss Governess, but I can see I was wrong," he called after her, his words and his husky baritone both a taunt.

A gauntlet.

Jacinda whirled about, picked it up. She was not a coward, and nor was she a spiritless miss who would cower when presented with a challenge. "I shall grant you one quarter hour, Your Grace."

"An hour," he countered, a smug grin curving his generous lips.

Lips she recalled working skillfully over hers.

Drat. She must not allow such deplorable thoughts. "Half an hour."

"An hour."

She gritted her teeth. "I believe you suffer from a misconception, sir. This is not the manner in which a compromise works. You made your offer, and I raised mine by fifteen minutes in an effort to appease you. However, your counter remained the same as your initial offer."

His grin grew, flashing a row of white, even teeth. How rare was the sight of his full, heart-clenching charm. For a moment, she could forget everything and everyone but him.

And then he spoke again, dispelling the fancy. "I am more than familiar with compromise, my dear Miss Governess. It is merely that I have no intention of engaging in it with you. I wish an hour of your time, and an hour is what I shall have."

The devil. "Half an hour is all I can spare."

He raised a brow. "Two half hours is what I require."

The utter *scoundrel.* "That is still one whole hour."

Whitley's grin only deepened, as if he were enjoying their banter, the knave. "Miss Governess, I do believe you are proficient at arithmetic as well as all the other requisite fields of study."

"Here is further proof of my aptitude in that subject: subtract one proficient governess from your household on account of your lack of compromise, and zero governesses shall remain," she pointed out, because she could not stifle her tongue, could not extinguish her pride.

He extended his arm to her. "I have a different sort of arithmetic in mind. Take one governess who needs to maintain her post, add one demanding duke who can easily dismiss her without reference, and what do you have? Forgive me if I am wrong, but I do believe what remains is a thoroughly routed Miss Governess and a duke who continues to eschew compromise. Allow me to escort you to the library."

She went. Because his arithmetic was painfully correct.

It was hers that was wrong, for she could not leave her position or this house until she had completed the loathsome task assigned her.

She needed to find evidence of his guilt or she and Father faced utter ruin.

Perhaps spending time alone with him was the sole means by which she could have her answers. She could only hope it would not also prove her downfall.

DRAGOONING MISS TURNBOW into joining him in the library was not one of his finer moments. Crispin was willing to admit this to himself if no one else as he poured brandy into a snifter, aware of her unsettling gaze upon him. Those golden-brown orbs of hers did not miss a bloody thing, and he spent half his time in her presence feeling as if she saw straight through to his marrow and half feeling as if she could not abide his loathsome presence.

"Would you care for a brandy, Miss Turnbow?" he asked with a calm he did not feel.

Ordinarily, whisky was his poison of choice, but somehow brandy seemed a safer, more gentlemanly spirit to consume in the presence of a lady. Curse it, when had he begun to concern himself with such nonsense? The ladies in his presence generally served one purpose.

"No thank you, Your Grace," came her soft, husky voice. "It would not be—"

"Proper," he finished for her, pouring a splash into a second snifter. "Propriety can go hang."

"Propriety would gladly hang a governess who overstepped her bounds with a duke," she reminded him quietly.

It was true, damn it. Of course it was, and the conscience he ordinarily drowned in whisky emerged. She was at the mercy of her reputation. No house of distinction would hire a governess who had been closeted alone with her employer in such a fashion. His time away from London had dulled him to the tedious vagaries of the *ton*.

He had spent so many years away from civilized society that returning was an anathema to him. He had never wanted to come back.

After Morgan had been taken by *El Corazón Oscuro*, Crispin had been determined to vindicate his friend or die trying. But then his brother's death had come as well, and he had been forced to return to England and a different sort of duty entirely. Also unwanted. Also grim.

He turned to her, a snifter in each hand, pleased beyond measure she was here with him now and yet disgusted with himself for all but forcing her to. "You are free to leave, Miss Turnbow. I will not hold you against your will."

She eyed him warily as he approached, offering her the glass. She made no move to accept it, but neither did she flee, and he took it as a hopeful sign. "I confess I do not understand your motivations, Your Grace. You press me for my presence here and now that you have it, you tell me I am free to go."

He knew a moment of shame. "You have always been free to go. I did not force you here."

She sniffed. "Coerced."

His brows shot up. By God, she was a forthright article, and it delighted and vexed him in equal measure. "I beg your pardon?"

But Miss Turnbow would not be intimidated. "You coerced me. I plainly exhibited to you a wish to find my chambers and retire. You intimated that if I did not join you, I would be in danger of losing my position. I need this position, and therefore, here I am, Your Grace. But that does not mean I need imbibe with you."

He lost his patience with her. With himself. "Let us be clear, then. You need not be present in this room. You need not accept this snifter of brandy, though it is of an exceptional quality and I highly recommend its bracing effects. You may retreat to your chamber and God knows what manner of book you read until the early hours of the morn. I shall not dismiss you or send you forth without reference. I am not so desperate or depraved yet that I will force a woman to spend time in my company. Therefore, if you do not wish to be in this library, be gone with you, and make haste so that you need not suffer my presence a moment more."

But Miss Turnbow surprised him yet again by refusing to move. She stared at him, her expressive eyes darkening. "How would you know that I am reading until the early hours of the morning?"

Blast. Now she would think he skulked about her door in the night, looking for an excuse to barge in and ravish her. Not that the prospect wasn't a fantasy of his... only in the fantasy, he did not ravish but rather plundered what she so willingly offered.

He swallowed and bit his inner cheek to stave off any unwanted surges of hunger. Seduction had not been his intention in inviting her here. His motivation was far more disconcerting. He had simply wanted her company.

"I have received reports on the inordinate expense of candles being supplied to you," he lied.

In truth, he roamed the halls at night when slumber could not even be achieved by drinking himself to oblivion. Pacing for hours was sometimes a means by which he might sufficiently weary himself enough to pitch into his bed for a scant few hours without being plagued by nightmares. When he closed his eyes, the day in the farmhouse returned to him, all the scents and sounds and fears. Inevitably, he lay in bed at night as a band of fear tightened around his chest until he could not breathe. Only exertion or drink could dull his mind enough to grant him rest.

If he saw a light beneath her door, it was because of the peripatetic journeys his ravaged mind forced him to make.

Thankfully, she did not see through his ruse. "The cost of the candles ought to be deducted from my wages, of course. I should have exercised more care than to so greedily burn them in the pursuit of my own distraction."

He had committed far greater sins than wearing candles down to nubs in his pursuit of distraction. "I do not mind the expense," he said curtly.

Her lips tightened for a moment's hesitation. "You only wish for my company and not for anything more?"

Of course he wished for something more than her mere presence. He wished for *everything*, but that did not mean he would not take up what she would give him like a beggar boy being thrown a scrap of meat.

He cleared his throat. "I wish for your presence, freely given. If you are offering it, Miss Governess, I accept. If not, run along and read your books all night long."

"I will remain." She was solemn as she plucked the snifter from his hand. "But you must promise me to maintain propriety."

There it was again, the thorn upon a rose. *Bloody hell*, if there was any word he was beginning to detest, it was surely that one. *Propriety.* He could not speak it aloud without the urge to spit. A viler epithet he could not countenance.

"Your virtue is safe this night." He gestured to the chairs flanking a fire that crackled merrily in the grate. "Please do sit, Miss Turnbow. It has been a long day, and I have a pressing urge to settle my bones."

She eyed him as warily as one might an enemy soldier who had just surrendered. Her distrust of him was apparent in her rigid bearing. Fair enough. He did not trust himself with her either.

"I expect my fichu to be returned to me," she surprised him by demanding.

In her haste to escape his evil clutches, Miss Governess had left behind her delicate, altogether too large, lace fichu. The very one that obstructed his view of her delectable bosom. Because he had a history with the cursed thing, he had stuffed it inside his coat pocket. And later, slipped it beneath his pillow for reasons he did not wish to explore.

The bloody atrocity smelled of her, and while he could not approve of its use, he was wholeheartedly in favor of having something that smelled of her close at hand.

"No." The answer left him of its own volition. For the same reasons he had stowed the adornment beneath his pillow, he was also unwilling to part with it.

His response made her brows snap together. "No?"

"It cannot be returned to you, as I have burned the thing." A prevarication he would gladly make as a mark upon what remained of his soul, for he would not admit to keeping her fichu so he could smell jasmine and stroke his cock when the need arose. Which had been once already that day, as it happened.

Sparks flared in her sherry eyes. "You had no right to destroy one of my garments. That lace was quite dear in price, I will have you know."

With his snifter, he gestured to the replacement fichu she wore now. "You seem to have managed in its absence with another abomination."

Delightful pink color kissed her cheeks. "For the purpose of washing, and in case any fichu requires mending, I own three."

He made a chastising sound with his tongue on the roof of his mouth. "Two now, I am afraid. None at all if I had my way."

Displeasure firmed her full lips into a tight line. "My *toilette* is none of your concern, Your Grace."

That was where she was wrong. Everything about her was his concern. From the moment she had turned up in his study in her drab, shapeless gowns and her fichus and her nonsensical caps, she had become the force propelling him through each day. He spent his hours alternately consumed with desire for her, hating his weakness, and fashioning the means by which he could spend more time in her presence.

"On the contrary." He took a sip of his brandy, timing his rebuttal to heighten her discomfit. He liked her when she lost her rigid grip upon the reins of her control. "If you are instructing Lady Honora and Lady Constance in the feminine arts, should you not demonstrate an aptitude for the fashionable?"

If it was possible to flay a man alive with a murderous glare, she would have done him in then and there. "Your Grace, forgive me, but my dress does not inhibit my ability to teach Lady Honora and Lady Constance French, Latin, and German. Nor does it limit my instruction on music or art or any other topic suitable for ladies of their distinction."

He had promised to behave, and yet something in him did not wish to honor that promise. There was no means by which she could reclaim the bloody fichu. And now that he had warmed to his subject, he realized he longed to see her in fine gowns that flaunted her glorious figure and displayed her beauty rather than cloaking it.

"I know of an excellent *modiste*," he suggested even though he knew what her response would be. What it had to be, as long as she continued to refuse his offer. "You need not settle for anything less than the best."

She laughed, but it was a mirthless, forced little sound and it made him long to hear her true laughter instead. "On a governess's wages, I must settle for what I already own, even if others see fit to thieve it from me."

"You need not live on the wages of a governess," he reminded her. "I have ample blunt to spare."

She had rejected him. Denied him. He couldn't lie to himself—her rebuff had smarted. But later, it occurred to him he had bungled his seduction rather badly. She was an unwed female, an innocent, and he had treated her in the same fashion he would any camp moll. He had waylaid her, savaged her with kisses, and half-stripped her bare in this study like the unstable beast that he was.

Sometimes, it was difficult for him to recall this was not war. That his time on the battlefield was at an end. After spending years away from polite society, engaged in the bloody, dirty, gritty business of death, returning to ballrooms and simpering misses seemed the world's cruelest joke.

But Miss Turnbow was no simpering miss.

And he wanted her still.

She had stiffened at his pointed words, and he noted her grip on her snifter had grown so tight, he could perfectly see the delineation of each knuckle. How delicious that she did not wear gloves, though her countenance suggested that was the only luck he would have this evening.

"It would not behoove a woman in my circumstances to accept such an offer, Your Grace," she pointed out, irritation rendering her tone pert. "Tell me, what would I do after you grew tired of me? No respectable house would open its doors to me. I would be forced to earn my bread on my back."

Her words were not all untrue, though it pained him to admit it to himself. But his need for her remained, and in his desperation to get what he wanted, he could not envision a time when he would ever grow weary of her in his bed. "The terms would be most generous. I would pay you handsomely. Leave you with enough funds to settle you quite comfortably."

If he had expected her acceptance, more fool he, for her eyes flashed and her lips thinned. "You told me you would be a gentleman, Your Grace, else I would not have joined you here. Such a despicable topic is not fit for further addressing, and indeed is best forever forgotten, as though it had never been spoken of at all."

Truth be told, her protest rather stung. He wanted her more than ever. Need was a fierce, hungry creature taking up residence in his blood. It ran thick and hot and heavy through his veins, setting him aflame.

"I am being a gentleman," he countered, taking a fortifying sip of his brandy. "Is this not an acceptable distance between us? I have not even attempted to touch or kiss you once, though there is nothing I long to do more on this earth than fling that cap from your head and pluck each pin away so that I might see the glory of your hair running unbound down your back."

Her color deepened, but she did not flee from his honesty as he had suspected she might. Instead, she brought her own snifter to her lips and took a tentative sip of the spirits he'd poured her. She gave a delicate shudder before returning her attention to him.

Her gaze was as pointed as a bayonet. "Words speak as loudly as deeds, Your Grace."

Yes, and all his words said that he wanted her. Of course he did, else he would not be so consumed by her. He wanted to believe it was the notion of securing the unattainable, a woman so firmly settled in her notion of seeing out her life in the thankless position of governess. He also wanted to believe her deliberate attempts to diminish her allure heightened his curiosity and arousal. That he had grown bored with his wastrel's life, and she was the diversion he required until the next comely, supple-breasted diversion appeared.

Certainly, her denial had sparked an answering surge of humiliation and anger in him. No one had denied him as he could recall, not before he was the Duke of Whitley, when he had been a soldier on the battlefield and sure as hell not afterward when he had returned to the undeserved praise of the masses. Ladies, strumpets, even lords and dowagers, former friends and enemies, and lovers, all wanted their piece of the Duke of Whitley.

Except for Miss Jacinda Turnbow, who was neither in awe of him nor susceptible enough to his rakish persuasion that she would give him what he wanted.

"Words are safer than deeds," he countered, watching closely for her reaction.

A wistful grin curved her lips, the first semblance of a true smile he had seen from her. "Sometimes words are far more dangerous."

He could not help but feel there was a hidden meaning to her words. He continued to study the paradox that was Miss Jacinda Turnbow, who had come to him in his time of need and accepted the Sisyphean task of molding his sisters into proper young ladies. Why had she taken the position? Surely, she could have found a better situation, if not a grander home. More money even, perhaps, than the twenty pounds per annum he was paying her.

"I have seen deeds that defy words," he said into the silence that had fallen between them, and he wished he had not. Speaking of the war aloud always made his gut swim with bile and his skin go slick with sweat. "Believe me, Miss Turnbow, deeds can be far more vicious, particularly when accompanied by bullets, bayonets, and swords."

"You speak of your time as a soldier, do you not?" she asked softly, drawing nearer at last.

He did not want to think of the horrors he had seen ever again. But they were never gone. Like the scent of the French captain's charred flesh, like the sight of Morgan's severed hand in a river of blood, like the enemy soldiers who had been buried alive, their eyes pecked out by ravens...they would remain a part of him forever. Sometimes, the memories swelled, pressing inside his skull, becoming insurmountable until he could do nothing but purge them by drowning himself in enough liquor to stupefy him.

His hand shook as he downed the rest of his brandy. "If there is any topic that is despicable conversation and not fit for further addressing, it is war."

Her gaze was wide, taking him in, *seeing* him, and he could not look away. "You must have endured a great deal, Your Grace."

Yes, he bloody well had, but nothing compared to the macabre end Morgan had faced. Crispin had not been vigilant enough that day at the farmhouse. He should have known better than to meet El Corazón

Oscuro with nothing more than a handful of men on the periphery who were easily slain when attacked from behind. He should have been the one who was killed. The one who was tortured.

Morgan was a brilliant soldier, a skilled intelligence officer, a bold and daring man with an intuitive wit. He had been too valuable to lose. Crispin should never have blundered that day. If he had been a better man, a better soldier, a better damned friend, Morgan would still be alive today. Guilt had not the capacity to heal. It only ate a man alive, slowly, from the inside, until nothing remained.

"I endured less than I deserved," he choked out, rising from his chair and stalking back toward his decanter. He kept his back to her, not wanting her to see the unrest coursing through him. Not wishing to see either pity or fear in her expression.

His heart beat faster now, a rapid staccato in his chest. His palms were sweaty, his mouth dry, hands shaking so violently he was almost incapable of refilling his snifter with brandy.

But it was the elixir he needed, as close to a panacea as he could reasonably get. He sloshed a more than generous quantity of brandy into the glass and raised it to his lips once, twice, thrice. Refilled the cursed thing. Drank more, gulping it down as though the stuff was air and he was a man who had been buried alive for so long, he could not inhale enough at one time.

His intention to go slowly this evening had dissipated. The need to numb himself became paramount.

"What happened to you, Your Grace?"

The quiet question, spoken in her soft, soothing tone, pierced the fog of fear and pain and horror cloaking his mind. He suspected he was on the edge of experiencing another fit. In the last year, they had become more and more frequent, vile spells during which he could not shake the memories of what had happened to him, what had happened to Morgan and so many of his comrades. And when he could not elude the memories, his body and mind became hopelessly confused, as though both were convinced he had returned to those dark days.

That could not occur. Would not occur. He could not afford for such an obscene burst of weakness to lay him low now, not before her. He had experienced fits before whores in the past—it was inevitable when a man spent his days and nights as he did. One had been terrified. Another had been intrigued, wondering if she could use his fears and the darkness residing within him to bring them mutual pleasure. The pleasure had been on her end alone.

He drank more brandy, inhaled deeply. The delicious scent of jasmine entered his nose and lungs. She had skirted nearer to him. He could feel her proximity like the charge in the air before a lightning strike. Still, he did not move to face her.

"Your Grace?" she persisted, her voice closer, softer. "Will you tell me?"

Was it his imagination, or did her hand pass over his shoulder blade in the ghost of a touch? He swallowed down another gulp of brandy before forcing himself to speak. "I fought the enemy until I could no longer fight him. Until my brother passed away and I was left with a title I never wanted and two sisters I can scarcely understand."

"You must have suffered in Spain."

Miss Governess had reached beyond her touch with the probing observation. Anger collided with the unrest within him, and he became a powder keg. Turning to her at last, he stalked closer, not caring that her eyes widened and her brows rose. Not giving a damn that her hand fluttered to her heart. Not even concerned he could read the fear sparkling in her sherry eyes. She ought to bloody well fear him.

He could not be trusted in her presence. His promise to play the gentleman had been smashed to bits by his inability to control himself. What nonsense had he fooled himself into believing? What in God's name had he hoped to accomplish with this infernal prolonging of his inner torture?

He did not stop until he had chased her to the opposite end of the library, and she had nowhere left to flee with a wall of books against her back. Embracing the rage, for it kept his demons at bay, he tossed his snifter into the fireplace. It exploded into glittering shards as it met with brick.

Crispin slammed his palms against the books, lowering his head so he invaded her air the same way she had attempted to invade his mind. "I do not speak of Spain, madam. If you value your position in this household, you will never again mention it in my presence."

Her long lashes swept down over her eyes, and when they raised, it was as if she had donned a mask. The fear was gone. Her gaze was steady and unrelenting as it burned into his. "If you think to intimidate me with your brutish ways and your superior size, you are bound to be sadly disappointed, Your Grace."

His cheeks went hot at her easy read of him, damn her hide. "If you think to remain beneath this roof one more night, you will conduct yourself with the humility befitting your station."

But she did not flinch. "Will you turn me out into the streets, then?"

Of course he would not.

He sneered. "Do not think my desire to bed you allows you liberties, Miss Governess. We are not equals. It is not your place to question me."

Her lips tightened almost imperceptibly, the only reaction she gave. "You were trembling," she observed.

Devil take it. "I do not tremble."

"You still are," she insisted, shocking him even further by touching his jaw in a feather-light caress. "Here."

He swallowed as a violent rush of need tore through him. Everything in him wanted to claim this woman as his. But he ground down the instinct and gritted his teeth. "There are other areas of my anatomy that require your attention, my dear, should you like to attend them as well."

She inhaled as though his crude suggestion had shaken her, and yet she did not remove her touch. "I think you do not need a mistress so much as you need a friend, Your Grace."

A bark of bitter laughter left him. "And you fancy you could take on that role, I gather? You may save your friendship for someone who wants it. The only thing I want from you is between your pretty thighs."

She jolted then, as if he had struck her, jerking her hand away from him. He felt the loss of her like a fist to the gut. Shame washed over him. He had been deliberately cruel and crude, but he felt no better for knowing he had finally bested her.

Her chin went up. "I will *never* give you what you want, Your Grace." She held her forgotten snifter to him. "Here you are. Perhaps you will find the solace you need in spirits just as you have done every day and night to no avail."

He pushed himself away from the shelving and accepted her mocking offer, tossing back the contents in one swift pull. "I have a different sort of solace in mind. If you will not oblige me, I have no doubt I can find two or three who will."

Her face went pale. "I shall bid you good evening then, Your Grace, and wish you all prosperity in finding two or three such inclined persons."

He watched her go, her bearing as regal as any queen.

After the door closed, he counted to fifteen before hurling her snifter into the fireplace to join the first.

CHAPTER ELEVEN

*T*HE DUKE OF *Whitley kissed her throat. His hands swept over her breasts as the stubble of his whiskers abraded her jaw. A pang of need surged between her thighs. His body was large and warm, dominating hers.*

"I want you," he whispered against her skin.

Her fingers threaded through his thick, soft hair. It seemed she could not get close enough. She wanted him deep inside her.

"I want you, too," she confessed, the words leaving her on a sigh as one of his big hands swept the hem of her nightrail over her legs. Higher and higher he went, and she was on fire with ecstasy, unable to deny either of them what they so badly wanted.

Nothing else mattered. It was as if they were the only two people in the world, lost until they had found each other…

The feral cry of a wounded animal hauled Jacinda from the depths of a feverish dream. Heart pounding, she jolted upright, the bedclothes falling about her waist. Cool night air kissed her skin, wringing a shiver from her. Inhaling a deep, steadying breath, she willed her thudding heart to calm, and listened.

Angels in heaven, that depraved dream. Shame washed over her. Where had it come from? Why did it plague her now when she must be more steadfast than ever in her determination to resist the lures of the Duke of Whitley? For days following their encounter in the library, he had avoided her, and she had been glad of his absence. Relieved when he had sent terse missives to inform her she need not attend their daily briefings. Satisfied when he carved out time for his sisters and requested she spend that same time otherwise occupied.

For even if he was innocent of the crimes laid against him as she had begun to believe, there was no future for the two of them. If she became his mistress, she would become a pariah forever. And he would never, ever wed her, she reminded herself. As a duke, he remained well above her touch. She was Mrs. Jacinda Turnbow, daughter of Sir Robert Smythe, simple soldier's widow, who lived in comfortable obscurity with her father. She preferred the company of books and ciphers to men. When the Duke of Whitley looked at her, he saw a woman he would make his mistress, not a lady he would take to wife.

And while Jacinda could not countenance the notion of becoming a wife again, neither would she even consider being any man's mistress. Especially not his. No matter how much his touch undid her, or how much her body ached for him. Alone in the darkness, she was keenly aware of the throbbing between her legs, the longing to be claimed that had not visited her in years.

Of all men, why had her traitorous body chosen to react to the Duke of Whitley?

Perhaps she had imagined the disturbance. Something had wrenched her from her slumber, but it was entirely possible the noise she fancied she had heard was part of her nonsensical dream rather than reality.

She exhaled. Inhaled again long and slow and deep. The night was still, unusually quiet for a London evening, though she supposed she had no notion of what hour it was. In the absence of sunlight, every hour was night, after all.

She still heard nothing. *There we are, then.* She had surely imagined the sound. Or it had been a part of an awful dream she did not care to repeat.

Either way, the horrible sound—real or not—did not repeat itself.

Until it did.

Raw and painful, the cry sliced straight through her even though it was muffled by the barrier of plaster and doors and distance. Only this time, she was awake. This time, she realized it was not the cry of a wounded animal at all. Rather, the strangled sound of pain had emerged from a human.

A dark, low-voiced human.

A man.

The Duke of Whitley, to be precise. She would recognize the husky, arrogant timber of his voice anywhere. She threw back the bedclothes before she could think better of her actions. Surely there was any number of other tactics she might choose when faced with such a predicament. Surely, she ought to remain safely and chastely abed where she belonged, free of scandal and ruin and, Lord help her, even worse.

The cry sounded again, keening and low.

There was such raw, violent need redolent in that long, suffering cry, as if it had been torn from him. Such pain. It struck her heart with the proficiency of a hundred tiny little picks. Digging deeper and deeper and deeper.

Without another hesitation, she rose from the bed, donning her dressing gown and belting it snugly round her waist. Her bare feet padded to the door. She opened it to the sound of another violent cry. The hall was empty, the servants and rest of the household long since abed for the night.

If she had a modicum of sense, she would return to her chamber, bolt the door, and forget she had ever heard a sound.

Her feet carried her before her mind could defeat them. Deeper into the darkness of Whitley House she went. She knew where the ducal apartments were thanks to her several trips to search for additional papers. Darkness did not deter her. Nor did reason and common sense.

All she knew was the duke was alone in his chamber. And he was suffering. And she could not bear it. She reached his door, hesitated while her rational mind attempted to convince her she was about to commit sheer folly. Her hand hovered on the latch.

Why should she go to him?

She did not even like the man.

He was arrogant. Frigid. Condescending. A drunkard and a rake-hell. She spent most of her day loathing him and the other part fearing the slivers of tenderness he could exhibit, so unexpected and sweet that they were like rays of sun after the coldest, darkest winter.

For he was also the man who had made time for his attention-starved sisters. Who had listened to her impassioned speech and implemented a change. Who had shed tears at the remembrance of his mother's death. Who kissed her so well, she knew no kiss that came after could ever compare.

She made her decision.

The door clicked open. She stepped over the threshold.

Into his dark world.

The door closed at her back. The air changed. Awareness hummed through her. She was in the Duke of Whitley's bedchamber. In the midst of the night. And for the first time, he was there as well. She could feel his presence, hear his rapid breaths.

He sounded like a horse that had just run its paces.

Though she knew she should go, her feet carried her the rest of the journey. Again, she knew her way, knew the lay of the furniture. One of the oddities of her mind was that she only needed to see anything once before she had it imprinted upon her memory forever. She knew his large bed dominated the far wall, and that it was flanked by tables on each side, that an armoire sat on the east wall, a small escritoire on the west.

His breathing increased.

Her courage flagged.

What had she been thinking, entering the duke's chamber as if she had the right? And what did she mean to do, shake him awake? Touch him? Her actions had been so reckless. So foolish. So stupid.

Jacinda spun on her heels, intent to retreat from the chamber before Whitley was ever the wiser. Her foot settled into a weak floorboard beneath the lush carpet. A loud creak spilled into the silence.

His breathing stopped.

Her heart stopped.

"Ripley?" the duke's sleep-roughened voice demanded.

Of course he would think her his valet. Jacinda had no desire to disabuse him of the notion. She pressed a hand to her heart, continuing her retreat wordlessly. The sooner she could manage to slip into the safety of the hall, the better she would feel.

Rustling bedclothes echoed through the chamber, followed by the unmistakable sound of two feet thudding on the floor. "Miss Governess."

It was not a question, but rather a statement.

She inhaled sharply and held her breath. How did he know? *It does not matter*, her mind argued. *Continue on your way. You must not falter.* In nine more steps, she would reach the door.

Heavy footsteps stalked toward her. "Jacinda. I know it is you. I smell jasmine."

For some reason, his words, which should have encouraged her flight, had the opposite effect. Perhaps it was his use of her Christian name. Perhaps it was he knew her scent, the sole luxury she allowed herself. Whatever the reason, she froze like a broken pocket watch, stopped on the last tick, unable to move beyond.

Hands settled on her shoulders, spun her about. In the darkness, she could not see him, but the lack of light only served to heighten her awareness of him. His heat blazed into her. She wanted to step into him, wrap him in her embrace. She wanted to turn and flee and never return.

"Perhaps, madam, you would care to explain why you are so adept at trespassing in the night where you do not belong," he growled. "And before you begin, do not dare to claim you fancied yourself in the library."

She swallowed. His grip on her shoulders was tight but not menacing, and his thumbs had begun to move ever so slowly, tracing the lengths of her collarbones. Almost in a caress. A frisson of something dark and delicious trilled down her spine.

"Forgive me for the intrusion, Your Grace," she managed to say, though her voice was irritatingly breathless. "I heard sounds, and I believed you were in distress. I should never have crossed the threshold. Indeed, I would not have, had I not feared you were in need of assistance."

"Sounds." His hands slid over the slopes of her shoulders, settling in the crook where her neck joined them. He toyed with the button on the high collar of her sensible nightrail that peeked out from beneath her robe. "What manner of sounds did you hear?"

Jacinda wetted her lips. "Sounds of distress, Your Grace. Groaning, moaning. I feared you were injured or otherwise in pain."

A low, wicked chuckle crackled forth then. "Did it not occur to you I may have been otherwise engaged, Miss Governess?"

She stiffened, knowing instantly what he suggested. To her great shame, she had not imagined such a depraved scenario, though she now had to admit to herself it was not far removed from reality. "I... forgive me for the egregious error, if you please, Your Grace. It was not my intention to intrude upon your solitude or privacy in any fashion. Please rest assured I will never again make such an inexcusable mistake."

"What would you have done, my dear, if you had entered the chamber only to discover I was not alone?" Wicked amusement underscored his tone.

Only he would pose such a shocking question. She supposed she would not have been at all surprised to find such a scene of corruption. Why, then, did the thought of the Duke of Whitley being *otherwise engaged* with a nameless, faceless female make her stomach clench?

"I have offered you my sincere apology, Your Grace," she said, coolly refusing to answer his query, for she did not wish to examine the answer herself. "If you will excuse me, I would very much like to return to the sanctity of my own chamber now that I am assured of your good health."

One of his hands moved from her shoulder to skim over her neck, settling at her nape. Long, thick fingers parted her hair, cupping the base of her skull. "No."

No? Surely, he could not intend to keep her here against her will, in his chamber?

"Your Grace, I beg you. It would be most improper for me to remain, and I—"

"Crispin," he interrupted.

Crispin. The name fit him, beautiful and stark. She longed to try it on her tongue. But she could not make her lips form it. "*Your Grace.* I must return to my chamber at once before my presence here is remarked upon. It would be quite ruinous indeed for the household to learn of my injudiciousness."

"Why did you come to my chamber tonight?" he asked, his voice vibrating with an intensity she could not decipher.

"You sounded as if you were in pain." The truth fled her, all she could give him. "You sounded... as if you needed someone."

To her surprise, he did not mock her or somehow render her words indecent. Instead, he did the most shocking thing of all. He leaned forward and lowered his head so their foreheads touched. His hot breath fanned over her lips.

The gesture was at once intimate and yet tender. He had not kissed her. He did not seem intent upon seduction this night. Her in the unlit stillness of his chamber, with no pretense or distractions between them, he seemed somehow different. Softer, perhaps.

"Do you know what the Spanish fighters do to their enemies, Jacinda?"

His low, bitter question, seemingly torn from him, shocked her. She expected anger from him, coldness and condescension. But harsh revelations—confessions, even—seemed incongruous for the man she had come to know.

"I am sure I do not wish to imagine," she began hesitantly, unsure of what to say.

"They bury men alive up to their necks. They nail them to church doors and trees. Rip their bodies apart and let the ravens peck them to death."

His words robbed of her breath and speech. She wanted to embrace him, but she was not sure if he would push her away. *Dear God*, the atrocities he must have witnessed at war. She was newly thankful she had never known what James had endured. His letters home had always been hopeful, filled with how much he missed her. She had always suspected he sheltered her from the vile truth of his circumstances, but he had done so knowing it would be easier for her.

"Battle is hell on earth, swords and cannon and blood and bodies, horses falling, the wounded screaming." A violent shudder tore through him, so strong she shook with the force as well. "But the savagery of the guerillas was different. They attacked field hospitals and hacked wounded French to death. They burned men alive."

The urge to comfort him could not be contained. It grew, a living thing, bigger than she was, until she could not keep herself from touching him. Her hands settled on his upper arms. Bare, firm male skin seared her palms. When she inhaled, it was his breath, and when she exhaled, hers became his.

"I am so sorry, Your Grace," she whispered, wishing with all her might there was some way she could take his pain from him and lock it away so it could never plague him again. But pain was not so easily removed once it had lodged itself in the heart, and she was not omnipotent. "I read many accounts of the war and your bravery, along with your comrades, but I cannot fathom what you must have endured."

"Ah, yes." His tone was grim. Cutting. Yet, he did not distance himself or reject her touch. "The reports of the fabled war hero. Such rot. And here I am, so sick with guilt that I cannot face my reflection in the glass. So shattered by the recollection of what I have seen and done I cannot even sleep through the night without drinking myself to oblivion or crying out like a babe in the night."

Her heart stuttered for a moment, her entire being curiously hit by the sensation she was balanced upon the head of a needle. A breath in the wrong direction and she would fall. Surely it could not be he was admitting his role in Searle's death after all, and in spite of her inability to uncover even one piece of evidence against him. "Guilt, Your Grace?"

"I am responsible for the death of my best friend." The low admission sounded as if it was torn from the deepest depths of him. "That bloody day will haunt me forever."

Trying to understand, desperate to believe she misunderstood his words, she cupped his face, wishing she could see his eyes and read his gaze. His beard stubble pricked her palms. "You cannot have been responsible."

"Oh, but I was. Searle and I were tasked with running intelligence with the Spanish guerilla fighters. The guerillero we met on the day he died was the most ruthless, untrustworthy blackguard on the entire Peninsula." He shuddered again, his breath catching. "I should have known something was amiss, that something about that day was different. I should have required a stronger force to accompany us. But I was too damned proud, and Searle and El Corazón Oscuro were arguing. Someone clubbed me over the head from behind with a musket. When I woke, the charred body of a French captain hung above me, and there was blood, so much blood. Searle's hand, still wearing his signet..."

Dear, sweet God. The tiny seed of doubt vanished, obliterated by the visceral hideousness of his recollections. No man as broken and racked with guilt as the duke could actually be guilty of arranging his friend's death. The two disparities did not equate. "Your Grace, you need not speak of it," she urged, hating the anguish in his voice. Hating he had been a witness to such barbarism.

Hating anyone would dare suspect him of treason when it was clear he had loved his friend like a brother. His desperate anguish could not be feigned. What he had seen could never be unseen, and it was a scar he would forever bear upon his psyche.

"Those murderous pigs *butchered* him, and I had no recourse. No bloody way of finding or helping him." His breath hitched. "By the time I woke on the floor, left for dead, he was already gone in every sense of the word. There was nothing I could do save remove the signet ring from the hand so I could send it to his mother. I never told her the manner in which I came to have it in my possession. And Christ on the cross, she cannot know. It would kill her as it has me. Each day since then has eaten me alive from the inside. I cannot forgive myself for failing to see we had been led to our slaughter, no better than cattle."

"It was not your fault," she said achingly, for it was what he need-ed to hear.

What she needed to say aloud. The Duke of Whitley had not mur-dered his friend. He was not colluding with the French or anyone else. His every correspondence suggested he was, at heart, a good man. A good man who spent his days numbing himself with drink and pleasure in an endless attempt to keep his mind from the weightier matters troubling him.

"Do you know I have not spoken of that day with anyone?" he asked suddenly.

She shook her head slowly, uncertain if she should be grateful for his trust or suspicious of it. "Your Grace, I—"

"Crispin," he interrupted with his renewed demand. "You're in my chamber, in my arms, in the blackest hour of the night. Surely you can say it now."

"Crispin," she tried, and swallowed, finding she liked it far too much on her tongue.

"Do I frighten you?" His question, issued in that velvet-soft drawl she had come to know so well—never failing to elicit gooseflesh—startled her.

Yes.

"No." Her answer was breathless. Simple. Another lie between them.

But she did not fear him in the manner he implied but rather in another altogether. He frightened her heart, for his vulnerability made her soften toward him in a way she had not before. Here was the man who loved his sisters and wept at his mother's memory. Here was the man who danced with wild abandon, whose touch was gentle, who...

Swallowing, she realized she had not felt such a magnitude of emotion for a man before. Her heart and life had been closed, and she had been happy to make Father and his work her world. She had loved James, but she had been a naïve girl when they had wed. And they had scarcely had the chance to grow together when he had gone, never to return.

"Damnation, woman," the duke groaned, and then he pulled her body against his so snugly there seemed to be not even a hint of distance between them. "I ought to frighten you. It would be wise for you to fear me."

Every part of her, from her breasts to her hips, pressed into his hard, masculine form. She ought to push him away, she knew. To break contact. End this madness. But her hands moved to his back from his arms, stroking over the hewn contours. His skin was smooth and hot, like silk and velvet and yet so much power rippled beneath the surface. She never wanted to stop touching him. To stop comforting him.

His arms banded about her.

She felt calm in a way she had not for as long as she could recall, as if she had just come home after a long journey abroad. As if she had found the place where she belonged.

How silly. How untrue, surely. And yet, she could not banish the sensation skittering along her spine, settling low in her belly.

He buried his face in her hair, and for a span of time, neither of them spoke. They held still, the ink of the night somehow dimming the harsh realities that would keep them apart by daylight. Jacinda did something foolish next. She lay her head against his chest, listening to the solid beats of his heart. His skin was bare and real and so very alive against her. And her heart answered. Her hands continued to glide over the planes of his back, absorbing his strength.

Awareness hummed in the air. The intimacy of this midnight-embrace far surpassed any they had shared before, and she knew instinctively they had crossed boundaries together they had not meant to. But in the darkness, he was no longer the Duke of Whitley, harsh and unyielding, libidinous rakehell.

Instead, he was just a man. A man who had endured the hells of war and returned home to two wild sisters and a duchy. To false accusations to which he was not even privy. To demons that haunted his sleep.

And for these few, stolen moments, she was just a woman. Not the woman who had been sent to scour his papers for cryptograms. Not the one who betrayed his trust even now by keeping the truth from him. Not a soldier's widow who had buried herself in her father's work and her studies.

But a woman who could not stay the swift river of emotion coursing through her. Who could not help but feel his pain and sadness.

Who wanted to help him to keep the horrors of his past at bay.

One of his hands traveled to her unbound hair, caressing the strands over her back with a gentleness that destroyed her. He was so much more than she had realized on the day she had first walked into his study.

Everything she wished she could tell him clamored to her tongue. *I am not a governess. I have been deceiving you. Sifting through your correspondence. Reporting your words back to another.*

What would he do if she revealed all to him? One breath was all it would take, and the truth would come spilling out like an upended tin of loose buttons. Would he send her away immediately? Would he wish to punish her? It was almost certain she would never see him again, and why did that thought leave her with such an empty anguish, a searing pain in her chest?

She should tell him. Regardless of the consequences. She would inform Father of her decision that she was no longer capable of remaining in Whitley's household and spying against him.

"Tears?" The duke's voice was a decadent rumble against her ear.

Her cheeks were wet. She wept for the man in her arms. For the impossible duke she did not dare like but whom she nevertheless felt so attuned to. For the broken man who could not sleep for the ghosts that hunted him even in his dreams. For the man who had removed a signet ring from his friend's disembodied hand so it could be returned to his mother.

Once they began, they would not stop. The tears rained down her cheeks, and she sobbed into his chest, marking his skin with the wetness of her sorrow for him. And she was so very sorry—for Whitley, for what he had experienced and witnessed, for every bit of suffering and anguish he had been forced to endure. He had woken to the horrible, unimaginable knowledge his friend had been tortured and murdered whilst he still lived and breathed.

That was the guilt that ravaged the Duke of Whitley.

It explained why he had become the man he was.

156

How very wrong she had been about him. How wrong everyone had been about him. For while it could not be denied his reputation was loathsome, every black mark against him was the direct result of what he had suffered. What he had seen. What haunted him still.

"I hurt for you, Your Grace," she admitted at last, though she knew all too well he could use such a confession against her later. "The horrors you have seen, the nightmares you have endured, should not be suffered by anyone. I ache knowing you suffer so."

"I am alive," he said bitterly, "and that is more than I can say for my friend. If my greatest complaint is a lack of sleep and some nightmares, I still remain on the correct side of the soil. And whilst I decidedly do not deserve to be here, nevertheless, here I stand."

Broken and sad and lonely.

"If I could take on the pain for you, I would," she said simply, and she meant it.

The Duke of Whitley was not at all as he seemed. She could not help but feel that here, in the blackness of the night, she had seen him—truly seen him—for the first time.

CHAPTER TWELVE

F OR THE FIRST time since his miserable return to England's shores, he wanted to hold a woman, to bask in her sweetness and comfort, bury his face in her hair and hold her soft body against his, every bit as much as he wanted to tup her.

You want to hold her more than you want to bed her, his heart whispered as it absorbed her words with an undeniable pang. *If I could take on the pain for you, I would,* she had said. And he believed her. Heard the note of sincerity in her dulcet voice, felt the tenderness in her tentative caresses. Up and down, her hands swept.

Consoling him.

Undoing him.

The wetness of the tears she'd shed for him coated his bare chest, and he could not think of a single, more humbling experience than the prim little governess holding him in her arms. Need swept through him with such violence his teeth ached. But it was not just a need to carry her to his bed and finish what they had begun on the night in his study. It was a need for her touch. For her concern. For her caring and gentleness. For her patience and grace with his sisters as much as with him.

He kissed the top of her head, for he could not stay himself. Her unbound hair was soft and smooth, falling in waves he longed to wrap around his fist. He inhaled, wishing he could keep her forever thus, bound to him, at his side. But she was his sisters' governess, and she was an innocent, and she was not for him. She deserved a whole man who could love her, who could make her his wife so she would never again need to work to earn her bread.

"Jacinda." He spoke her name with great reluctance, for there was nothing he wanted more than to strip her bare and lose himself inside her this night. Somehow, in the absence of light, she had become his sun. And he did not wish to dim her brilliance. "You must return to your chamber now."

Her hands stilled in their slow ministration, and he wished he could recall the words at once. As if suddenly remembering their stations and the impropriety of remaining in his bedchamber *en déshabillé*, she withdrew from him. "Yes, I suppose I must. Forgive me for the familiarity. I do not know what I was thinking, entering your chamber."

"Do not run from me." He reached blindly for her, finding her hand and holding it when she would have retreated. He could not allow her to rush away, not in embarrassment or shame. Gratitude welled up within him, spilling forth. "I... thank you for..."

Caring.

His lips would not form the word.

He licked them, his fingers tightening over hers, his heart thumping as wildly as it had when he'd been wrenched from the nightmare. He did not dare to presume that someone as good and patient and kind as Miss Jacinda Turnbow could care for a man as jaded and depraved and ruined as he. They shared an attraction. She had heard a sound in the night. And he had raved on like a madman, unburdening his soul to her as if she could absolve him of all his sins. Little wonder she sought to escape him now.

"You are most welcome, Your Grace," she said firmly, giving his fingers a tentative squeeze in return.

He stood there stupidly, holding onto their linked hands. Her bare skin against his was a cooling balm and a roaring flame all at once. He could not let her go, and yet he could not beg her to stay. It had been selfishness, pure and simple, to think he could make this lovely, fierce woman his mistress. Selfishness to think he could keep her for himself, like a bird in a cage.

Crispin released her. He had no choice. It was either that or haul her into his bed. "Naturally, neither of us shall remark upon this occasion ever again. I do expect your silence and loyalty."

"Naturally, Your Grace, you need not fear. Your confidences shall remain private," she said quietly, using his title again. "I bid you good evening."

It rankled, not hearing her call him by name now that she had. Just as it rankled to send her away from him, to remind her of her place in his household, to demand her fealty when she had never exhibited a hint of anything but a strict discipline and an adherence to her duties. She had disposed of a mouse carcass on his order, by God.

Shame swept over him as he thought of his treatment of her. He had been callous and cold, cruel and demanding, because her presence nettled him and her denial infuriated him, and because from the moment he had seen her in her dun weeds and lace and hideous caps, he had wanted her for his own. He had known she was different. That she was someone who could make him weak.

She had not been like any of the governesses who had come before her.

Nor would she be like any who came after.

Because she was more than a governess to him, and she always had been. She was a woman, daring and intelligent and proper and feisty. Yet even when he had tried to force her to hate him, he had longed for her still. And no matter what he had done or said, she had still come running to him in the night, defying her iron-hard sense of propriety, taking him in her arms, crying for his pain.

If I could take on the pain for you, I would.

Her footfalls crept over the carpet, taking her father and farther from him.

"Wait." The single word emerged like a shot, and it took him by surprise, for he had not meant to speak. He had intended to keep his peace and listen to her leave.

Her movement ceased. "Your Grace?"

His legs moved, eating up the distance between them, bringing him to her in a few long strides. He stopped just short of touching her. "What if you did not go?" he rasped.

"I beg your pardon?" Her voice had acquired a breathless quality that told him everything he needed to know.

He inhaled slowly, exhaled, gathering his wits, wondering if he dared when he had so newly decided to listen to his conscience. *Beelzebub and hellfire.* He had no choice. He needed her, damn it. "What if you were to spend the evening here in my chamber?"

Her sharp gasp cut through the heaviness of the night air. "I already told you I will not be your mistress."

And he was about to make a devil's bargain, for he would gladly sell his soul for one night with Miss Jacinda Turnbow in his bed. "I do not want you to be my mistress."

That was, admittedly, a detestable lie, for he would like nothing better than to make her his and keep her until his body no longer hungered for her as if she was the feast presented to a starving man. But not in this instance, for the madness in his mind wanted instant appeasing. It wanted her now, any way he could have her, just as long as she wished it, too.

His heart thudded so loudly, he swore she might hear it as the silence stretched. Still, she did not speak. Nor did she move.

Until at least, a swish of fabric and a cool burst of air told Crispin she'd spun to face him. "I am afraid I do not understand what it is that you wish from me."

What he wished of her.

His cock stirred to life as he thought of just how much he wished from her and how very depraved those wishes were. But for the moment, all he knew was he could not bear for her to go. Could not bear to face the empty darkness of his chamber, to lose the heat of her touch, the alluring reassurance of her curved body aligned to his.

He needed her.

She could not heal him. Nothing and no one could. But perhaps, just perhaps, one night with her in his bed could diminish some of the restlessness in his soul. Perhaps they could lose themselves in each other and in the passion sparking bold and true betwixt them.

"Your Grace?" she prodded. "I cannot remain here. Already, I have made a ruinous mistake in coming to you, and I risk disastrous consequences the longer I linger."

"One night in my bed," he bit out. "That is what I wish from you."

"I cannot."

Her response was swift, though not convincing. He took a step closer. "You cannot or you will not?"

"Both."

But still, she did not move to leave.

"Touch me again," he invited.

"Pardon?" She sounded shocked but also, unless he missed his guess, tempted.

"Just as I said, Jacinda." Another step, and her dressing gown brushed his drawers. Her warmth singed him. Her generous breasts grazed his chest. "Touch me again, and then answer my question."

"I do not... I cannot... this is absurd, Your Grace. I must return to my chamber before your little games land me in a desperate situation."

Her words should have sounded frosty—he suspected they were meant to sound thus—but her husky tone belied her attempts at dismissing him. "Do not, cannot, will not. Or dare not? Methinks the lady is afraid."

"Of you?" She made a dismissive sound that had him grinning. "I can assure you I do not fear you, Your Grace. What I fear is foolishness. Haste. Making mistakes from which there is no return. Which is why, as you can see, there is no more prudent recourse than for me to return to my chamber and forget this brief moment of indiscretion ever occurred."

She was lying to herself. He heard the hesitance in her tone. But his pride was a thorn he could not overlook. If she wanted to cling to propriety and pretense, he would not stop her. Though every part of him wished she would stay, mayhap she was not wrong in her wish to flee.

For, one night inside her would never be enough. He would inevitably want more. And what more could she give? She had made it more than clear she would not become his mistress.

"Go, then," he urged lowly. "Return to the safety of your chamber. Forget you were ever here, and I shall do the same."

But she did not go. She lingered, unmoving, a shadow in the fragment of moonlight that drifted beyond the window dressing. He held his breath, willing her to remain. Her hesitance set off a new flare of need. Around them, the night was quiet.

Her hand flattened over his chest above his heart, setting his body aflame with a hundred thousand fires of raw, desperate want. He settled his left palm over hers, holding her fast lest she think to withdraw. Their fingers intertwined. Still, neither of them spoke.

Words had never been more superfluous.

He cupped her nape, guided her head back, and slammed his lips to hers. He knew she was an innocent and he should be tender and slow and gentle, but his body ached to claim her. He could not control himself, could not quell the vicious ardor that made him want to take everything she would offer.

And then take more.

But his inner battle over reining in his inner beast became moot the moment she kissed him back. She was fierce in her response as she was in all things. She opened, sighing into his mouth, clutching at his shoulder as if she could not get him close enough. Her tongue tangled with his, battling him, it seemed, for dominance.

What a sweet skirmish this would be. His cock went rigid. He ground it against her softness, letting her feel him, letting her know who would ultimately win in this bedding. Letting her know it would be her flat on her back, him inside her, taking what was his.

Damnation.

His ballocks tightened at the thought of knowing Jacinda Turnbow so intimately, loving her so well she would never forget the way he tasted on her tongue or the way he felt atop her. That she would never bed another man without wishing it was him.

Nay, strike that thought. That she would never bed another man. Ever. He wanted this—*her*—beneath him, astride him. He wanted her hair unbound, its glorious red strands a curtain over his chest as she kissed a path to his cock. He wanted her on her knees as he drove into her from behind. He wanted pleasure her with his tongue until she came undone. To wake up with the scent of jasmine in his nose and her lush breasts in his hands.

He wanted her to be his always, and he knew it now with a finality that should have alarmed him, but somehow, it settled into his gut with an air of rightness. One night would never be enough. Nor would one week or one month or one year. Jacinda was a conflagration in his blood, coursing through him. She made him...

Beelzebub and hellfire, she made him feel alive again.

He nipped her lip, licked into her mouth. She met him kiss for kiss, her hands roaming his body, tentatively at first and then with greater urgency. Her fingers glided over his shoulders before running down his arms. Trailed over the planes of his abdomen and made a scorching path back up to his chest.

They kissed until his lips were tender from the bruising force of their mutual, mad passion. His mouth found her jaw, her ear. He caught the fleshy lobe between his teeth and tugged, a fresh surge of satisfaction unfurling when she moaned his name.

"Crispin."

There was her capitulation, in her kiss, in the breathy exhalation of his given name, in her refusal to leave the chamber. But still, he needed both of them to be sure. To know that she went willingly to his bed because she wanted him as much as he wanted her.

"Jacinda," he whispered into the shell of her ear before kissing the sweet hollow just below. "Tell me why you did not go."

"Oh," she sighed as he licked her there, working his tongue over her silken flesh in much the same manner he intended to between her legs.

He kissed down her throat. "Tell me."

"You never say please."

He chuckled against her skin. She was an odd little thing, this woman. Intelligent and brave when she needed to be, firm and proper yet fiery in his arms. Passionate in her kiss. And she was not wrong. He supposed he had not much use for pleasantries or manners or even humanity in the years he'd been at war.

For her, he would try, because he liked to give her contentment. Though it was a foreign notion, his head was clear, and he could acknowledge the truth. "Please, Jacinda. Tell me, *please*, why you are still here. Why you're still in my arms. Because I have longed for this moment from the very first time you crossed the threshold of my study, but I would not have you here if you remain out of some sense of obligation or fear for your position."

He found the line of buttons on the front of her nightrail through the darkness and flicked open enough that he could pull it and her dressing gown aside to reveal the soft skin he sought. He dragged his nose over her collarbone, inhaling her scent and following with a line of open-mouthed kisses.

"I did not go because it has been years since I have lain with a man, and I… I want to lie with you." She paused. "I wish to remember what it feels like to be wanted in such a way. Just for tonight."

Her confession gave him pause, for it was unexpected. She was not an innocent after all, and though that fact surprised him and caused an unwanted twinge of jealousy for the unknown man who had taken her maidenhead, Crispin knew an instant, sobering sense of relief. She was here because she wanted him. She was experienced enough to understand desire, to acknowledge what was happening between them.

But he had to know something first, for the very thought she had been taken and abandoned by some thoughtless cad was enough to make violence stir in his soul. "Why are you not wed, Miss Turnbow?"

"He... he was a soldier." Her voice was hushed, steeped in sorrow. "He died on the winter march through the Galician mountains on the Peninsula."

The retreat to Corunna. He knew it well. Thousands of men had died on the impossible journey through the mountain range with the French at their heels. He swallowed down the rising bile at the memory.

"I am sorry," he said hoarsely, meaning it to his bloody bones. War was hell. Anyone who said otherwise had been fortunate enough to never have lived it.

"Please." Her hands framed his face, gentle and tender, sending a wave of soothing to battle the agony that threatened to rise within him. Her thumbs traced his cheekbones, and the tempest abated. "Let us not dwell on past pains. Let tonight be free from everything. Free from past, present, the separations between us."

The breath left him. There was nothing left to say. He pressed a kiss to each of her palms, and then he bent, scooping her into his arms in one swift motion. No more waiting. No more of anything. Tonight, they were Jacinda and Crispin, not governess and duke. And tomorrow... tomorrow could go to Hades for all he cared, but he would worry about it when the morning sun rose over the city. One way or another, he would convince her to see reason, and that was simply that.

For now, there was this. He lowered his head, his mouth finding hers in the darkness. He kissed her as he walked until his knees pressed against the mahogany side rails of his bed. Kissed her still as he lowered her gently to the mattress. Tore his mouth from hers to light the lamp on his bedside table.

A soft glow brought the chamber alive, and suddenly he was blinking owlishly, his eyes adjusting to the change in brightness. Slowly, slowly, his gaze settled back upon the woman lying in his bed. His heart thudded.

Without a hideous cap to rob him of the sight of her hair, those glorious, silken skeins swirled over his bed in a riot of red. Her cheeks were charmingly flushed, her lips swollen from his kisses and the hue of a freshly ripened berry, her breasts straining against the slim constraint of her nightrail and robe. The nightrail itself was already undone halfway to her navel, and the dressing gown parted so that a mouthwatering sliver of her skin was bare for him: the valley between her breasts, the smooth sweep of her chest to her perfectly lush belly.

His mouth went dry. He had never seen a more beautiful sight than Jacinda Turnbow on his bed, heated from his kisses and touch, blinking with an adorable frown into the illuminated chamber. She was even more beautiful bereft of her cap, lace, and abominable gowns.

"This is your last chance to change your mind," he warned, throat thick. Desire pulsed through him. His fingers went to the fastening at the waistband of his drawers, hesitating.

Her cheeks darkened to a deeper shade of red. "I am certain."

Thank Christ.

He thumbed open his drawers and dropped them to the floor, aware of her rapt gaze upon his straining arousal. Eyes on her, he stroked himself, watching her reaction. Her lips parted. His cock grew harder, a drop of seed weeping from the crown. He slicked it over the engorged head. Her tongue flicked over her lower lip, and she swallowed.

Yes, he was heartily glad she was no virgin. Because the way her eyes devoured him, the intense pressure in his ballocks, and the painful state of his cock could not be rectified with a slow, gentle introduction to lovemaking. He joined her on the bed, hands going to the knot on the belt of her dressing gown and making short work of the knot. Gently, he helped her to shrug the unnecessary barrier away.

When it was gone, he caught the hem of her modest nightrail, dragging it over her knees to reveal her trim calves, and then higher still, to the lush curves of her hips.

She stayed him, catching his hands in hers. "Do we need the light?"

"Yes." He released her hem reluctantly, and traveled back down her delicious body to her tapered ankles. He was a man who dwelled in the darkness, but for this, his first time seeing Jacinda, his first time sinking home inside her, making her come, he wanted light. *Nay*, he required light. The sight of her, the sounds of her, the smell of her. He did not want to miss a single, blessed moment. Not a hitch in her breath or her lashes fluttering against her cheeks. Not the arch of her back or the moan from her lips.

Gently, he caressed an ankle, raised it to his lips so he could press a kiss to the protrusion of her bone. Even this was somehow glorious. Forbidden. He licked her because he could, because tomorrow morning as they broke their fasts, her ankles would be hidden from him behind a drab gown and stockings. Because he would not be free to touch her or kiss her. Because tomorrow, they would go back to being Miss Governess and the Duke of Whitley.

Unless he could convince her otherwise.

He *had* to convince her otherwise.

Crispin brought her other ankle to his lips. Another kiss. She made a delicious hum in her throat. Emboldened, he slid his hands higher.

Over her calves, his fingers tracing every inch of her smooth skin, following it to the twin dips behind her knees. He kissed each kneecap, guiding her legs open.

"Your Grace," she protested as he bunched her nightrail higher still, so that it rested around the perfect swell of her hips, just barely shielding her mound from his hungry gaze.

No, he would not allow a return to formality, though her embarrassment was delicious. She was a delectable dichotomy, hot then cold, in his arms and yet about to flee, passionate but hiding herself behind drab weeds and silly caps. What had happened to Miss Jacinda Turnbow to fashion her into the woman she had become?

He could not help but wonder as he kissed the hollow on the inside of first her right knee and then her left, allowing his tongue to flick against her skin for another taste. Here, she mirrored her personality, a perfect blend of salty and sweet. His effort wrung another sound of satisfaction from her, and so he licked the hollow of her other knee as well before raising her hem and kissing her inner thigh.

"Say my name," he ordered, his fingers tightening on her hips, guiding them farther apart.

His mouth found a smattering of freckles on her inner thigh in the shape of the constellation Cassiopeia. Unlike the queen that was the namesake of that cluster of stars, however, Jacinda was anything but conceited. Quite the opposite, as she did not seem to be aware of her own beauty. Her hesitance and shyness were lovely, a welcome and marked difference from the endless string of women he'd bedded since his return.

He worshiped those freckles with his mouth and tongue, traced her curves with his hands as he coaxed her legs wider. The air was redolent with the musk of her arousal, humming with her soft sigh of surrender. Everything in him screamed to flip her nightrail up the rest of the way and taste her. But he did not want to rush this or her, and now that he had her where he wanted her, he wanted to prolong their joining so it would last on the nights when he no longer held her in his arms.

She said it at last. "Crispin." A whisper he scarcely heard above the din of his pounding heart. Then louder, a moan that vibrated in his ballocks, hardened his cock. "Crispin, please."

He smiled against her silken flesh and raised her hem another inch. Glancing up from his quest, he caught her gaze and fresh bolt of lust hit him with lightning intensity. This was how he wanted to see her forever, her glorious blazing locks on his pillow, her lips dark and swollen from his kisses, her gaze tender, her pupils dilated, a rosy flush on her neck and high cheekbones.

The need to tell her, to fill the heavy silence between them with something meaningful, was new. He had no whisky to cloud his thinking tonight, and his mind was free, unencumbered. There was a lightness he could not ever recall experiencing in his chest.

"You are the most beautiful sight I have ever beheld, Jacinda," he rasped. And she was, for no woman had ever been lovelier. No woman had stirred him as she did, and whether that was a blessing or a curse, he could not say in the moment.

All he knew was he needed her. She filled the cold, broken places inside him with sunshine and warmth, and he had not realized how damned tired he was of living in the darkness until her.

"No," she denied softly. "I cannot be."

"Indeed." He lowered his head, kissed one inner thigh and then the other. "You are."

Her hem bunched up higher still. One more tug, and he could devour her.

"Crispin, you must not." Her fingers found his, squeezing gently. "This is too wicked."

"I assure you, love, this is not wicked at all." He kissed her left hand, nibbled on the right. "Wicked has yet to begin."

"Your Grace." She had reverted to formality again, but her thumbs rubbed circles atop his hands, and her tone lacked firmness.

"Crispin," he reminded her, taking one of her fingers into his mouth and sucking as he longed to do on her pearl before releasing it. "The time for talking is over. Lift your nightrail and show yourself to me."

"I…" a breathy exhalation left her. "I cannot."

He nipped her knuckle. "Yes." Then he laved the lines there with his tongue. "You can. You are brave and kind and good, Jacinda. Too good for me. But for tonight, you are mine, and I wish to see all of you. I want your bravery and your kindness and your goodness. I want you on my tongue so I will always remember what you taste like long after tonight. So, when next we see each other, you will think of the pleasures of my tongue between your thighs, and I will recall how exquisite it was to fill you with my tongue before I filled you with my cock."

"*Oh.*" Her eyes widened. She licked her lips.

He had her attention now, and it was not without a great deal of satisfaction he realized his prim little governess *enjoyed* his crudeness. She liked hearing of all the naughty things he wished to do, the myriad ways in which he would so thoroughly debauch her. Had it made her wet? *Damn*, but he hoped he would find her slit soaked with her juices, slick with need for him. He would lick up every drop.

"Remove your nightrail." His tone was guttural with need. This prelude to lovemaking had affected him in ways he could not control. And if he didn't have her on his lips and tongue soon, and if he did not sink home inside her flesh, he was going to spend on his stomach like a callow youth.

She released her grip on his hands, caught the fabric of her nightrail in her fists, and hauled it upward, not stopping until it was over her head, and she tossed it in a seamless arc to the floor. It landed on the Aubusson in a soft thud, and that quickly, Jacinda was bared to his ravenous gaze.

Her hips were wide and full, mouthwateringly curved. Her mound was a decadent temptation so near to his lips, glistening and pink and made for him. Her belly was lush, her waist nipped inward for a figure as womanly and perfect as he had imagined, leading to breasts that were even fuller than he had imagined. They would spill over his palms in their abundance, topped with erect nipples the blush-pink of a rose.

And then her elegant neck, her face. My God, she was a diamond of the first water. The loveliest creature. A study in innocence and wanton desire.

His.

Holding her stare, he nudged her thighs open even more before dipping his head to suck her pearl into his mouth. Her eyes went wide, mouth opening to form a soundless exclamation. Keeping their gazes locked, he used his tongue on the sensitive bundle of flesh, licking lightly and then with long, intentional sweeps. She tasted sweet yet complex, the salt of the ocean mixed with the sweetness of Portuguese strawberries and a tinge of exotic musk.

Her hips undulated against him, rocking, seeking more, and he knew he had won. He had her precisely where he wanted her, trapped in the maws of a pleasure so divine that nothing could tear her away save complete release. He licked her, harder, faster and then slow and gentle. He used his teeth until she shuddered against him, crying out with her first spend, his name on her lips.

And then he ran his tongue along her slit, delving inside her. She bucked, jerked, her fingers finding his hair and twining themselves in it. For a time, he gave himself up to the intoxicating joy of giving her pleasure. She was all he smelled, tasted, and saw, his hands digging into her hips, guiding her against his mouth as her sated cries split the air.

He pleasured her until he could not bear to continue lest he embarrass himself. With a final kiss to her quivering mound, he made his way up her siren's body, over her rounded belly to her generous breasts. He sucked a nipple until she moaned, those frenzied fingers of hers raking his shoulders.

She was wild, his Miss Governess, and he could not be more delighted at the discovery. She could gladly tear him apart, claw him up, bite him, suck him, lick him, ride him, and he would forever be her willing slave.

But they did not have forever. They had one night, and dawn had already begun to arrive with its unwanted early light pricking his chamber and with its reminder he could not keep Jacinda in his bed for the next decade as every part of his inner savage wished.

He kissed higher still, over her throat, all the way to her chin. There, he stopped, suspending his weight over her body with his forearms, her lovely face framed in his hands. "Tell me what you want, love."

His rigid cock was between them, nestled against her slick cove. She had him so ready that one false twitch of her hips, and he would come all over her mound as if he had never before seen a cunny. But more than anything, he wanted to be sure. He did not want her regrets or her bitterness. He wanted her to know precisely what devil's bargain she was entering. To decide that it—*he*—was worth it.

"I want you," she said then.

The brazen acknowledgment of her desire undid him. As did her simple acceptance of him, for he knew what it cost her. Knew that Miss Jacinda Turnbow was not the sort of woman who would lie with just any man.

He dipped his head, fusing their mouths. She opened instantly, her tongue dueling with his. What she lacked in skill, she possessed in enthusiasm. She kissed him with a wild abandon that brought him to his knees. Desperation snarled through him. He kissed her harder, deeper. Shifting his weight to his left forearm, he reached between them with the right, his fingers dipping into her sex to tease her engorged nub. She moaned into his mouth, and he swallowed her cries, her need, wished he could tuck it so deep inside himself that he would carry it with him always.

She was so wet, so ready, and he could not wait another breath. Guiding himself to her entrance, he sheathed himself in one swift thrust. Nothing could have prepared him for the welcoming heat of her. She was so tight. So incredibly bloody tight. And right, so very, very damn *right*.

He tore his mouth from hers, his breath coming in harsh pants as he sought to hold himself back. He was keenly aware she was not experienced, and he had never before bedded a woman of her ilk. "How does it feel, love?"

She blinked at him, her sherry eyes glowing into his. "Wonderful. *You* feel wonderful." She looked as if she was about to say more but swallowed instead, either too self-conscious or too afraid to give further voice to her desires.

He did not mind her shyness, even as they were joined in the most intimate way a man and woman could be united. If anything, it made him want her more, for he knew her. He knew all too well how much her honesty and uninhibited behavior would cost her by full morning light.

He kissed her long and slow, reassuring her as best he knew how before retreating to drop kisses on her jaw. "I will go slowly, love. Tell me what you want. What you like."

"Everything." She cupped his face and kissed him so sweetly and tenderly it undid him. No one had never touched him thus, as if he were important. As if he were essential. "I like everything you do to me."

Beelzebub and hellfire. She did not need to say a single word more. He withdrew from her almost entirely before sliding home again in a hard, steady thrust. He kissed her. "How about this?"

"Yes."

He did it again. "And this?"

"Oh, yes." She sighed and her channel clenched, tightening on him, drawing him deeper still.

He was mindless now. Mindless in his need to satisfy the raging fires in the both of them. Mindless to take her. Mindless to possess her. Mindless to fill her with his cock so deep and so hard she would never want another man. That she would want to stay with him, in his bed, and at his side forever.

He sank home inside her again and again. Damn, but she felt so warm and so tight and so wet. He could not deny the rightness of it. The rightness of her. He knew to his bones he could have her beneath him, that he could lose himself inside her, a thousand times or more, and it would not be enough. It would never be enough. She was the only woman he wanted. She was the reason he could not even summon half an interest in the whores at The Duke's Bastard.

She was the only woman he wanted in his bed, in his life. Now and forever.

Now and forever?

Good God.

He could not possibly be thinking of…

There was no way…

Marriage was out of the question.

He was not the sort to make a proper husband. *Damnation*, he was too jaded, too broken, too haunted by the past. Why, he could not even sleep through the night without going mad. He would never inflict himself upon another.

Why then did the thought of marrying Jacinda and having her in his bed each night make him so hard that he almost spent deep inside her womb when he knew better than to leave his seed where it could grow? Furious at himself, confused, hungrier for her than ever, he kissed her with the fires of passion raging within. Kissed her and kissed her. Reached between them once more to stimulate her pearl, listening to her throaty moans and taking note of each jerk of her hips as he learned how hard and how fast she wanted his touch.

Suddenly, she tightened on his cock, crying out, her body stiffening beneath him as she reached her pinnacle. He pounded deeper, finding her leg and hooking it over his shoulder so he could angle himself to advantage inside her. She came again, shaking and shuddering and crying out with her release. It was all he needed. The tightening of her channel, the wet rush of her spend on his cock, compounded. One more thrust, and he pulled out, holding his prick in a tight grip as he came all over her, painting her belly and the valley between her breasts with his seed.

He kissed her again, and it was done.

But Jacinda and Crispin were far, far from being done. He had been lying to them both when he had said all he wanted from her was one night. One night was not enough. As he collapsed against her, his heart pounding, he knew it as surely as he knew his own reflection in the glass. They had only just begun.

CHAPTER THIRTEEN

S HE WOKE TO the strange, buoyant sensation of floating through the air in the fashion of a bird. Strong arms banded around her, holding her as if she were as fragile as the finest piece of china. Her heart gave a pang at that, for she did not deserve his tenderness. Nor did she deserve him.

Misgiving rushed through her, chasing the sleep from her body. She had made a foolish lapse in judgment last night, going to his bed. For with each day, each hour, each minute, each breath, she lied to him. She was not who he thought she was, and though that deception was bad enough on its own, she was also here to find evidence against him that could well send him to prison or even the gallows.

She stirred in his arms, needing to be released, to feel the firmness of the floor beneath her feet, to put some distance between them. But then he did something so very unlike the Duke of Whitley.

He kissed her temple. "Hush. I have you. Be still."

That simple whisper on her skin affected her in ways she could not comprehend. So did his words. *I have you.* As if in that one, succinct sentence, he could allay all her worries and fears. How she wished he could.

But he did not have her. He could never have her. Nor could she have him. She was a fiction. A pawn in the Earl of Kilross's game. He was a duke, far above the reach of a common soldier's widow and the daughter of a knight. Their paths should never have intertwined.

"Please," she whispered. "Let me go."

She meant it literally as well as figuratively. This madness could never be repeated. She would not be his mistress, and she needed to find evidence of his guilt. The two were insurmountable obstacles.

"Do not be so stubborn," he ordered without heat. "I am taking you to your chamber, and that is that."

Indeed, unless she was mistaken, there was a note of something else underlying his tone. Something warm and affectionate. Something that spoke to her heart. Sent a molten trill straight through her.

She told herself it was because she wished to avoid detection that she remained silent as he carried her down the hall through the darkness. That it was why her arms linked around his neck, why she nestled her face into the heated skin of his chest. Here, he smelled like him, musk, and citrus and so very good, she could not help but to press her nose close and inhale.

The hitch in his breath told her he noticed her sudden interest. "You would be wise to cease, madam, if you do not wish me to take you back to my chamber and keep you there for the next sennight at least."

Though he issued it as a warning, his voice was husky with sensual promise.

Her heart beat fast enough to rival the wings of a butterfly. She kept silent, resisting the urge to press her lips to him one last time. If her fingers toyed with the silky ends of his hair as he carried her, it could not be helped. How she wished they were different people, in a different place, a different time.

But they were as lost to each other as they had ever been.

He stopped, jostling her a bit as he opened a door, and crossed the threshold before closing the door quietly at his back. Slowly, he lowered her to the floor, his hands going to her waist to steady her when she wobbled.

"You must go at once," she blurted, needing to somehow banish the unwanted emotions threatening to overwhelm her. Needing to banish *him*. His presence in her chamber so near to dawn would be fodder for belowstairs gossip, and she had no wish to make a pariah of herself or invite undue scrutiny. She still needed to find a way into the locked drawer of the desk in his study.

At the thought, hot shame swept over her. What had she done? She had granted the man she was betraying the greatest liberty of all. She had given him her body. He had kissed her, worked his knowing hands over her. He had used his mouth upon her. How would she look upon him by morning light, knowing she had lain with him?

"I will go," he said softly, his voice a delicious rumble that did not fail to produce a frisson of something wicked down her spine. "But this is not done between us, Jacinda."

"It is," she insisted. For it was. It had to be. Indeed, it had never begun, for she was deceiving him. Plotting against him even as he touched her with such tenderness that she longed to cry.

"Nay." He caressed her waist, keeping her anchored to him, and yet not attempting further seduction. "It is not. You came to me tonight."

She swallowed. *Yes*, she had, for her weakness for him knew no bounds. Even now, her heart gave a pang at what could never be. But she could not forget that even without the shadow of Kilross dogging her, she was naught but a need to be assuaged for Whitley. He would grow weary of her. She was merely a woman he would bed, not wed.

"I should never have done so," she forced herself to say, for it was the truth, stark and bitter, torn from her.

"I am glad you did." His hands slid up her back, warming her through the layers of her nightrail and dressing gown.

Her cheeks heated at the realization he must have dressed her. When she had fallen asleep in the warm, soft cocoon of his bed, she had been naked, sated, and tired. He had held her to him, his heart thumping with steady reassurance beneath her ear, and she had been too sated and content to move.

How could she have so thoroughly lost sight of what she must do? How had she allowed herself to become so vulnerable to him? Her hands stole to his shoulders, but instead of pushing him away as she knew she must, she remained as she was, absorbing his quiet strength. He had donned a robe for their journey down the hall, and she missed his skin.

She trod on most dangerous ground, just one more kiss from ruin. "I do not regret coming to you, but we cannot engage in such folly again."

He shocked her then by drawing her to him in a tight embrace and burying his face in her hair. "The only folly would be in never holding you in my arms again. I need you, Jacinda."

With the faint light of dawn stirring beyond the window dressings and the jingling of tack, a sign of London coming to life on the street below, reality intruded. His gentleness disarmed her. How she wished for his bite rather than his purr.

But she could not forget that at any moment, the servants would stir. "The domestics will soon be about. Please, I beg of you, leave me."

He kissed her crown before releasing her. "I will do as you wish, but do not think I will concede defeat so easily. We have only just begun."

With that promise, he left her standing alone, mourning the loss of his comforting presence and touch. The realization of what she must do next left her colder than she had ever been.

THE MORNING HAD dawned grim and gray and raining, forcing Crispin to take his curricle to The Duke's Bastard. Foul weather never failed to make the wound in his thigh ache and his disposition to turn sour.

But the drizzle and the chill were not the sole reason for Crispin's sullen mood as he stalked into Duncan's office unannounced, slamming the door at his back. He had finally had Jacinda Turnbow where he wanted her most—on her back in his bed—and yet by the light of day, it was as if she'd never been there.

He had nothing but the lingering scent of jasmine on his pillow and one long, unruly strand of sunset hair in his sheets as proof that making love to her had not been a strange fabrication of his war-maddened mind.

Duncan looked up from the ledgers he'd been reviewing at his desk, raising a golden brow. "Whitley, you look as if you have just attended your own funeral."

Crispin threw himself into an overstuffed chair opposite Duncan's desk, sighing. "Do I resemble a corpse to you, Duncan?" he asked irritably.

His friend studied him silently for a beat. "Whisky, Cris?"

"In the morning?" he returned, continuing their little game as if he hadn't given many a bottle the black eye before midday with nary a speck of guilt.

Duncan sat back in his elaborately carved seat. Hades rose in stark relief from the polished walnut at his right shoulder and Persephone at his left. The dichotomy seemed appropriate. Hades certainly represented Duncan, though his Persephone had yet to be discovered. "You have yet to tup the governess, then?"

Crispin's ears went hot. "You have tongue enough for two sets of teeth, Duncan."

"Astounding." His friend grinned. "I never thought I would see the day you would wear your heart on your sleeve for a prim and proper governess."

"I do not have a heart," he growled, "and if I did, I most assuredly would not wear it upon my sleeve for Miss Turnbow or anyone else. I would toss the worthless thing into the fire grate and see it turned to ash."

Duncan's levity only deepened. "You look well aside from your formidable frown, Cris. I am happy to see it. And I daresay you smell a great deal better now than you did on the last occasion upon which we crossed paths. Perhaps your little governess is good for you."

"She is not mine," he gritted, forcing his mind to his reason for coming to The Duke's Bastard, which was certainly not to be hounded by Duncan about Miss Turnbow. His inner irritation on that score alone was enough to make him itch. "Did you receive the packet of letters I had my man deliver here last night?"

"I did." Duncan's countenance sobered at once. "You mentioned only having uncovered them in your household. Where the devil did you find them?"

"In my study, inside the locked drawer of my desk." His fingers tightened on the arms of his chair, his knuckles going white beneath the strain. "Tucked betwixt the pages of my journals."

Duncan's jaw hardened. "Bloody hell, that is deuced odd."

The misgiving he had felt upon the odd discovery the day before returned tenfold. "My thought precisely."

"Clearly, they are ciphers," Duncan said, depositing his quill in its inkwell, his dark gaze sharpening. "What secrets they contain is anyone's guess. I have already put out inquiries into the matter. One of my gentlemen is familiar with deciphering. If there are answers to be had, I will obtain them for you. Have you any inkling as to who might have done such a thing or why?"

He shook his head, still as perplexed all these hours later as he had been last night upon his initial discovery. What purpose could enciphered missives hidden in his desk possibly serve? Who would have hidden them there? The only enemies he had ever possessed were the French soldiers he had faced in battle.

Along with one soulless Spaniard. The guerillero's face rose in his mind, for he had committed it to memory. If he ever saw El Corazón

Oscuro again, he would gladly make that bastard pay for what he had done to Morgan. Crispin would begin by severing his hand. And after that...

With a shudder, he forced himself to return to the present. He was no longer at war, and there was no means by which he would ever again see the Spanish cutthroat who had earned his reputation in spilled blood.

"I haven't an inkling who might be behind this," he admitted to Duncan. "As for motive, I cannot speak to it without knowing what the cursed things say."

Duncan inclined his head. "I will have answers for you, Cris. Fear not on that account. Whoever he is, we will run the bastard to ground."

Humility was a new sensation for Crispin in the life he had cultivated since his return from war. He felt it now, a sharp twinge in his chest. An ache in his gut. Duncan was a loyal and trusted friend, and he knew better than anyone money could not buy such a privilege. "Thank you, Duncan. Have you any cutthroats you can spare? I dislike the notion of some scoundrel slipping into my home and acquainting himself with my personal effects."

"Here now, Cris." Duncan made a flourishing gesture with his hands. "My men are not cutthroats. They are gentlemen of the first stare."

"Just as your lightskirts are ladies," he grumbled, wondering anew why his friend quibbled over such trivialities. The entire staff of The Duke's Bastard wore livery. But then, Crispin could not deny the genius of the club that Duncan had built, located on St. James and appealing to all the vices of the *ton's* supposed gentlemen, from gaming to quim. It had certainly made him a hideously wealthy man, far greater in riches than the man who had sired and denied him. "Does referring to a criminal as a gentleman render him any less a criminal or any more a gentleman?"

SCARLETT SCOTT

"If he believes it himself, then it does, and that is all I require." His irascible friend grinned again. "I shall gladly provide you with some of my *gentlemen*, however. Whisky now? Or will you be returning home to Miss Turnbow's—"

"Damn you," he interrupted Duncan's lewd bent of thought. "Do not say another word about her."

Duncan blinked, an expression of feigned innocence pinned to his face, the blighter. "Dear me. I was about to say 'careful tutelage of your sisters' but if you had something else in mind, you randy devil..."

Gritting his teeth, Crispin rose from the chair. "If only everyone else thought you as droll as you find yourself, friend."

"I have it on good authority that most do." Duncan winked as he stood as well. "Particularly those of the female persuasion. It would seem, at any rate, that they find me far more entertaining than they find you these days."

He scowled. "If you refer to your ladies of dubious morals..."

"I refer to your governess," his friend interrupted smoothly.

The man was like a dog with a bloody bone. "Curse it, Duncan, I already told you that she is not mine."

Duncan stalked to the sideboard and poured a finger of whisky into a glass. "Are you sure I cannot tempt you?"

Crispin shook his head, for he needed his mind sharp and unclouded. "My mind is enough of a cesspool today without the devil's brew."

His friend shot him a glance, his brow raised. "Turning down whisky and mooning about like a lovesick lad? What will happen next?"

He scowled. "I do not moon."

Duncan cupped a hand to his ear in a theatrical gesture. "Did you hear that sound? I do believe it was the parson's mousetrap."

"I am not wedding the governess," he snapped with more force than necessary. Unbidden, the foolish bent of his thoughts whilst he had been deep inside her sweet cunny returned to him. His cheeks heated.

Duncan tossed back the content of his glass and let out a slow exhale, observing him all the while in that uncanny way of his. "God's blood, I never thought I would see the day the Duke of Depravity was brought low by any woman, let alone a spinster governess."

He winced at the reminder of the mocking title he had been christened with in the scandal sheets. "I am not depraved, and neither is Miss Turnbow a spinster. She is lovely, with fiery-red hair and warm sherry eyes that crinkle in the corners when she is amused. Her nose has the most distracting smattering of freckles, and her mouth is made for..." Suddenly aware of his friend's grimly amused countenance, he stopped himself from further waxing poetic about Miss Turnbow's endless attributes and cleared his throat. "That is to say, I am sure she could have her choice of any gentleman."

Not for the first time, it occurred to him that she had likely been forced to become a governess because she'd been ruined by some cad who had taken her maidenhead and then run off to war only to get himself killed. The notion of some young buck so misusing her did not sit well with him. She had been reduced to a life of purgatorial servitude, left to be preyed upon by unscrupulous masters who...

Damnation, left to be preyed upon by *him*.

It was a sobering realization. *Devil take it*, how was he any better than the bastard who had bedded her and left her? He, too, had taken what he wanted without offering her anything of substance in return, for the lady had made it abundantly clear she would not be his mistress.

Duncan had poured himself another drink while Crispin prattled on. He took a sip, pinning Crispin with a considering stare. "I do believe you have fallen in love with the lady."

His friend's quiet pronouncement rocked him even more than his inner musings had. "Do not be daft."

For how could he be in love with anyone when he did not believe in such rot? Never mind he had only known her for a short span of time. Never mind she did not share the same station as he. That she had refused him at every opportunity.

But she had also come to him when he had been in the throes of one of his violent nightmares. She had touched him with a tenderness that undid him even now as he stood in The Duke's Bastard with Duncan looking on, a witness to his inner chaos. He could still hear her sweet voice, the utter conviction underlying her words.

If I could take on the pain for you, I would.

And she had not left him. She had given him one night.

He wanted *all* her nights.

Every single damned one.

"I do not think I am daft, Cris." Duncan's contemplative voice plucked him once more from the thoughts that threatened to drown him. "You care about this woman."

"Yes," he rasped, the admission torn from him but nonetheless true. "Bloody, sodding hell. Much good it does me."

"Woo her," his friend suggested, shocking him, for it was the least likely sentence to emerge from the mouth of Duncan Kirkwood, devil-may-care, black-hearted gaming hell owner.

"How?" he asked before he could stay his wayward tongue. "One does not escort a governess to a ball or take her for a drive. Good God, I am not the sort of man who can stomach such nonsense even if I wished it."

"I am hosting a masque here tomorrow," his friend pointed out.

"A Cyprian ball," he argued. "I can hardly escort her to such an event, and even if I could, Miss Turnbow would never agree to such a thing. Propriety is the woman's middle name." Except for when she was in his arms. The unwanted thought made heat flare inside him.

"Tsk, Cris. It is a *masquerade* ball."

Bloody Duncan and his love of wordplay.

Crispin could not suppress his wicked grin. "No doubt attended by *ladies* and *gentlemen*."

"You are learning, Duke," Duncan mocked. "Slowly but surely. You need have no fear she will be seen. Guests are to remain discreetly masked at all times."

He knew he ought to be appalled by his friend's suggestion. There was no means by which he could persuade Jacinda to attend such an inappropriate gathering. But since it was a masque, no one would know her identity. And the thought of escorting her to one of Duncan's wild balls gave him a flutter of pleasure. How he would love to see her cheeks flush. To watch her watch the other couples engaged in amorous play. To take her to a private room and strip her bare.

He swallowed. "Perhaps if I can convince her, it would suffice."

Duncan raised his glass in mock salute. "You will think of a way. Of that, I have no doubt."

CHAPTER FOURTEEN

HOLDING A BOUQUET of hothouse flowers in one hand, Jacinda rapped on the duke's study door with the other. It had been twelve hours since she had last seen him. Since she had last *touched* him.

Twelve wretched hours.

But who was counting?

"Who is it?" he called from within his lair.

How odd it seemed to be separate from him now. To be the servant at his whim, standing on the other side of a portal that denied her entry without his explicit consent. Just that morning, he had held her in his arms, carrying her to her chamber as if she weighed no more than a babe. *We have only just begun*, he had promised her, only to disappear for the majority of the day.

She had been unable to sleep following his departure from her chamber, alternately horrified at her lapse in judgment and aching to repeat the mistake in equal measure. Instead, she had performed her own perfunctory ablutions with water gone cold the night before and dressed, pacing the floor and wondering how she would face him after going willingly to his bed.

But she need not have worried, for he was not present at breakfast as had recently become his custom. Nor did he return for hours afterward, his arrival so near to dinner she had scarcely time to change after completing the day's lessons with Lady Con and Lady Nora before seeking him out.

She should not have been hurt by his defection, for he had promised her nothing, and she had given him one night. She could not allow anything more to transpire between them for the sakes of her heart and future. Already, she had begun to feel far too comfortable here at Whitley House. She could not deny she had developed feelings for the duke and his sisters. They had burrowed through the callused part of her to the softness she'd no longer believed she possessed.

"Who is it?" he asked again, reminding her she had lingered, holding her breath in the hall, unknowing how she ought to proceed.

His voice, dark and decadent and promising sin, made a trill lick down her spine despite her every intention to remain unaffected.

She stiffened, forcing all such nonsense from her thoughts and body. "It is Miss Turnbow, Your Grace."

"You may enter."

Stifling the retort that rose to her lips, she did as he bid, securing the door behind her back before approaching him, the flowers outstretched as if in offering. "I believe these belong to you, sir."

He had stood upon her entrance, unfairly handsome in his dark coat, snowy cravat, and breeches that had been fashioned to fit his muscled legs like a second skin. "You brought me flowers, Miss Turnbow? How could you have known that roses are my favorite?"

She flattened her lips into a grim line of displeasure. "How did they get into my chamber?"

A slow, sensual smile curved his lips. "I am sure I have not an inkling, Miss Turnbow."

The thought of him in her chamber when she was not there unsettled her. What if someone would have witnessed his trespass? And furthermore, what else had he done and seen? How long had he been there? Had he riffled through her belongings? Did he suspect her of the treachery she was bound to perpetrate against him?

She swallowed against the knot of uncertainty that threatened to rise and close her throat altogether. "You had no right to enter my chamber. If you had been seen, or if a servant had noted the flowers before I saw them, the conclusions would have been as obvious as they would be erroneous."

"Obvious?" Raising an imperious brow, he slowly skirted his desk. "What do you mean to suggest, Miss Turnbow?"

Her cheeks flamed. Last night, this wicked, arrogant, perfect duke had been deep inside her body. He had pleasured her with his tongue. But she could not say any of that aloud. And she must not note how strong his thighs were, no doubt the product of his years at war, or how broad his chest. *Nay*, nor should she recall how he had felt, filling her, possessing her.

She forced her gaze back to his. "What I mean to suggest is, if the lord of the house is entering the chamber of the governess with a bouquet of flowers, it only suggests one thing."

He came nearer still, not stopping until he was so close his heady scent washed over her, sending a pang of need to her core. With a negligent air, he leaned his hip against his desk, crossing his booted ankles. His gray gaze consumed her. "What thing would that be, my dear Miss Turnbow? Would you care to elaborate?"

"No," she snapped, tiring of being his game. His levity coupled with the dangerous gift of his flowers nettled her. He could play the cat all he liked, but that did not mean she was required to be his mouse. She pressed the flowers into his chest. "You must take these, Your Grace."

"No," he echoed, the ghost of a smile flitting over his sensual lips.

"Yes." Determined, she pressed them deeper into the solid wall of his chest, not caring the petals crushed against his coat and scattered to the floor.

"I said no." He caught her wrist in a firm but gentle grip, his thumb caressing a circle of delicious fire along her eager skin. "I do not give a damn who sees the bloody flowers, Jacinda. Let anyone draw what conclusion he will. I do not owe anyone beneath this roof a single cursed thing except for my sisters." He paused, turning her hand over and raising it to his lips for a lingering kiss. "And you."

Whether it was his action or his words that robbed her breath, she could not say. All she knew was she gawped at the Duke of Whitley as if he had begun speaking in a foreign tongue. Confused and flustered, she attempted to regain possession of her hand, but he held fast, continuing to deliver those slow, tiny touches with his thumb.

The heat in her body spread, turning to a fire in her veins.

And yet, she could not allow herself to succumb to either her body's traitorous wants and needs or to the Duke of Whitley himself. *But you can to Crispin*, whispered a wicked voice inside her.

Nay. Doing so would be ruinous. Dangerous. Foolish.

Impossible.

"You do not owe me anything, Your Grace," she forced herself to say. "If you harbor a guilty conscience for... for what transpired between us, allow me to absolve you now. What was given was given freely, but it will not—nay, cannot—bear repetition."

"It cannot, or you cannot?" he asked softly, continuing the deliberate caress that wreaked such havoc upon her ability to resist him.

A simple touch, his bare skin on hers, was all she required.

"Both." Her voice was breathless. She tugged her wrist to no avail, but it was a halfhearted attempt anyway for the truth. She loved his touch. She craved it, hungered for it, and the wickedest part of her answered to the darkest part of him.

But that did not mean she could indulge in such a selfish, ruinous fashion ever again. She was an honorable widow with a reputation above reproach. She was not fast. She had never once taken a lover, having neither inclination nor opportunity, being so ensconced in her work with Father.

Not until the Duke of Whitley, that was.

But lover was far too intimate a term to describe him. Rather, he was an indiscretion. A mistake. A regret. He had to be. Reason warred with desire.

"But you can, Jacinda," he said low, scarcely using any strength at all to tug her into his strong, lean form.

Weak-hearted fool that she was, she fell into him, bracing herself with a palm flattened to his chest. The bouquet remained between them in her other hand, and she could not be certain whether it represented a flag of surrender or truce.

He took the bouquet and tossed it aside with a growl, hauling her to him, his lips slamming down on hers.

Surrender it was, she decided. *Yes*, she could. If she dared. She opened for him, her arms twining around his neck. It had been twelve hours, and if the viciousness of their kiss was any indication, they were both starving for each other. He cupped her face, holding her still for his tender onslaught.

He smelled of leather, the crispness of the outdoors, citrus, and a faint hint of smoke. She wondered where he had been, but then his mouth was hot and demanding as it blazed a trail of fire down her throat. She thought of the flowers and her heart clenched. At least part of his time away had been spent in thinking of her.

Her fingers tunneled into his thick, silky hair of their own accord, traveling over his skull, and that, like the rest of him, was shaped to perfection. Her fichu disappeared, revealing her modest décolletage to him, and she recalled the missing scrap of lace he had yet to return to her.

"I only have one more fichu," she protested weakly as his tongue settled in the hollow at the base of her throat. "You cannot steal that one, too."

"Mmm." He kissed to the top of her breast, flirting with the neckline of her gown. "Buy a hundred more if you like."

His words startled a laugh from her that ended in a squeak when his strong hands caught her waist and lifted her atop the polished surface of his imposing desk. He stared down at her, his expression warm and unguarded in a way she had never seen it before. He seemed younger in that moment, the weight of years and war gone.

She did not remove her arms from about his neck, though she knew she must. The selfish part of her wanted to wait another breath, another beat of her heart. To drink in the sight of him and tuck it into her memory for later when she could never look upon his countenance again. When she would look back on the stolen moments during which she had been the Duke of Whitley's lover.

Reality intruded then, as it always did, in the form of her conscience pricking her. She had no widow's portion, and Father had gambled away everything they owned. And she had no choice but to betray Whitley to save herself and Father from ruin.

But she could say none of that. "I could not buy a hundred fichus even if I wished to do so, Your Grace," she reminded him instead.

His gray gaze darkened. "I will buy them for you as long as you agree to never wear them in my presence."

"I cannot accept your gifts," she said, breathless as his hands snagged the simple muslin of her gown and bunched it upward.

Cool air washed over her heated skin through her stockings. He settled himself between her thighs, his touch slipping into the hollows at the backs of her knees. "Will not," he corrected, frowning. "First the flowers and now my offer of lace. Perhaps you will accept something else from me instead, Jacinda?"

Unadulterated want pulsed between her thighs. She swallowed, suspecting the something else to which he referred was the length of him, rigid and thick and long, a temptation pressing against her mound through the layers of clothing and respectability separating them. He caressed behind her knees, lowering his head so their mouths almost brushed.

She stared back at him, unable to look away, unable to move. He was everything she wanted and everything she could not have. "I gave you one night."

Ever so tenderly, he laid a kiss upon the corner of her lips. "What if I want more?"

She inhaled, rubbing her cheek along the bristle of whiskers on his jaw that had already begun to grow since his morning shave. "I cannot give you that."

But neither could she release him.

Nor could he release her, it seemed. His hands, still clenched in her skirts, traveled higher, not stopping until her hem landed about her waist. Chemise, petticoats, and muslin pooled. Strong fingers traced the curves of her hips, guiding her thighs apart. He kissed the other corner of her mouth, his lips feathering over hers in a tantalizing caress.

"Will not," he repeated. Gently, he gripped her hips and slid her forward until her bare mound brushed the swell at the fall of his breeches. "You're soaked, darling."

She could not deny his statement when the proof coated his breeches. They were buff, and the economical part of her mind wondered if there would be a stain. Would his valet spot it and know the cause? Her cheeks went hot at the thought.

"You are wicked," she scolded.

He gave her a smoldering grin, his mouth a scant distance from hers. "Depraved. You never did answer my question, Cin."

The sobriquet was unexpected. On his tongue, it sounded deliciously wicked. Not unlike the word. *Sin. Yes,* the worst part of her liked it well. All her life, she had been Jacinda. Jacinda the good daughter, Jacinda the loyal wife, Jacinda the quiet widow. For the first time, a wild sense of possibility flitted through her. She saw herself, just for a flash, as someone she might be instead with the shackles of her responsibilities removed.

But the shackles remained, loosened rather than removed, and she could not escape. "What was your question, Your Grace?"

"Crispin," he prodded, one of his knowing hands dipping between her thighs to trace her most intimate, sensitive flesh. "Will you accept something else from me, Cin?"

Long fingers found the bud of her sex, just the whisper of a touch, so light. She swallowed the moan that rose in her throat but could not keep her body from responding. Her hips undulated, seeking, longing for more pressure.

She should tell him to go to the devil. Should recall what she was about, what she was meant to do, and push him away and flip down her skirts. But her greed superseded duty. She wanted those fingers on her. Wanted those fingers inside her. Wanted his mouth and his tongue and his...

Oh, Lord in heaven.

Jacinda expelled a humid breath. "Crispin."

He hummed a sound of approval, still stroking over her slick nub enough to tantalize but not satisfy. "Tell me what you want. I am your servant to command. Whatever you order me to do, I shall do." He kissed her again, lingeringly, his tongue swiping across her bottom lip. "I promise."

She should know better than to believe the promise of a rakehell. A man she dared not trust. And yet, her resolve had been stripped away as surely as her skirts. *One more time*, wheedled the wickedness inside her. *What can be the harm?*

"Tell me what you want," he prodded. "Take what you want, Cin."

Jacinda wetted lips that had suddenly gone dry. He was giving her what she had never had in all her life. The twin prizes that eluded every woman thanks to her sex. Things she had not even realized she longed for until this very second.

Power.

Freedom.

She knew what she wanted, and it was the Duke of Whitley on his knees before her, pleasuring her with his mouth. It was a pleasure she had not known existed, and even now, the mere remembrance of his tongue dancing over her sensitive flesh, alternating with the suction of his mouth and the nip of his teeth, sent a thunderbolt of arousal straight to her core.

But she did not dare say what she wanted aloud. Instead, she guided his mouth to hers. When she would have deepened the kiss, however, he withdrew. His gray gaze bored into hers. "Tell me what you want," he urged again, teasing her with his fingers relentlessly.

The steady ache between her legs had built into a crescendo with his clever digits exerting just enough pressure to arouse her without allowing her to reach her pinnacle. Her body longed for the release he denied her.

Still, she could not speak aloud the new iniquity that ran through her. "Crispin."

"Cin." He kissed her again, and it was a kiss that claimed, a kiss that made certain no other kiss that came in its wake could ever match it. "You can." *Kiss.* "You will." *Kiss.* "Say it now."

His fingers traced her seam, and when she would have twisted her hips to bring him inside her, he withdrew his touch altogether. She was bereft, denied of the one thing she needed the most.

Holding her gaze, he raised fingers glistening with her dew and sucked them into his mouth. When a guttural sound of appreciation rumbled from him, something inside her broke.

She was in control.

She knew what she wanted.

And she was going to take it.

"I want your mouth," she said. "On me."

The look he gave her was enough to set her aflame. The words had scarcely left her lips before he guided her bottom to the edge of the desk and sank to his knees. Hot, smooth hands swept over her thighs. She held her skirts in place, taking in the sight of the Duke of Whitley obeying her wish. This was decidedly not what she had intended to happen in seeking him out, but she had never seen a more pleasing sight in her life.

Until his dark head dipped. His handsome face pressed against her mound. His tongue played over her pearl expertly. The bite of his teeth had her moaning, and then she gave in entirely, keeping her skirts in place with her left hand while allowing the right to burrow into his thick, sleek hair. She cupped his skull and raked his scalp with her nails in appreciation when his tongue followed her slit.

She could not stifle her moan. Full-bodied and loud, it would announce to anyone passing in the hall what she was about. What the duke was about. She knew she had toed a dangerous line between passion and ruination, but now that she had cast caution to the wind, she could not stop.

Would not stop.

His fingers tightened on her hips. He buried his face deeper, using the pressure of his mouth to stimulate her, and when he once more found the nub of flesh that sent pleasure hurtling through her like lightning, she knew it would not be long. He sucked. Those masterful fingers left her hip to sink inside her. He stroked, curling his fingers, probing deep inside as his mouth sucked.

Jacinda lost control. Lost herself. Her head fell back, her mouth going slack. Pleasure ricocheted from the apex of her thighs to every far reach of her being. She rippled like a still lake that had been hit with a boulder. She shook and cried out. The pleasure was so intense, she could do nothing more than grit her teeth and ride it.

Abruptly, he stood, his gaze hooded as it settled upon her. Jacinda could not help but to notice his lips were swollen and wet, and the sight sent a surge of need through her. He cupped her nape, tilting her head back so he could take her mouth as he wished, and when their lips connected, their kiss was as feral and desperate as it had ever been. She tasted herself on his lips and tongue.

She loved the manner in which he kissed her, as if he could not get close enough, could not feel enough. As if his next breath depended upon it. And she kissed him back with the same fervor, the same unrelenting desire. Their push and pull was a delicious dichotomy that aroused her senses in a way she had never previously imagined possible.

He broke the kiss, his breaths falling harsh and hitched across her lips. His forehead pressed to hers, their noses rubbing like old lovers reunited. "What do you want now, darling? Tell me."

"You." This time she did not hesitate. She was too swept away by the passion and pleasure he incited. Too far gone for him. "I want you inside me."

With a guttural sound, he plucked open the fall of his breeches, and in the next breath, he was inside her. Deep, hard, demanding. He stretched and filled her, and the air left her lungs as she shifted to accustom herself to this new invasion, so different from the last time when he had been atop her. His cock was hard and long, and he felt so very right inside her. So good.

He withdrew almost entirely before sinking inside her again. She was so hungry for him, so wet, that it heightened her every sense. Mindless, she wrapped her legs around his waist, arching into him, meeting him thrust for thrust. They did not even kiss now. Their embrace was a primitive one, arms clasped about one another, his face pressed to her throat as he slammed into her again and again.

His fingers, so cunning, went between them once more to work her. It didn't take much to send her careening over the precipice. She tightened over his rigid cock as she lost herself, shattering into a thousand shards of delirious pleasure and spending in a flooding release that left her limp and sated atop his desk.

Crispin angled his hips, pounding into her harder and deeper, an-gling her so he fitted to her perfectly. Steady and hard, he thrust into her until she spent again, crying out and tightening on him. He buried himself inside her, withdrawing at the last moment to come on her skin.

CHAPTER FIFTEEN

*B*EELZEBUB AND HELLFIRE.

Not one blessed part of his day had gone according to plan. As Crispin buttoned the fall of his breeches, sanity intruded. He had meant to woo Jacinda, and instead, he had tupped her atop his desk without even bothering to lock the blasted study door. They could have been interrupted or discovered at any moment.

Discovered.

He winced at the unfortunate word, which somehow lent a tawdry tarnish to what they had just shared. She was not his secret to keep, and he disliked feeling as if she was. His gaze settled back upon her, noting the pretty blush on her cheeks, the marks his mouth had left upon her creamy throat, her gorgeous legs still spread wide, skirts pooled around her waist. His seed was smeared upon the softness of her inner thigh.

The sight made his cock harden again. He wanted to assemble his domestics and announce she was his. Curse it, he wanted to assemble all London and shout it from the roof of Whitley House. He wanted to know everything about her. He wanted to be the source of her smiles. To coddle and protect her. To take care of her. To have her in his bed each night.

He was obsessed with the woman.

Mad for her.

He feared it was far worse than he had admitted to Duncan.

Shaken, he reached into his coat and extracted a monogrammed handkerchief, using it to wipe the evidence of his recklessness from her. Her fingers found his.

"Stop, Your Grace." Her voice was quiet with an emotion he could not discern. "You need not tend to me. I am perfectly capable of seeing to myself."

Her reversion to his title stung. His gaze snapped to her lovely, flushed face. "Damn it, Jacinda. My tongue and my cock were both inside you."

She gasped at his vulgarity. "Crispin, please."

"Bloody hell." He knew a spear of shame, for despite the alarming and unprecedented warmth he felt for her, he seemed to be perpetually inept at charm. He finished removing the traces of their lovemaking and balled the handkerchief in his fist, flipping down her skirts with his free hand. "Forgive my coarseness. I am afraid I am not a gentleman but a wild man, and I cannot control myself where you are concerned."

Wide, sherry eyes searched his. "You have the same effect upon me."

"What if I wish for more than one night?" he asked solemnly.

"Do not, I beg of you." The sadness underlying her mellifluous tone pricked him.

Was he the source? He hated to think it. "You cannot deny what is between us. We want each other too badly."

She drove him to distraction. He found himself haunting the halls of his own home in search of the far-off trill of her laughter. Joining her and his sisters in a chamber so he could smell the faint scent of jasmine and drink his fill of the sight of her. But it wasn't just the physical connection they shared, undeniable though it was, for something in her called to a primitive part of him that said this woman was his. Would be his. Had to be his in ways no other ever had.

It was also her. She was kind and good. The progress she had made with his sisters was as much a relief as it was warming to the depths of his cold heart. Jacinda glowed from within, radiating warmth and compassion and caring. She was like a lost ship's treasure the ocean had washed onto the Portuguese sands during his stint on the Peninsula. His to claim from the deep. A prize beyond measure.

But he was losing her. She slipped from his desk. "I ought not to have acted with such a careless disregard for my circumstances once more."

Her back was to him, her head down, and she seemed to be searching the Aubusson for something. What, he had not an inkling. He longed to protest the retreat of her warmth and her soft, sweetly curved body. Instead, he turned, watching the soft play of light in her gleaming hair.

Ah. He must have removed her hideous cap in the throes of passion, and she sought to find it. "One more day," he said, darkly amused when she could not seem to locate the bloody thing anywhere. He could only hope he had tossed it somewhere she would not look.

"One more day, and then what shall it be next?" She spun back to face him, her expression pinched, her tone rife with exasperation. Her dun gown fluttered about her, and even in the shapeless, joyless sack, he could not help but be stirred anew at the sight of her.

He started toward her. "One more day, and then the next shall worry about itself."

"But I shall worry about the next," she said softly as he reached her. "For I am the governess to your sisters, and I... there is much about me you do not know."

Of course there was. She had a past. So did he. Hers intrigued him rather than repel him. He longed to know everything there was to know about her, and he could not recall ever being so inclined when it came to a female. Before her, women had been for pleasure and distraction, first at war and then at home. But she was different. She was not like all the rest.

Crispin could not resist cupping her pale cheek and strumming the delicate line of her jaw. Here was a stray freckle, just the one, and he was endlessly fascinated by its solitary presence. "There is much about the world I do not know, Cin, and yet I go about each day continuing to live in it."

Her breath hitched. The golden flecks in her eyes darkened. "That is different and you know it. We could not be farther apart. I am your servant, and you—"

"And I am *your* servant, my love," he interrupted, continuing his slow and steady strokes—nothing but the pad of his thumb. "That is all I am, here and now, to you."

"Now," she argued, "but there will come a day when that changes. If not tomorrow, then the next, or perhaps the fortnight after."

He could not quell her fears, it seemed, and he wondered what had happened to her—who had hurt her—that she could not trust enough to take a chance on what he offered: companionship, passion, his purse and person at her command. Perhaps the only way was to leave the choice in her hands and hope she made the right one.

Crispin withdrew his touch although it pained him to have her so near and yet keep his hands at his sides. "I want you to have tomorrow to yourself."

Her forehead wrinkled with confusion. "But tomorrow is not my scheduled day."

He raised a brow. "In my household, I make the rules, madam. You shall have the entire day to yourself tomorrow, to do with as you wish. Con and Nora shall do fine with a day's break in their studies. One can only hope they do not revert to their old ways of sledding down the grand staircase, of course. Think of it as a test of your efficacy thus far, if you must."

When he had initially planned for her to have a day of rest tomorrow, he had not envisioned giving her *carte blanche*. Rather, he had hoped he might send her to a discreet *modiste* so she could acquire a costume for Duncan's masque. And then he had envisioned squiring her away in a carriage, feeding her hothouse strawberries, drinking copious wine, and dancing with her until the candles sputtered out before fucking her so hard and deep, he was imprinted upon her memory and her body forever.

But in truth, he did not want to take her day from her and make it his. He wanted her to choose it for herself. He wanted her to choose *him*, damn it.

"All of tomorrow to do with as I see fit?" she asked warily.

He suppressed a wince, for he well knew what his compromise could cost him. "Yes, though there are any number of choices available to you, should you wish to investigate them."

Her eyes narrowed. "Please elaborate upon these… choices."

"My carriage will be at your disposal. If you choose, it will take you to the finest *modiste* in London, where you can choose a gown and mask to wear to a masque ball in the evening." He gave an indolent shrug of his shoulders as if he hadn't a care. "Or, you could choose for it to go anywhere else within London. You may also remain here at Whitley House. Your enthusiasm for the library, while a trifle geographically inept, leads me to believe you may find any number of tomes within of interest. Or keep to your chambers if you prefer." Here he paused, and he could not help himself. "Better still, come to mine."

She was silent, studying him, and how he wished he could read her thoughts. Everything within him longed to haul her back into his arms and take her all over again. To ply her with kisses and caresses until she capitulated to his every wish.

"A masque ball?" she asked softly, finally.

He had piqued her interest, it seemed. Was it possible that beneath her atrocious brown gowns and ridiculous caps and generally hideous spinster attire, there beat the heart of a woman who longed for a beautiful gown and a turn about the ballroom? He would not have supposed Miss Jacinda Turnbow's head could be turned by a masque ball, but perhaps there was hope for his plans yet.

Crispin cleared his throat against a sudden thickness that had taken up residence there. "Tomorrow evening. I would be honored to have you accompany me as my guest, but the decision is yours alone."

She pursed her lips, calling his attention—never far from them—back once more. "I shall consider your offer."

A surge of triumph streaked through his chest, but he fought to keep the foolish, ridiculous joy from his expression. How much power she wielded over him. It was astonishing to think only two months ago, he had not known of her existence. How bloody horrid. The notion left him with a stark and hollow feeling in his chest, as if a gaping chasm had opened up. He resented each day he had spent in his life without her in it.

But he schooled his features into a cool mask, bowing. "Again, the choice is yours. I shall not expect you at breakfast or for the rest of the day, for that matter. But if I shall see you in the evening for the ball, we leave at eight o'clock."

Her lips tightened. "You will attend whether or not I accompany you, Your Grace?"

A hiss nearly left him at her return to formality, but he managed to suppress it. Perhaps this was the nudge she required. "Yes."

"Of course." Her gaze lowered. "Oh, there it is."

To his utter dismay, she snatched up her ugly cap and replaced it over her glorious hair, covering it from view once more. With a hasty curtsy and nary a word more, she fled from his study.

JACINDA RESISTED THE urge to tug at her alarmingly low décolletage as she took in the masked revelers swirling about the ballroom. The bodice of the gown she had chosen for the masquerade fit her as if it were a second skin, and the corset Madame Ormonde had insisted she wear beneath it only served to further the effect. Her bosom was lifted high, her ordinarily large breasts on shocking display. How she longed for the blanketing comfort of one of her fichus.

But the Duke of Whitley did not seem to mind.

She caught his pale gray eyes—more arresting than ever with his black mask emphasizing them—upon her bosom. Warmth skittered through her before she chased it away. When he had insisted upon her day to herself, she had intended to ignore his suggestions. Her objective had been to engross herself in the library or to have a delightful afternoon nap. Something proper. Something *safe*.

Instead, her feet had seemed to have a mind of their own, carrying her to the waiting carriage to the taunting echo of his impassioned plea. *One more day. One more day. One more day.* The Duke of Whitley was a difficult man to refuse, and despite her objections to the contrary, she could not resist the temptation of more time in his presence.

Or more time in his arms. One more night in his bed.

Because she could not keep delaying the inevitable. She had less than a fortnight remaining to uncover the ciphers Kilross claimed were in his possession and spare herself and Father from impending ruin.

"You are somber for one surrounded by so much gaiety," he observed, his voice a decadent rumble in the raucous din of the assemblage.

She pursed her lips, grateful for the presence of her golden half mask, which complemented the diaphanous pink silk gauze of her dress. "I should never have agreed to come here with you. It is horribly—"

"Improper?" he interrupted, his tone one of dark amusement.

Jacinda frowned. "Precisely. My gown is far too low to be seemly."

"It is perfect, Cin." Again, his stare lowered, glinting with appreciation.

"Furthermore," she continued, ignoring him, "this is no ordinary ball."

"Indeed." His sensual lips twisted into a wicked grin, making her wish his mask also did not draw so much attention to his mouth. "It is a masque."

"At a house of ill repute," she could not resist pointing out.

It had not taken long for her to make the alarming discovery. The licentious murals and ribald marble statues in the front hall, along with the daring décolletages of her fellow female revelers, had made the conclusion easy to reach. She supposed she ought not to be surprised the Duke of Whitley would escort her to such a depraved soiree. Little wonder everyone in attendance wore masks.

"This is not a house of ill repute but a gaming establishment." He grinned, flashing white, even teeth.

She was scandalized, she told herself. But she was also… intrigued. "You are a scoundrel," she said, but the accusation lacked heat. "You should have warned me of the nature of this ball."

His grin deepened. "If I had, would you have agreed to accompany me?"

"Naturally not." Her ears went hot as a couple floated past them in the scandalous hold of the waltz. The lady's skirts were dampened, her miniscule bodice cut so low that a hint of pink peeked from the top of each breast.

"Then I wholeheartedly do not regret my decision." His gaze flitted past her shoulder at the same moment she felt a presence. "There you are, old fellow."

Jacinda turned to find a tall gentleman, garbed in black from breeches to cravat. He was handsome in a classic sense, his golden hair and bright blue eyes an ironic foil to his penchant for darkness. At odds with the rest of the merrymakers, he wore no mask.

"Miss Turnbow, Mr. Duncan Kirkwood, owner of this fine establishment," Whitley introduced them.

Her mind processed the knowledge he was a gentleman whom it

would ordinarily never be possible for her to meet. Mr. Kirkwood offered an elegant bow that Jacinda met with a curtsy.

"A pleasure, Miss Turnbow, to make your acquaintance." He took her gloved hand and raised it to his lips, lingering longer than necessary. "Would you care to dance?"

The duke stepped forward, scowling. "I am afraid you are too late. I have already claimed this dance with Miss Turnbow." He muttered something beneath his breath that sounded like *and every bloody other one.*

Mr. Kirkwood grinned, his good humor unaffected. "Perhaps the next dance, then."

Whitley's gray gaze narrowed to slits behind his mask, his jaw going rigid. "Haven't you an unsuspecting patron in need of fleecing somewhere?"

The other man's good humor remained unaffected by the duke's insult. Despite Whitley's irritation, the two shared an easy air that suggested a close friendship. Mr. Kirkwood's grin deepened, the disparity between his boyish charm and his dark apparel more notable than ever.

"As a wise man recently said to me, if only everyone else thought you as droll as you find yourself, friend." His grin faded when his gaze settled upon someone in the crush of dancers. "What the devil is *she* doing here?"

"She?" Whitley's expression turned wolfish. "Is something amiss, Duncan?"

Mr. Kirkwood's countenance darkened, his eyes fixed upon the unknown female that so confounded him. "Nothing I cannot manage, Cris." He bowed. "Enjoy the evening, lovebirds."

With that, he stalked off, the milling guests parting for him as if a giant, invisible hand preceded him. What an odd, interesting fellow. Jacinda watched him for a moment before turning to the duke. "You are friends with Mr. Kirkwood?"

"I was friends with him until he held your hand far longer than necessary," he growled.

Jacinda suppressed a smile at the possessive note in Whitley's voice, for she knew she could never truly lay claim to him regardless of how much part of her wished it. "For tonight, I am yours," she said softly.

Even if it was all they had.

His eyes blazed into hers, glittering with sensual promise. "If I had known how greatly it would please me to see you wearing a beautiful gown, I would have directed Madame Ormonde to make you two dozen more than the handful I chose. Pink suits you, my dear."

She felt removed from herself in the dress, almost as if she were someone else. How freeing it was to pretend, to live in the moment rather than worry about tomorrow and all the pain and uncertainty it would bring. But then his words settled in her mind, and her earlier puzzlement at the modiste possessing a small cache of gowns that seemed suited to Jacinda's figure made sense.

"Do you mean to tell me the gowns I saw today were commissioned for me by you?" she demanded.

"You are too beautiful to hide yourself in colorless sacks," was his mild response as he snagged two glasses from a passing servant who bore a tray of beverages. He presented her with one and kept the other for himself. "Drink. It will do wonders to ease the frown wrinkling your brow."

She fixed him with a stern look, the one she usually reserved for his wayward sisters. "When?"

"Preferably now," he muttered before taking a sip from his own glass and wincing. "Bracing stuff. I do wonder what concoction Duncan has ordered for this evening's festivities. A warning, before you begin. Moderation is required in all things at The Duke's Bastard."

Good heavens, even the name of this dubious establishment was sinful. But Jacinda was not going to allow him to distract her so easily.

"I meant to ask when you commissioned the gowns for me, not when should I drink this dubious brew."

As she said the last, she gave her glass a discreet sniff. Ratafia, it was decidedly not. He considered her with his cool stare, and she wished she could see his entire face without the hindrance of his half mask.

"Yesterday. Fortunately, Madame Ormonde possessed some dresses made for a lady who was not able to afford them after her wastrel husband lost everything in a game of hazard." He paused. "Her form was propitiously similar to yours, it would appear. But I will not deny that whilst I was there, I requested she create some more suitable gowns for you. Seeing you in brown grows hideously tiresome."

"You cannot buy me gowns, Your Grace," she hissed, reverting to his title as a reminder to herself as much as it was to him that this enchanted evening was all they had.

His jaw flexed. "It pleases me to do so."

"It is wrong," she argued, feeling she must. She could not afford to allow herself to think what was between them was anything more than fleeting. For heaven's sake, even without the deception she was forced to perpetrate against him, she had too much pride to become his mistress. What she had given of herself, she gave freely.

"I want to take care of you," he said softly, the admission sounding torn from him. "Will you not let me in this small capacity? Is it truly so hateful to accept something from me?"

She stared at him, realization hitting her with the force of a blow. No, of course it was not hateful to accept his gifts. She wore a gown that had been paid for with his coin at that very moment. But the reason she could not allow him to buy her gowns was not her pride alone. Rather, it was far more troubling.

She had fallen in love with him.

There, in the midst of the den of iniquity to which he had brought her, surrounded by masked lords and ladies of the night, she knew without a doubt her heart belonged to the Duke of Whitley. To the Duke of Depravity. To Crispin. Whoever and whatever he was, she was his. The thought of leaving him left her with a physical ache in her chest and a swirl of nausea in her stomach.

It was why she could not accept more than this gown and this final night. As it was, she considered the gown a loan. She would leave it in her chamber when the time came for her to depart Whitley House in less than a fortnight.

"Damnation."

His gritted epithet woke her from the spell that had seemed to settle upon her, and it occurred to her she stood gawping at him, no rejoinder at the ready. What could she say? She was afraid if she attempted to use her tongue, it would reveal her every secret.

I love you.

I am betraying you.

Please forgive me.

"I do not wish to argue with you, Jacinda." His lips compressed into a firm line that she longed to coax away with a kiss. "Come. Let us find a place where we can have some privacy. The dancing can bloody well wait."

Clenching the stem of her glass, she allowed him to guide her away from the ballroom, mind whirling with the implications of the emotions that could no longer be contained. How could she bear to remain at Whitley House and perpetuate her deceptions?

CHAPTER SIXTEEN

H E HAD WELL and truly muddled his attempt at wooing her. In recriminating silence, Crispin led Jacinda to the private chamber on the second floor that Duncan had reserved for his use, sliding the lock home once they were on the other side lest anyone attempt to intrude. The chamber was familiar to him, with dark walls and red silk drapery, dominated by a large bed and a wall outfitted with one-way viewing portals to the chamber adjacent should one be so inclined.

He had often been inclined in the past, but the prurient view beyond the chamber did not call to him just now. All he cared about was Jacinda. She had been so damned silent and pale in the ballroom he had feared she would flee into the night.

He turned to find her standing a few paces from him, sipping from her glass. She was so bloody beautiful in her ethereal rose dress that it robbed him of breath each time he truly drank his fill. The short, capped sleeves had been fashioned into silken petals of flowers, leaving her creamy upper arms bare above her buff gloves. Her bosom was high and full and mouthwatering, her lean waist perfectly accentuated by the gown's fitting. A gown that had been commissioned solely for her could not have been more perfect, and he could not stop staring.

But he had not brought her here to the privacy of this chamber to ogle her, he reminded himself. He had brought her here because she was angry with him, and he could not bear to be the cause of her displeasure.

"If you wish it, I will cancel the gowns," he said into the silence.

"It is not the gowns but the expectation." Her tone was quiet.

Her words were not. He needed her to understand he was not attempting to buy her favors. He wanted to woo and win her, not to force her into anything she did not want. His need of her was so strong and so pathetic, he would be willing to accept anything she gave him, any part of her, however small.

"I have no expectations. The gowns are a gift, much like the flowers you crushed into my chest and left upon the floor of my study yesterday." He could not quite expunge the bitterness from his words. "All I want is to make you happy, Jacinda, however I may, and in whatever manner you will allow."

Because she made him happy. She filled the hollowness inside him. Chased the darkness with her light. She was as compulsory to him as air.

"Becoming your mistress would not make me happy, Crispin." Sadness underscored her words, and he felt the weight of the emotion sink into his marrow. "I would be miserable."

He understood her pride would not allow it, and he accepted that. What he could not accept was not having her. One day, one night— this bloody borrowed time she allowed him, was not enough, damn it. In the short time since she had come into his life, she had wrought so much change. She had helped to free him from the dark depths to which he had sunk in the wake of Morgan's death.

The truth of it—of how much he required her—choked him. He swallowed down the knot rising in his throat, and went to her, staring down into her eyes, willing her to see it for herself. "I do not need a mistress. I need *you*."

Curse it, he had never said such a thing to a woman before. Had never before been or felt so bloody vulnerable.

Her eyes widened, molten honey glittering in the warm depths.

Her lips parted. "You already have me."

Restlessness surged inside him, mingling with a churning brew of too many other emotions to count. He had spent years of his life at war, hardening himself to all sentiment. He had killed without compunction, had faced enemy fire without fear. And yet, this one petite woman who had swept into his study one ordinary morning, had the power to make him feel. So much power in her small, fine-boned hands, in her lush pink lips, in her every word and deed.

It was fucking terrifying.

Too terrifying to continue contemplating. Instead, he plucked the glass from her fingers, depositing it on a table before returning to her. The time for talking was done. Tenderly, he cupped her face, lowering his mouth to hers. She opened for him with a sigh, clutching his shoulders. Her breasts, full and high in her glorious gown, pressed into his chest.

They kissed as if it was their last, as though they had been starved for and deprived of each other longer than a mere day. Lips and teeth and tongues collided. What remained of his control snapped, and she was every bit as desperate as he was. Their hands tore at each other's clothes. Buttons and fastenings opened. Knots came undone. Kisses and caresses punctuated each revealed swath of skin.

Naked at last, they came together atop the bed. She urged him onto his back, tearing her mouth from his to kiss down his neck, to his chest. His already rigid cock went even harder as she kissed down the taut plane of his abdomen. In his fervor to get her nude, he had neglected to take down her hair. As she kissed to the jut of his hipbone, finding his puckered scars and placed reverent kisses upon them as well, he plucked every pin he could find until her tresses rained down in glorious, silken fire.

Lower still she went, settling between his thighs, looking up at him shyly. "Tell me what will please you."

Good, sweet Lord. He should not ask it of her, and yet he could not

SCARLETT SCOTT

resist. "Touch me here." He guided her hand to his ballocks.

She palmed him in a feather-light caress. "Like this?"

"Harder." As one, their hands moved. He showed her how he liked to be touched. Her movements grew more confident. Desire licked down his spine. "God, yes, love. Now take me into your mouth."

Her lips parted without hesitation, and she did as he instructed. The warm wetness of her mouth engulfed him, and he lost the ability to think. He wrapped a hand in the lush skeins of her locks, the breath hissing from him when she flicked her tongue over his crown. The sight of his engorged prick between her petal-pink lips was enough to undo him. "I am going to spend in your mouth if you do not stop," he cautioned through gritted teeth.

The only acknowledgment she made of his warning was a deep, rumbling purr of feminine satisfaction that he felt all the way to the base of his cock. A groan tore from him. He was helpless beneath her, her willing slave. His hips pumped, seeking more, wanting release. And she obliged him, prolonging her sensual torture until he could hold back no more. He lost himself, his ballocks tightening in a violent release down her throat.

Heart thudding, he hauled her over his body, arms clamping around her to hold her to him. He buried his face in the sweetly-scented hair at her crown, pressed a kiss there, and wished he could keep her there forever, in the moment, naked and his alone.

She kissed his chest directly above his heart. "I am in love with you, Crispin."

Bloody hell. No one had ever said those words to him before. And far from igniting a panicked sense of dread in him as he might have supposed they would, they had the opposite effect. A pervasive sense of warmth blossomed in his chest and possessiveness roared through him with such fury he had to grind his teeth.

As one, he rolled them so that he was astride her. He was already hard for her again. He took her mouth in a long and steady kiss as he fitted his cock to her slick cove, and when he slid inside, he knew he was home.

SHE WOKE TO chill-night air licking at her bare skin and large, hot hands on her hips. She had not moved from the sated sprawl in which she had fallen asleep on her stomach, legs outstretched, head cradled by her pillow. The hands caressed her, thumbs drawing slow, steady circles of seduction on her skin. She gave a low moan of appreciation and undulated her hips, seeking Crispin. His reverent touch roused her from sleep. In the blissful darkness, she did not have to worry about tomorrow and what it would bring.

Though she had not meant to confess her feelings for him, she was glad she had. Even if they could never have anything more than these stolen moments together, she wanted him to know how strong and true her feelings for him were. This, along with her body, was all she could give.

"My sweet, Cin." The rasp of his whiskers as he rubbed his cheek over her bottom made a fresh surge of wetness pool between her legs. He kissed first one cheek of her bottom and then the other, humming his pleasure as he went along. The kisses moved to the cleft at the top of her backside, traveling up her spine. He spoke in between each well-placed press of his beautiful mouth. "You." *Kiss.* "Are." *Kiss.* "Mine."

Part of her knew the gravity of the folly she had committed in falling in love with him. In responding to his knowing touch and wicked lips. In wanting him with such a rampant, desperate ferocity that she ached and throbbed and even now let out a low moan, arching her back so as his lips reached her shoulder, her bottom pressed against his long, hard length.

Every intimacy she permitted dragged her deeper beneath his spell and farther from the reason she had come to Whitley House. She longed for this man. She had no defenses against him. Not even her sense of honor or her desperate loyalty to her father, could shake the way she felt for him.

She was wicked, and this was wrong. But wrong had never felt more right.

He licked her shoulder blade, then caught her skin in his teeth and gave her a nip that was more pleasurable than painful. A sigh escaped her.

"I never want to leave this bed."

Ah, if only they could remain thus forever. Just the two of them, free of the shackles of their pasts and presents and futures. If only she could confess all to him, reveal her duplicity and the reason for it. Ask him for his forgiveness, help him to clear his name and emerge unscathed from the cloud of suspicion haunting him. Find a way to save herself and Father from ruin.

He kissed a path to her nape. "Or rather," he growled against her skin, "I never want you to leave *my* bed, for that is where you belong."

Nor did she, but such thoughts inevitably led her back to the utter hopelessness of her situation. But she had determined not to allow the outside world to intrude upon them for the remainder of this blissful night, and it was not yet dawn. She moved her bottom instinctively against his rigid cock.

"Did you mean what you said?" he asked, his voice rough with sleep and desire. The thick length of his arousal slid against her from behind.

She bit her lip to keep from speaking. Raw need settled in her core as a pulsing ache. She wanted him again. But still, she would not admit her feelings for him again or even think it, for she could not bear to fall any deeper in love with him than she already had. If he ever found out how deeply she had betrayed him, he would never forgive her.

Nay, all that belonged to them—all they could have—was this final, stolen night of passion. It would have to be enough to warm her for the many long, cold years ahead of her. Years without him.

The notion left a hollow, desperate sensation inside her breast.

"I want to be inside you now, love, and I know you want it, too. But I will not give you what you want until you tell me."

"Please," she begged, squirming against him, wanting him inside her, wanting to tell him she loved him again and yet too desperately fearful to admit it.

He kissed her ear. "Are you going to say it or do I need to punish you?"

His low voice made desire trill down her spine. But she could not capitulate. Already, she was drowning in her love and need for him, in her desperation to keep him. She could never have him in the way she wished, and one day she would lose him forever.

"It does not mean what you think it does," she forced herself to say. "I will not change my mind and become your mistress."

He kissed back down her throat, nibbling on the curve of skin where her throat met her shoulder. His fingers dipped inside her folds at the same time, long and strong and sure. "You are so wet for me."

She was, and though his frank assessment brought a fresh wave of heat to her cheeks, it also sent a new pang of desire straight to her core. She opened her legs wider, moving against his hand.

"I want you," she whispered, still denying him his wish, for she needed to maintain a barrier between them more than ever.

His clever digits played over her flesh before sinking inside her.

"Mmm," he murmured his appreciation, crooking his finger so that it reached a secret place that sent a surge of desire rushing through her. Her passage tightened, and already sensitized by their earlier, frenzied bout of lovemaking, she was painfully close to release. "That is not enough, I am afraid. Tell me, and I will give you what you want."

He withdrew, and she squirmed restlessly, seeking his questing touch or his hardness, whichever she could have. But she would not say the foolish words again. "I want you inside me."

He bit her shoulder. "Say it, Cin."

I love you.

It was there, in her heart. In her mind. It was a feeling that consumed her, one she would never forget, even after she would be forced to leave him. And that was the real reason why she could not do as he asked. She loved him so much it hurt, and he had destroyed her for any other who would ever dare to come after.

"The words," he urged, kissing back down her spine. "Say. Them." Kiss, kiss, kiss.

Oh.

Something inside her unraveled. His mouth sent gooseflesh over her. A tremor of something wicked and wonderful licked its way straight to her core. She ached for him, and not just physically but... everywhere. Her heart, her mind, her body. In a short amount of time, this man had become so much to her.

He had become everything.

He palmed the left mound of her buttocks, fingers tightening just enough. "I want it on your lips, on your tongue. I want to hear it again, just once more if it is all I can have."

His palm connected with her bottom. The sting was not strong, but just enough to jar her free of the weighty musings holding her down. "Tell me again. Say it, Cin."

Good sweet heavens, the way he abbreviated her name. Sin was precisely what she wanted to do with him. Tonight, tomorrow, and every day thereafter. She had fallen in love with the man she had to betray. The man she continued to deceive with each word, each touch, each breath.

His palm connected with her flesh again. This time, it stung.

"Say it," he demanded. His teeth sank into her flesh. The sensation of his mouth upon her rump was so wicked and foreign and unthinkable, she could not help but want more. But despite her wantonness, she would not bend.

"I cannot," she insisted, defying him.

He delivered another swat, just as stinging as the last.

His mouth moved over the flesh that had just received his hand. Open-mouthed kisses worshipped her, making a lie of all his threats. "Damn you, Cin."

She felt as if her heart had been gutted with the finesse of a fishmonger plying his trade. "I cannot."

"Cannot?" He spanked her bottom again, inciting a deliciously wicked ache. "Or will not? It feels as if we have tread on this tired ground before, my love.

"Both?" she asked, half question, half response.

He gripped her hips again, guiding her onto her knees, bottom thrust upward. His fingers splayed on her thighs, urging them to part. And then his tongue was upon her, inside her. He worshipped her with his mouth, his fingers finding their way through her folds to the wanton bud within. She was slick and engorged, and the combination of his tongue and gentle, knowing pressure wrung a sudden, violent climax from her.

She surrendered. Gave in to him. To everything. To her heart.

"I love you," she moaned. "I love you. I love you."

With a satisfied groan, he replaced his tongue with his cock, sinking deep inside her in one swift, hard thrust. "Finally, my love," he gritted, withdrawing slowly only to slide home again.

And again.

And again.

And nothing had ever felt so real. Nor had it ever felt so perfect. If only the morning sun never needed to rise.

CHAPTER SEVENTEEN

"OH, MISS TURNBOW, orange cheesecakes," said Nora with a sigh. "How lovely!"

Whilst Nora's enthusiasm for the dessert plated before her was decidedly unladylike, Crispin had to admit Jacinda had managed a great deal of improving transformation with his hoyden sisters. Indeed, the entire household was ablaze with the light of her presence, and it seemed that no one—not even the ordinarily stalwart Nicholson who currently presided over dinner with an uncharacteristic smile—was immune to her charms.

"This is even better than the Portugal cakes, Miss Turnbow," added Con, her eyes rolling in imagined bliss.

Jacinda flushed, her gaze meeting his for a moment before flitting wildly about the table, as if she searched for a safe place to look. He was staring, but he did not give a damn. All he could think of was her sweet voice telling him she loved him in the night.

She loved him. How impossible. How wonderful. She. Loved. Him. *Him*—the most imperfect, unlovable, unlikable bastard in the realm. He had spent the entirety of the day since their secret return from their night of indulgence reliving every second of it. His besotted mind had complete control over all the rest of him. It seemed that he could only see, hear, and smell her.

How he longed to be tasting and touching her as well.

But that would have to wait for a more opportune moment than when he sat at the table with his maiden sisters, servants hovering at their elbows. How he longed for privacy. To have her alone. For her to be his alone. If she loved him, surely there was a way he could convince her to give them both what they wanted.

"Crispin, will you not try Miss Turnbow's cheesecake?" Nora asked him then, tearing him from the wicked bent of his thoughts—a constant state, he was afraid, whether he was in Jacinda's company or removed from it. "I promise you, it will be the very best thing you have ever eaten."

Oh, he very much doubted so. But he wisely kept that reflection to himself.

Slowly, his sister's words pierced the perpetual fog of lust clouding his brain. He looked down at the creamy dessert before him. Ordinarily, he did not eat desserts, preferring spirits to sweets in an effort to preserve his flat middle. But this—what Nora had just said—gave him pause.

His gaze fell back upon Jacinda. Damnation, she was lovely even back in her governess weeds and that infernal cap. Hers was a beauty that burned from the inside out, uncontainable. "You... *made* this, Miss Turnbow?"

The notion was almost impossible to comprehend. Rusty as he was in the ways of polite society, he knew that ladies did not toil in the Cook's domain. His mother had never stepped foot inside the kitchens of Whitley House in her entire tenure as duchess. How was it that whilst he had been thinking of her and moping about like a love-starved greenhorn, she had been baking a bloody confection?

"Yes, Your Grace," she said softly, her brilliant gaze still avoiding his. The pink kissing her delicate cheeks deepened.

He could not look away. She had been belowstairs. In the kitchens. *Working*. Like a servant.

Because she was one. Or at any rate, she was a slight step above one. Such was the place of the governess, not truly part of the family and yet not completely a servant, hovering in social purgatory. Belonging nowhere and to no one.

He knew all this, of course. But the stark evidence of it, lying seductively on a plate before him, gave him pause. As did the thought of her toiling in the kitchens, her capable hands whipping together her ingredients. For a brief, shameful moment, he imagined approaching her from behind as she was distracted by her task, lifting her skirts and gripping her hips, sliding his cock home inside her. Kissing her neck, tearing open the front of her gown so that he could palm a breast and tease a hungry nipple.

"Crispin?"

He tore his gaze from Jacinda, settling it instead upon Con. "Yes, Con?"

"You have yet to take even a forkful," she pointed out. "Do you wish to pay Miss Turnbow insult?"

He cleared his throat, wondering when in the hell the minx had begun chiding him for his cursed manners. "Forgive me." He forked a small portion of the cake and brought it to his mouth.

The instant the creamy sweet reached his tongue, he suppressed a moan of delight. *Beelzebub and hellfire*, the woman knew how to make a divine dessert. But of course she would. Did her skills know no bounds? Would her allure never end? For while he had certainly never imagined that a woman's culinary skills might give him a cockstand, hers did. That she could use her dainty hands to produce something so masterful and delicious appealed to him in a fashion he could not have previously envisioned.

She was not just intelligent and kind and good and beautiful, not just giving and compassionate, but also capable and useful. She was the sort of woman who was unstoppable, and he wondered how in heaven's name she had ever found herself in her current predicament, earning her bread at the mercy of others. It occurred to him while he knew her body quite well, he had yet to learn her story.

He swallowed the bite of soft, rich decadence. "Miss Turnbow, this is indeed perfection."

Much like you.

He left those three, troubling words unspoken.

If his gaze was overly fond and warm when it found her once more, he did not give a damn. He wanted her to see the way he felt for her. Hiding it felt more and more like a travesty with each day that passed, particularly when she had been so generous with her heart.

A pleased smile curved her lips. "Thank you, Your Grace."

He would have said anything just to be the recipient of that smile. Damnation, she took his breath.

"Miss Turnbow makes the best sweets," Nora said, recalling his attention to her. She grinned like the imp she was.

A foreign sensation settled in his chest as he sat there, forking up another bite of Jacinda's heavenly cheesecake, his sisters happier than he had seen them since his return from war. He was filled with so much bloody pleasure and yes—damn it all—happiness that a realization struck him.

This was *right*. The four of them, seated round the table, smiling and joyful and content. It was a family. *Family.* The word echoed in his mind. He had not been part of a family since before he purchased his commission and left for war. But now, the notion took root like a seed, sprouting.

And that was the precise moment he knew, on his second bite of orange cheesecake with Jacinda's sherry eyes twinkling into his, he was going to marry her. It was the only way. He could not let her go, and she belonged here at Whitley House. She belonged with him, at his side, as his equal.

As his wife.

The realization sucked the breath from his lungs. He ate the rest of the bloody cheesecake in a haze as he worked out the particulars of what he needed to do.

JACINDA STOOD ON the threshold of Crispin's study, the knowledge of what she needed to do swirling a sick tide of bile in her stomach. Had it just been a mere day ago she had dressed in a gown she could never dream of affording and made love with him as though their days together were endless? It was so far away now, so far removed and untouchable it could have been a lifetime ago instead.

How easy it had been for her to hold the inevitable at a distance, to pretend the devil would never come calling, asking for his due. But by the harsh morning light when she had dressed in the gown of the day before and ridden in secret with him back to Whitley House, slipping back to her chamber through an old corridor the servants did not typically use, her shame and guilt had threatened to consume her. She had known then something must be done.

She could not bear to remain in Crispin's life and in his bed, to love him as she did, and continue deceiving him. And so, she had managed to disrobe and hide her beautiful gown, replacing it with a serviceable brown muslin, and headed to the kitchens where she knew she could find a spare corner to craft a dessert and put her mind at work finding a solution.

Jacinda had attacked the problem in much the same way she approached ciphers: with careful deliberation, application of logic, knowledge of possible outcomes and likelihoods. No matter how many ways she looked at her situation, and no matter how much she had loved basking in the quiet happiness of Lady Constance, Lady Honora, and Crispin at dinner, there was only one answer.

Only one way for her to put an end to it all.

With a deep, steadying breath, she lifted the latch, careful to avoid detection. The hour had not yet grown so late that she was confident other servants were not yet about, but she had no notion of when Crispin would return from his sudden departure for his club, and she could not afford to wait.

His disappearance had made the decision much easier. For while she had hardly expected him to follow at her heels like an adoring puppy, neither had she anticipated his indifference. Or just how much it would cost her to sit at the table as his servant once more, unable to call him by name or touch or kiss him. Once more the secret that he kept, the woman he would take to mistress but never to wife.

And despite herself, despite knowing she was not being truthful or even fair to him, the ache in her chest would not dissipate. They had always been doomed, and neither her love for him nor his lust for her could alter that.

She entered his study, closed the door at her back, and found her way to his desk in the darkness by heart. Once there, she lit a candle, beginning the thankless task of riffling through the private correspondence of the man she loved. Her hasty inspection yielded nothing new: innocent correspondence with the steward of his country seat, yet another fond letter from the dowager Marchioness of Searle, a note of gratitude from a foundling hospital.

At last, she reached the locked drawer. Her heart beat a rapid staccato as she withdrew a pin from her hair and set to work attempting to unlock it. She had never before picked a lock, but she understood the way the mechanism worked, and it did not take long for her to feel the lock give way.

The drawer slid open. She knew a fresh wave of shame for invading his space so thoroughly. Her fingers hovered over a small collection of leather-bound volumes, knowing instinctively she had reached the point from which there would be no return.

But she had no choice. If she unburdened herself to Crispin, he would loathe her for her deception, she would return to Kilross empty-handed, and she and Father would be cast into penury. If she did as the earl bid her, she at least had a chance of keeping a roof over her head. She had no widow's portion from James, and the one man she had depended upon had somehow squandered everything. Her sole hope was that this search, like all the others, would yield no fruit and she could return to Kilross with an honest heart and report Crispin was not in possession of any enemy ciphers.

She extracted the first volume from the drawer, thumbing through it. She recognized his neat scrawl, dates and places, and knew it must be a journal he had kept during his time at war. Naturally, he would wish to keep the content private. How horrible it was of her to intrude upon his innermost thoughts.

A folded paper fluttered to the thick carpet.

Frowning, Jacinda retrieved it, unfolded it, and her heart sank to her slippers. Written in clear script was a collection of letters that formed no coherent words or meaning. *No.* It wasn't possible the man she had come to know so well could have been lying to her. She refused to believe it.

Frantic, she sifted through the rest of the pages of the journal, finding another loose page. It too contained a cipher. Sick, Jacinda removed each volume from the drawer, sifting through it. All told, she found seven enciphered letters. Hands shaking, she tucked them all into the secret pocket she'd sewn into her gown.

She returned the journals to their drawer, locked it once more with her hairpin, and snuffed the candle. The leaden weight of dread hung on her chest as she carried her ignominious loot back to her apartments. She had candles aplenty, and nothing and no one would stop her from discovering the contents of the ciphers this very night.

For either she had just betrayed the man she loved, or he had been deceiving her all along.

DESPITE THE INORDINATE amount of time and funds he had spent within its walls, the last place Crispin wanted to be that evening was

The Duke's Bastard. But when he had received Duncan's urgent summons as Con and Nora prepared to retire for the evening, he had known he must go. Much as he would like to ignore the troubling papers he had found stowed in his desk drawer, he could not.

And so, it was that he found himself ensconced in Duncan's office once more, this time with a whisky in hand because his friend had insisted upon it. The news his friend had for him could not possibly be good. Duncan settled into his Persephone and Hades chair, his unnerving blue gaze unreadable.

"I can bear the suspense no longer," he drawled as if he had not a care. When in truth, he had every bloody care. He did not like hardness of Duncan's expression, as if it had been hewn of granite. "I assume you have had word from your little birds. Tell me, what have you discovered?"

Duncan was solemn. "I am afraid it is not good, Cris."

Crispin's blood chilled. Dread sank its fangs into his gut, and the tension spread throughout his body like poison. His hand tightened upon his glass, but he did not raise a drop of the poison to his lips regardless of how tempting it was. "Tell me."

A muscle in Duncan's jaw ticked. "It has been brought to my attention a lord who serves the Foreign Office was deep in his cups this evening. He was crowing about his impending glory to anyone who would listen at the hazard table, claiming he had evidence that would prove there had been a plot against the Marquess of Searle. That he was going to be a bloody hero."

The words defied Crispin's expectations so severely for a moment, they rattled about in the air and his dumbstruck mind could not ingest them. Could not make sense of them. Taken apart, they made sense. Foreign Office. Plot. The Marquess of Searle.

He could not have been more shocked had Duncan withdrawn a bayonet and proposed to run him through. "A plot against Searle? What in the bloody hell? I was there the day in the farmhouse when the *guerillero* turned on us."

"That is not all," Duncan said quietly. "Following his decimation at the hazard tables, he turned his attention to one of my ladies. She sought me out after their encounter because he mentioned your name."

"In what fashion?" he demanded, his grip upon the glass so tight he feared it would shatter into a thousand angry shards.

Duncan tossed back a long swallow of his own whisky, grimacing and exhaling before continuing. "He told her you were responsible for the plot against Searle. That you led him to his death because you were colluding with the French."

Silence descended. Words floated through his mind, but he could not make sense of them. They made no cursed sense when strung together.

Plot against Searle.

Colluding with the French.

You were responsible. You were responsible. You were responsible.

Crispin closed his eyes as a wave of unwanted memories returned to him. The pain exploding in his head, the darkness, waking up to the grisly sight of the captain who'd been burned alive. The corpse's face had been scorched into a contortion of agony. All the blood. Morgan's hand, neatly hacked off and lying in the pool. Heat prickled him, then cold, then heat again. His heart pounded. It was as if a band had been fashioned around his chest, squeezing the life from him until he could scarcely breathe.

Everything returned at once, full force. His entire body tremored beneath the force of it.

There had been so much blood. The scent of death and burnt flesh. A raven had flown in through one of the broken windows, ready to peck at the dead. *El Corazón Oscuro*'s threat returned. *You will regret your words, Searle. I will take great pleasure in making you eat them before I let the birds peck out your tongue.*

Bile clamored up Crispin's throat.

He slammed his fist into the desk, banishing the memories, beating them back with the pain that radiated up his arm. Silencing them with the rage that coursed through his veins. He had been helpless on that day, unprotected and taken unaware. He had not been able to help himself or Morgan.

But he would be damned if he would not defend himself now. "I was beaten and left for dead," he told Duncan tightly. "I woke with a roasted enemy captain hanging above me, with a broken rib and a badly beaten skull."

Duncan winced, the pity in his eyes as undeniable as it was unwanted. "According to my lady, your accuser suggested your injuries were elaborated upon, and that they were staged as part of the conspiracy."

"My accuser," he spat. "Who the hell is he, Duncan, and when did this supposed information make its way to the Foreign Office?"

Duncan held up a staying hand. "Before I tell you, there is more you must hear. And I will also have your promise that you will not tear into his private chamber and demand satisfaction. I love you like a brother, but this club is only as good as its reputation. If one lord were beaten to death or challenged to a duel here, it would ruin me."

"He is still within these walls?" Every part of him itched to rise. To tear apart plaster and brick until he located the rotter.

"Yes. Sleeping off his drink, as it were."

Crispin raised the glass to his lips at last, taking a long pull of whisky. It simmered down his throat but did nothing to dull the maelstrom rising up inside him. This was not what he had expected. Not what he had needed. By God, he was blindsided. He could not have been more shocked had an entire brigade of enemy troops poured into The Duke's Bastard at that very moment, bayonets and musket fire at the ready.

He slammed his glass down upon Duncan's desk, realizing belatedly he had drained the content and still, he felt nothing. "I promise you.

Give me his name, Duncan."

"The Earl of Kilross," Duncan said.

And once again, he found himself flummoxed. Utterly confounded. He could not recall one occasion in his life upon which he had ever crossed paths with Kilross. "I have never met him. How can he possibly have evidence against me of a crime which I never committed?"

Duncan refreshed both their glasses from the decanter he had left upon his desk. "The man is a braggart in addition to sporting a limp prick, apparently. For while he was more than willing to sing his own praises, according to my lady, he could not perform. But she is loyal to a fault, and she primed him with additional drink so she might encourage his loquaciousness. He claimed you continue colluding with the French, and that you are in possession of ciphers to prove it. He also said one of the domestics at Whitley House is in his employ, reporting back to him. He told her that within the next fortnight, you will be exposed and he shall be hailed as a hero."

Bloody hell, if the nonsense Kilross had spouted to Duncan's lightskirt was to be believed, he was being *spied upon* in his own home as if he were some sort of vile traitor. Worse, should the spy in question locate the planted ciphers, he would look guilty as sin.

"My God," he said aloud, marveling at the ease with which his life could potentially be torn asunder. Mere hours before, his only concern had been how he would convince Jacinda to become his bride, how quickly he could obtain a license, and whether or not it was appropriate to marry her since his year of mourning for Phillip was not yet concluded. "Someone planted those ciphers in my study to make it look as if I was a conspirator against Morgan. To implicate me in his death."

Someone was trying to prove he was a traitor, damn it all.

And they were doing an awfully bloody good job of it, too.

"All evidence points in that direction." Duncan was grim. "My man working on the ciphers you brought me has yet to decipher them, but he feels he will soon have answers. Without knowing what the ciphers say, we cannot be sure of how they implicate you."

"I need to remove them from my desk," he said. "And destroy them."

His friend nodded. "The sooner you are able to do so, the better. I suggest burning them to ash. Then turn every inch of your study upside down in an effort to be certain there are not more lurking elsewhere. You cannot afford to be caught unawares."

His shock gave way to anger then. Someone was conspiring against him. Planting evidence against him. Plotting to see him imprisoned or worse. This disgrace was not to be borne.

He had risked his life for years, had been the best damn soldier he knew how to be, had been shot and stabbed and nearly killed. Had suffered the sights, sounds, and smells of so many atrocities he still could not sleep at night. And now some whoreson's baseless accusations had rendered him suspect by his own Crown?

He shot to his feet, for he could not sit civilly for one moment more. The beast in him raged. His hands were trembling with a violence that had not occurred in some time. Stalking the length of Duncan's office, he paced to the window and then back, feeling so helpless and impotent and furious he could not speak.

His mind whirled, galloping at the speed of a runaway stallion. He needed to calm himself. Needed to think. Form a plan of attack. This was no different than a battle formation. The enemy thought it could penetrate his line of defense and slay him in his sleep, but he was no longer unaware of the danger. He would defend himself to the death if necessary.

"Did the bastard suggest who in my employ was spying against me?" he asked then, knowing it was unlikely, but needing to ask the question all the same.

Duncan eyed him. "Have you hired any new domestics within the last two months?"

By God, Whitley House was crawling with any number of domestics, none of whom he took note of beyond their peripheral presence. It could be any damned one of them. "Not that I am aware of, though admittedly, I leave that sort of thing in the capable hands of my housekeeper."

"Think carefully, Cris. If you must ask questions, do so with discretion," Duncan cautioned. "Should it be discovered I provided you with such damning information…"

"You need not say more." Crispin was grateful to his friend for warning him of the impending storm, and he well understood the reputation of the club was paramount for Duncan. At least he could face what lie ahead of him prepared. He could search the ranks of his domestics, isolate the traitor, and go about building the case for his innocence. "You have my promise no one shall be the wiser. I greatly appreciate the favor you have done me. Your loyalty as a friend is unparalleled."

Duncan gave a jerky nod. "I know you are innocent, Cris, else I would not have come to you and compromised myself in such a fashion. No man in London is your equal, and any enemy of yours is an enemy of mine."

His friend's unshaking belief in him humbled him. "Thank you. Your trust means more to me than you can know."

Duncan sighed. "You must think. The charges against you are serious, if what Kilross spouted off tonight is to be believed. Given you found planted ciphers in your study, I cannot imagine there is not a legitimate threat against you. If there is a traitor in your midst, you must weed them out. Your reputation could well be used against you, should the right *ammunition* come to light."

He thought of all the carousing he had done, the endless drinking and whoring. For six solid months, he had been convinced that numbing himself was the only way to survive what he had endured.

The only way to quiet the ghosts that would not cease haunting him.

"Ammunition," he repeated. "Yes, I have created more than my fair share of that since my return to London."

He had not earned his sobriquet as the Duke of Depravity by living the life of a monk. How easy it would be for an unknown enemy to turn his demons into the noose that would tighten around his neck.

"Cris." Duncan stood, rounding his desk, his countenance lined with worry. "I hesitate to say this, but I would not be your friend if I did not. You have one new domestic beneath your roof, and you must not forget it."

Air roared in Crispin's ears.

Yes, there was one new domestic beneath his roof. But he had fallen so deeply beneath her spell, so helplessly in love with her, he could not see her as a servant any longer. When Duncan had first posed the query, it had never even occurred to him to include her.

Because it could not be her. Not his Cin. He needed her far too much. She had but to look at him with her wide, sherry eyes, and all he could see was warmth and light and everything good. Not to mention redemption. She was his future duchess, damn it all.

Yet, his mind swirled with questions. Was she not the newest addition to Whitley House? And had he not found her in his study?

No.

Damn it all to the devil.

It could not possibly be Jacinda.

No, curse it, no.

Doubt began to swim through him, making him ill all over again.

She had not been forthcoming about her past apart from mentioning a dead soldier. He'd dismissed it as something that did not affect him, a part of her that had come before she had known him just as he had not come to her an innocent either. Their pasts were their pasts, and he had not questioned it. But now, for the first time, he wondered what else she could be hiding from him.

He could not bear to contemplate her duplicity, and yet he needed to, for his good name and possibly even his freedom depended upon his impartial review of everyone in his midst. Even her.

"Cris?" Duncan's concerned voice shook him from his turbulent thoughts.

He blinked, took another shuddering breath. "Jacinda came highly recommended by the Earl of Aylesbury, and she has worked wonders with Con and Nora."

She had also asked him about Spain. Had questioned him about Morgan.

Damn it all to hell.

His vision darkened, his reaction to the notion of her betrayal so visceral and raw he did not even know how he would react should it be proved a reality. She had made him feel whole again. He had slept through the night for the first time last night without a nightmare because she was at his side. And yet, the evidence against her was too strong to be ignored.

"Trust no one until we can be more certain of what is at play here," Duncan advised, his tone harsh. "Suspect everyone. Investigate her to the fullest, Cris. This will not go away. It will come to a head, and I very much fear what shall become of you if you are ill-prepared to defend yourself."

He tamped down the bile rising in his throat. "Bloody hell, you are right, and if it is indeed her, then I am the worst sort of fucking fool. I will do as you suggest and make a thorough examination of everyone, Jacinda included."

Especially Jacinda.

In the morning, he needed to pay a call to the Earl of Aylesbury. But first, he needed to get back to Whitley House so he could destroy the ciphered letters. Even if everything in him longed to hunt down the Earl of Kilross and slaughter him in his sleep, he could not, for it was entirely possible the earl was nothing more than a pawn or an emissary. This was not a battlefield but his life, and he had to do everything in his power to uncover who was trying to tear it asunder.

CHAPTER EIGHTEEN

J ACINDA BEGAN PORING over the ciphers the moment she returned to her apartments. Unlike the incredibly intricate numeric ciphers from the Peninsula that she and Father had been attempting to decipher, the messages from Crispin's desk were alphabetic. A cursory examination of them led her to believe they relied upon a key phrase known by the sender and recipient. All she needed to do was study the pattern of the letters, watching for telling sequences and repetitions, and she would be able to make an educated guess at the phrase.

As afraid to discover their contents as she was to remain in the dark, she sketched out an alphabetic square much like the one she had used to decipher the message Kilross had provided as her test. While she worked, her mind fretted. Her hands trembled, dread churning her stomach into a sick sea. The more she considered the information Kilross had initially given her about Crispin versus the man she had come to know, the less sense it all made.

Why would Crispin plot against his friend? Why would a soldier who had fought with honor for years secretly collude with the enemy? She had witnessed the agony of his grief when he had spoken of the Marquess of Searle. It had not been feigned. The Crispin she knew was not capable of such treachery. Beneath his tortured exterior beat the heart of a good man.

No matter how she looked upon it, there were only two possible scenarios that made sense. Either the ciphers were not from the

French, or they had somehow been planted to make Crispin appear guilty. But who would want to harm him, and why? How would Kilross have come upon his knowledge of the ciphers?

The more her mind spun with questions, the more frustrated she became. She made several guesses at the key phrase to no avail. Just as she settled upon a new phrase, a discreet tap sounded at her door, and she froze.

She knew at once it was Crispin.

Shaking, she scrambled to gather up the ciphers and the paper upon which she had been scratching out her attempts to break them. Folding them all, she stuffed them inside a book she had borrowed from the library but had yet to read. With a deep breath, she stood, smoothing the skirts of her brown muslin she had yet to change out of.

Another knock.

Would he take one look at her and see the guilt written on her face? Would he know she had gone through his personal effects yet again, that the evidence of her sins were tucked into a book he owned some scant few feet away? Willing her frantic heart to slow, she crossed the chamber and opened the door a sliver.

Crispin stood in the hall, candle in hand, bathed in a warm glow. He still wore his evening clothes, his cravat snowy-white perfection, his long, muscled thighs perfectly delineated in his buff breeches. Their gazes clashed, his burning with an emotion she could not define.

"Let me in, Jacinda."

Not a question, not a lover's plea, but a demand.

A cool prick of warning slid down her neck, but she stepped back wordlessly, watching as he stalked into the room, commanding it with his mere presence. She closed the door softly and spun to face him, girding herself for what he would say. Had he discovered her treachery? Had he realized the ciphers were missing from his desk?

He placed his candle on the writing desk where not even a minute before she had been scouring the correspondence she'd stolen from him. Shame skittered down her spine as she forced herself to meet his gaze.

She had never felt more wretched in her life.

"You baked the cheesecake," he said into the silence, his low baritone doing unsettling things to the flesh between her thighs.

It was not what she had expected. Not at all. She blinked. "Yes." She paused, wondering if she had displeased him. "I hope I have not overstepped my bounds. I enjoy making sweets, and I will own that plying Lady Constance and Lady Honora with the efforts of my labors has gone a long way toward making them more amenable to our studies."

A brief smile flitted over his lips. "You are most adept at making those around you *amenable*, Cin."

There seemed to be a warning hidden in his words, or perhaps a judgment. She could not be sure. "It is my duty as governess."

"I do not refer to my sisters alone." He moved toward her, stopping only when he was near enough to run a finger along her jaw. "But to me."

She held herself still as he trailed his caress down her throat. "How have I made you amenable, Your Grace?"

His gray eyes darkened as it dipped to her mouth. "You make me forget everything and everyone but you. You walk into a chamber, and you are all I can see. All I want. Sometimes I even smell your scent when you're not there. In my study just now, for instance."

Her heart thudded with so much force she feared he could hear it. How was it possible the strains of her perfume had lingered behind when she had gone? Was he testing her? There was an almost imperceptible change to him as she studied him from beneath lowered lashes. He seemed harsher, the angles of his beautiful face sharper than normal.

"You should not have come here," she whispered instead of responding directly to what he had said. For what could she say?

Incriminating herself, confessing all, would do her no good now.

"No," he agreed, his fingers going to the ties that fastened her gown in the back and tugging on the ends. "I should not have."

Her gown loosened, the bodice gaping. "Crispin, what are you doing?"

"How did you come to be a governess?" he asked suddenly. "You never did mention it."

She licked lips that had gone dry, feeling as if she were caught in an impromptu interrogation but for what purpose and why, she had not an inkling. "I suppose you could say it was forced on me."

He plucked away her lace fichu, and then his fingers slid beneath the muslin at her shoulders, grazing her skin as he raked it down. He watched his progress with a glittering, predatory stare that heightened her foreboding. "Your soldier ruined you and left you to fend for yourself?"

"I... he did not ruin me," she murmured, thinking of James, the familiar old pang in her heart. He had been a good man, kind and patient, and he had loved her. She could not allow Crispin to think he had ruined her even for the sake of her lie.

"He was not the first, then?" he asked, sounding almost detached as he dragged her bodice and sleeves to her waist.

"Yes, he was. My past is complicated, and as it has no bearing upon the present, I would prefer not to discuss it." She realized belatedly that he had caught a fistful of fabric in his grip, banding her arms, trapped in her sleeves, to her sides. Her breasts spilled from the top of her stays. "Crispin, what are you doing? I cannot move my arms."

"Do not worry, darling," he said, his tone silken with promise and something else that she could not define. "I would never hurt you."

He pulled the pins from her hair one by one, sending curls falling about her shoulders. His lovemaking was always fiery and ferocious, which was what made this cool, calculated approach so disturbing. "Why are you doing this?"

His pale gaze bored into hers. "A test, my love. Do you trust me?"

She did not hesitate with her answer, for while he had filled her with misgiving, it was not because she feared him. Rather, it was because she feared what he might have discovered about her. "Of course I do."

"Good." His head dipped, his mouth finding her throat. He sucked her skin, nipped it with his teeth. "I trust you as well, Jacinda. With my sisters, with my heart." He kissed to the place where her neck and shoulder joined. "I trust you would never betray me."

Her hope caught on one sentence. He trusted her with his heart. But before she could bask in that revelation, the rest of what he had said hit her. *That you would never betray me.* The breath caught in her lungs, a lance of fear cutting through her anew. He suspected her. There was a reason for his change, she felt certain of it. And what could she say? The evidence of her betrayal sat carefully tucked away not four feet from him.

She did the only thing she could conceive of doing, bowing her head to press a kiss to the top of his head, inhaling deeply of his scent, masculine and beloved. "I love you, Crispin."

That was the only truth she could give him. Tears pricked at her eyes and she fought to keep them from falling, leaving her face pressed into the silken strands of his hair. God, how she loved this man. More than she could have imagined possible. It was bigger than she was, so easily capable of destroying her. And she did not care. Loving him was worth it.

He was worth it.

She knew in that moment without a doubt she would never give the ciphers to Kilross. She would uncover their contents and cast them into flames. If Crispin was somehow, against all reason, guilty of such treason, she would do her utmost to save him. She loved him too much. Even though he could never be hers, she could not bear to be the one who betrayed him.

She would face anything else.

Even penury.

There had to be another way for her and Father. Whatever it was, she would find it. Tonight, she would go without sleep until she discovered how great a chasm she would be forced to leap.

A sound tore from his throat, more a growl than a groan. With one more open-mouthed kiss to her bare skin, he withdrew to look down at her, searching her face. "Damn you, Jacinda. You have so much power, do you know that?"

How wrong he was, for in truth, she was powerless. Powerless to keep from hurting him, to keep from losing him, to stop what was about to unfold. Day by day, she had given him more and more of her heart and herself. Tonight would be the last.

She shook her head. "I have no power. I am at the mercy of the world."

"As are we all." He released his hold on her gown and gave it a savage tug. The sound of fabric tearing filled the air. Down it went, past her hips, falling to the floor in a whisper. "And as I have been at your mercy, Jacinda Turnbow."

His hand slid to her nape, cupping her skull as if it were fashioned of fragile porcelain, a touch that belied the sudden ferocity that blazed from him. And then his lips were on hers. Molding. Melding. His kiss crushed and bruised. It took with a savagery that stole her breath. His tongue sank into her mouth. His teeth caught her lower lip and bit.

She understood the raw need in him because she felt it herself, the blossoming desperation. The need to mark and be marked. The steadfast knowledge this was to be their goodbye. She felt it in his kiss, heard it in the words that lay unspoken.

He broke the kiss, panting, his jaw rigid. "I have given you every chance to unburden yourself, wanting—nay *needing*—to believe the best of you. And yet you have not. So, tell me, madam, what were you doing in my study tonight?"

The question and the stinging accusation in his tone made her blood go cold. He knew. Somehow, he knew. Here was his test, revealed to her. And she had failed it miserably. *Tell him everything*, her heart urged. *It is not too late. You have not yet gone too far.*

But the ciphers mocked her from where they lay hidden, reminding her she did not know their contents, how they had come to be locked inside his drawer, or why. If she told him the truth, he would not stop until he hunted down Kilross. That much, she was certain of, and it would only give the earl precisely what he had wanted all along: Crispin. Whether he was guilty or innocent, she needed to protect him. What was one more lie in a sea of so many?

She raised her chin, meeting his gaze. "I was waiting for you."

He brought his lips perilously near to hers once more. "And helping yourself to the contents of my desk, darling?" his voice was low and soft. Deceptively soft.

There was no way he could have known she had taken the ciphers unless he had gone to his study upon his return and sought to retrieve them, which meant... which meant he was not innocent at all, but guilty just as Lord Kilross had claimed. Her heart foundered.

"I do not know what you speak of," she lied defiantly.

Crispin brushed his mouth over hers, a featherlight caress. Once. Twice. "Do not lie to me."

Her eyes were wide upon him, her hands—free of the imprisonment of her sleeves—settled upon the tensed muscles of his upper arms. "I am not lying."

"Yes." His fingers tightened in her hair then. "You. Are." He sneered. "What a stupid bloody fool I am, believing in you for a moment. Tell me, what was your intention in coming here to Whitley House? What devil's bargain have you with the Earl of Kilross?"

At the earl's name, everything in her turned to ice. "I came here because you hired me as governess," she forced past lips that had gone numb. "Please release me."

"Are you fucking him?" His question was a vicious snarl.

She flinched. "Release me."

"Tell me the bloody truth, Jacinda." He was breathing heavily, his eyes darkened like thunderclouds in an ominous sky. "Who are you and what are you doing here?"

"I am the woman who loves you," she said. "If you wish to punish me or to hurt me, I will not stop you."

It was the most truth she could manage to reveal. For she did love him. Even if he was guilty. Even if the ciphers proved Kilross' theory. She could not love him less. Her heart did not function in such a capricious fashion, one moment helplessly in the thrall of a person and the next not. Here was the truest part of her life over which she had no power, her heart. She could not control who she loved.

"Damn it." He gripped her chin, tilting her head back. His eyes plumbed the depths of hers. "I have no wish to hurt you. All I want is the cursed truth, madam."

"Do what you will to me," she said quietly. "Go on, Crispin."

"Where are the papers?" he bit out.

She met his gaze, unblinking. If she had to, she would save him from himself. That was how much she loved him. "What papers, Your Grace?"

"Shall I tear apart this chamber until I find them?" he gritted.

He would find them with ease. But she had nothing left to lose. "Tear apart this chamber if it pleases you. You shall not find whatever it is that you seek."

He set her from him as if he could not bear to touch her for another moment. "If that is how you wish it, then I have no choice. In the morning, I will be seeking an audience with the Earl of Aylesbury. When I return, I shall expect your cooperation. You will answer my every question. Until then, you are barred from leaving this chamber."

Already, it was as if he was a stranger to her, and how it crushed her inside. She had known it may come to this. Only her foolish heart had propelled her onward, naïve in the belief that one more day and one more night would be enough. But this, the awful finality, his harsh coldness and barely suppressed rage... nothing could have prepared her for it.

"How do you propose to keep me within this chamber?" she dared to ask. "I have duties in the morning, and Lady Constance and Lady Honora will wonder—"

"Do not dare to speak their names," he interrupted, his lip curling as if she were beneath his contempt. "You are dismissed from your post, effective immediately. And until I can discover just how deep your treachery runs, you will find yourself confined to this chamber."

Uncertainty merged with outrage. "Do you intend to lock me within this chamber?"

"I have a man stationed outside the door. You will not be permitted to leave without my approval," he said coldly.

The words settled in the vicinity of her heart like an ice-cold blade. "You have had a man stationed outside the door from the moment you entered?"

He inclined his head. "You stole from me. You lied to me. Even now, you continue to prevaricate when we both know I have caught you at your games. I do not trust you. Nor have you given me cause to do so. Until I can determine how great a risk you are to me, I cannot allow you to leave this chamber."

He had planned this, then. Had known from the moment he entered that she had been within his study, had opened his locked drawer, and had taken the ciphers. But how he knew about Kilross was a matter of question. And if he truly thought he could contain her in a chamber, and that she would meekly remain, awaiting him to mete out his punishment to her, he was wrong. She loved him, and she could not fault him for being angry with her. She had lied to him, after all. But she had only his best interests at heart, and his best interests did not lie in her remaining trapped in a chamber. But he could not know that, for she could not tell him.

Perhaps it was better this way. They had been doomed from the start. Better to end it now rather than later, when she had fallen even more in love with him.

"Very well," she managed to say. "I think it best you leave now, Your Grace, for your lingering will only be cause for speculation and rumor. Unless you wish to tear my undergarments away as you did my gown and ravish me?"

He grimaced, raking a hand through his hair, her taunt hitting its mark. "I would never have to ravish you and you damn well know it."

It was one of the few truths that had been spoken between them that evening. He turned to go, and for some reason she could not suppress the need to have the last word.

"I would never betray you," she called after him softly, meaning the words more than she had meant any she had ever said, aside from when she had told him she loved him. Nothing had changed for her. She loved him, and she would fight to protect him, however she must.

He paused, his broad back still to her, and for a beat, she thought he would spin about and come back. But he did not. Instead, he stalked from the chamber, slamming the door behind him with so much force, the pictures hanging on the wall shook and swayed from side to side.

Only after he was gone did she allow her tears to fall. After an indeterminate span of time spent wallowing in her own loss and despair, she finally forced herself to return to the ciphers. It was going to be a long and ugly night, but she would not rest until she had the answers she sought.

SHE WAS LYING. Damn her beautiful, treacherous hide.

Crispin stalked the confines of his study, feeling like a beast locked inside a cage. His fists itched to pummel something. The demons inside him roared and clawed, demanding to be unleashed. He longed for a whisky, but he knew the devil's brew would not soothe the ache in his soul or the agony in his heart. Indeed, it never had, and he had relied upon it far too much in the misguided belief that it would.

He had nowhere to go and no one upon whom he could rely. Even on that dark day in Spain when he had woken to the realization that his best friend was dead, he had not felt so numbingly alone. The blackness he had been holding at bay beckoned, calling him with its siren lure.

If he went back to The Duke's Bastard, he would thrash the Earl of Kilross to within an inch of his misbegotten life. Perhaps he would not even stop until he was covered in the man's blood and watching him breathe his last.

And if he returned to Jacinda's chamber, he did not know what he would do. He had never been as filled with rage and betrayal as he had been when he had returned from the club, unlocked his drawer, and found the ciphers missing. He had sworn he could smell the sweet perfume of jasmine lingering in the air, a suspicion that blossomed into a vicious poison when Nicholson confirmed he had seen Miss Turnbow exiting his study earlier that evening.

He had gone to her instantly, furious and yet desperate to believe she was not capable of such deceit. That the woman who owned his heart was not also abetting an enemy he had not even realized he possessed. His frenzied mind had returned, foolishly, to the cheesecake she had baked. How could a woman who had betrayed him so thoroughly also be capable of such domestic care? Who lovingly crafted a dessert for a man while plotting his downfall?

He had clung to the thought, to the hope.

But she had not assuaged his fears. Rather, she had proven them accurate.

Her denials had been futile, for he had read the flash of truth in her eyes. He felt the finality in her kiss. The frantic beating of her heart had given away her guilt. There he had stood, the woman he loved in his arms—bloody hell, the woman he had been determined to make his damned duchess—and he had *known*.

How desperately he had wanted to be wrong. Part of him had wanted to throw her upon the bed and lose himself inside her one more time. Part of him had been so disgusted, he could not bear the sight of her. He had not imagined her capable of such perfidy, but now he knew the truth, he questioned each moment.

Had everything between them been a carefully crafted lie?

Had her initial protestations of propriety been cultivated to make him want her all the more? My God, even her drab dresses and fichus had to have been part of the role she played. Her figure was lush as any courtesan's, her beauty undeniable. How had he thought for a moment such a creature as she would be accepted in any household by a wife who wished to keep her husband's eyes from wandering?

Who was the real Jacinda Turnbow? Was that even her bloody name?

How dare she do this to him? To *them*? To what they could have been?

With a cry of animalistic fury, he took up the beckoning decanter of whisky and hurled it against the wall. The resulting smash was not satisfying enough, so he reached for a glass and heaved it as well. Still not enough. He stalked to his desk, slashing his arm over the papers neatly stacked on its surface, sending a ledger, an ink pot, and his quills flying.

Chest heaving, he stared at the destruction he had wrought, the broken shards of glass, the dripping stain running down the wall, the scattered papers and spreading blot of ink on the Aubusson. Not enough. Her words taunted him, churning through his mind.

I would never betray you.

I am the woman who loves you.

Lies, damn her. He slammed his fist atop the polished surface of his desk. Once. Twice. Thrice. The last time with so much force, pain rattled up his arm and lodged itself in his gritted teeth.

She had swept into his life, lifting him from the darkness and into the light only to cast him asunder once more. But if she thought she could win this battle, she was wrong. He had faced musket fire and bayonets, sabers and thundering cannon. He had no fear, and where she was concerned, he would also have no more weakness.

By the time he was done with her, Jacinda Turnbow—or whoever the hell she was—would be begging for mercy.

CHAPTER NINETEEN

T HE FLAME ON her last candle sputtered out, sending a single plume of smoke curling into the air. It mattered not, for the sun had risen in the sky, and the familiar sounds of London coming back to life filled the street below. Jacinda reread the letter she had written for Crispin one final time.

Dear Crispin,

I cannot say how sorry I am for deceiving you. Please know I would never have done so had there been any other way. My father is but a humble decipherer in service to the Crown as his father was before him. In recent months, however, he has not always been himself, and his gambling debts left us at the mercy of the Earl of Kilross, who not only owns Father's vowels but threatened to remove my father from service and take our home if I did not do as he asked.

He claimed to have knowledge you had conspired with the French, and were responsible for the Marquess of Searle's death. All he required of me was that I take on the role of governess to Lady Constance and Lady Honora and search your belongings for ciphered messages, which I was to then decipher and provide to him.

I was desperate to save my father and myself, and though I know it is not a sufficient excuse, I hope you will one day forgive me for my part in this injustice. I could not have known what I would find within Whitley House was not evidence of your guilt but instead the other half of me I had not known was missing. I could not have known I would fall in love with you, or that I would come to love your sisters as though they were my own.

Nor could I have known the Earl of Kilross brought me here under false pretenses. I have destroyed the original ciphers that were placed in your drawer—not by you, as I know now, but by the earl or one of his emissaries. I will not rest until I can right the wrongs I have aided in perpetrating against you.

Most affectionately yours,
Jacinda

Swallowing against a fresh rush of tears, she folded the letter into thirds. There was so much more she longed to say, but she was running out of time. Deciphering the messages from Crispin's drawer had led her to a discovery all its own. The ciphers bore the same errors as the test cipher Kilross had given her. Words were transposed, jumbled out of order alongside one another. The mistakes were too many in number to be overlooked.

And as she had stared blearily at the deciphered messages in the early hours of the morning, what had never made sense to her at long last did. Crispin was not guilty of anything. The ciphers had been written by Kilross himself.

But going to Crispin with her evidence was out of the question. As it was, she doubted he would believe her. Even if he did, he would seek out the Earl of Kilross, demanding answers. A man so intent upon bringing about another's downfall that he planted false evidence against him was a desperate man indeed. Perhaps even an unhinged one, and Jacinda could not bear for anything to happen to Crispin.

In her naïveté, she had brought this misery upon him, and it was now her duty to undo all the damage she had done. She did not dare hope Crispin would ever forgive her, but if she could lift this curse from his shoulders, she would.

With a shaking hand, she addressed the missive to him before standing.

All that remained for her to do was leave Whitley House without anyone being the wiser. First, she needed to dispense with the guard at her door. Once he was out of the way, she could escape via the same passageway she and Crispin had made use of the night of the masquerade. Taking a deep breath for fortification, she moved across the chamber, setting her plan into motion.

CRISPIN STARED AT the breakfast he could not stomach eating. Exhaustion mingled with the anger that would not be ameliorated by any number of smashed objects. He had not slept but had spent the night alternately pacing in his study and breaking nearly everything inside it to bits. The culmination had been his chair, which had been surprisingly difficult to destroy. But he had finally accomplished it by holding the legs and swinging it into his desk. The legs had made excellent kindling, as had the arms.

Still, he was not satisfied. Nothing healed the gaping wound inside him. Nothing could chase the sickness swirling in his gut. Nothing could change the fact the woman he loved had betrayed him so thoroughly and viciously, that he did not know how he would ever recover from the staggering treachery of it.

He would have to face her today.

Would have to craft some sort of plan for dealing with her. For dealing with Kilross as well, a man he had spoken a scant handful of words to if his recollection served. Thus far, he had no notion of why such a man would be so invested in seeking his downfall. Nor had he any inkling why a woman who had been tasked with orchestrating it would also go to such great lengths to do so. Had bedding him been necessary?

His hand clenched, the knuckles sore from the abuse they had received in the night. Had telling him she loved him, writhing beneath him, and sucking his bloody cock been necessary? Her betrayal was personal. It ran him through like a lance.

Nicholson appeared suddenly in his peripheral vision, clearing his throat. "Forgive the interruption, Your Grace."

"I bloody well told you I wish to be alone," he snarled at his butler, slamming his fist upon the table with so much force the cutlery danced.

Nicholson remained stalwart, not even wincing. "Yes, Your Grace. However, there is a Sir Robert Smythe at the door, and he is most adamant about an audience."

"I know of no Sir Robert," he said, making a dismissive gesture as if to shoo an unwanted fly. "Send him away."

The butler cleared his throat again. "He is asking for an audience with Miss Turnbow, Your Grace."

It was no secret *Miss Turnbow* was currently a prisoner in her apartments, with a rotating guard courtesy of Duncan positioned outside her door. The action had been met with perplexity by his domestics. He had not given a damn. The woman was a viper, and she needed to be contained whilst he decided what he would next do with her.

His gaze narrowed. "Explain to Sir Robert that Miss Turnbow is not at home."

"I already have, Your Grace, and I am afraid he is quite adamant."

Beelzebub and hellfire. He rose from his seat. It was not as if he was going to eat the bloody breakfast before him anyhow. And if Nicholson could not chase the blighter away, Crispin would. There was also the possibility a visitor for her might have some information regarding her that would prove useful.

His strides lengthening at the notion, he stalked to the front hall, surprised to find a tall, thin bespectacled gentleman with a shock of hoary hair that looked as if he had been raking his fingers through it. He held a hat in his hands that looked as if it had seen its heyday some thirty years earlier. But there was something familiar about the man's face. The shape of it, perhaps, and he possessed a warm brown gaze with such unique striations of color that Crispin had only seen it before on one other person.

Her.

Good God, could it be possible the man before him was her father?

"Sir Robert," he clipped out abruptly, offering a curt bow. "I am the Duke of Whitley. What brings you here?"

"I have come for my daughter," he said in a booming voice, eschewing a return bow altogether. "Where is she? What have you done with her?"

"Who is your daughter, sir?" he returned tightly. "I cannot answer your query until you answer mine.

"My daughter is Jacinda Turnbow, you blackguard," the older man snarled with a startling amount of vigor. "I demand to see her at once."

He hissed out a breath of displeasure. "Perhaps this is a dialogue better conducted in private, Sir Robert. Nicholson shall see to your hat and coat. Come with me."

Crispin wisely refrained from leading his unwanted guest to his decimated study, opting instead for the small salon where his mother had favored receiving callers. He waited for Nicholson to close the doors before gesturing toward a settee. "Please, Sir Robert."

But Sir Robert stood firm. "I will not sit until I see my daughter. Do not think for a moment I am unaware of your black reputation. If you have harmed her in any way, you will answer to me."

He had gone all night without sleep and felt as if he had been picked apart by ravens from the inside out. His patience was nonexistent. "And what do you propose to do to me, Sir Robert? Do tell."

"I shall pummel you with my fists if I must, you scoundrel," huffed

Jacinda's father, raising his wizened hands as if in warning.

Crispin could not contain the dark mirth at the image Sir Robert's threat brought to mind. Had she somehow gotten word to her father that she was his impromptu prisoner, he wondered? Surely this could not be a coincidence. Perhaps Sir Robert was a part of the machinations against him.

"If you do not mind, sir, I would far prefer for you to answer some questions before the pummeling commences," he quipped, careful to keep his tone flippant when inside, he was a maelstrom. "What do you know of her association with the Earl of Kilross?"

The elder gentleman paled. "How much do you know?"

A fresh stab of betrayal sank into his gut. If any part of him had foolishly continued to believe that proof of Jacinda's innocence might somehow emerge, her father's words crushed it. "I know she has been here in my household under false pretenses. Whether she had been tasked with planting false evidence against me or discovering it, I cannot yet say, as the lady in question continues to deny knowledge of it."

"Good God." Sir Robert ran a hand through his already disheveled hair. "She is not to blame. I am at fault for everything. Please, Your Grace. Allow me to explain, I beg you. Jacinda must not be held accountable for my sins."

On that point, he would beg to differ, but he would not quibble now when it seemed that some much-needed answers could possibly be at hand. "Go on, Sir Robert."

"I have lost everything," Sir Robert revealed, pausing as he seemed to collect his thoughts. "I do not know when the downward slide began or even how, but a few hundred pounds one night and then a few more the next...I kept thinking to win back what I had lost. But the hole became deeper. The Earl of Kilross holds all my vowels. He promised he would forgive my debts in exchange for Jacinda doing as he asked."

The breath left him. If Sir Robert was to be believed, Kilross had committed extortion against Jacinda. "Go on."

Sir Robert's gaze fell to the floor. "Because Kilross works for the Foreign Office, he is familiar with the fact that I am a decipherer. My eyes are no longer what they once were, and I have been relying upon my daughter for assistance in my work. Jacinda is an excellent decipherer in her own right, and Kilross knows it. He arranged for her to become governess here so she might have access to your correspondence, where she could then read any ciphered letters you received from the French and report back to him."

The very notion he would be receiving ciphers from the enemy made Crispin so bloody angry, he wanted to tear apart his study a second time. *Hellfire*, but there was only one person who could be intent upon making it look as if he were guilty of treason.

Kilross himself. Not Jacinda. His heart rejoiced. She had been forced to deceive and betray him, and while that did not mean his forgiveness would come easily, it meant there was hope for them yet. That all was not lost. That *she* was not lost.

That everything they had shared had been as real and true as he had believed.

But there was more to this sordid tale, he could smell it, and he needed to know precisely what faced him.

"There is just one problem with the earl's misguided pursuit of me," he drawled, feeling an icy chill settle deep inside him. "I am not guilty of conspiring with the enemy. Nor would I ever do so. I did not dedicate years to being a soldier, risking life and limb, just to assist Boney in his desire to conquer the bloody world."

Heaving a sigh, Sir Robert met his gaze once more, and though it was distorted behind the lens of his spectacles, the resemblance to Jacinda's rare eyes once more gave him an uncomfortable jolt. "I am aware of that now, Your Grace. You may be a rakehell and a despoiler of innocents, but you are not a traitor. Nor are you a murderer."

With a bitter smile, he inclined his head in acknowledgment. "I thank you for the glowing report of my character."

"There is good news to be had in all of this, however, and it is the reason for my precipitous arrival here," Sir Robert continued. "Jacinda need not be at the mercy of Kilross any longer, for I have used her notes to break the great cipher we received from the Peninsula."

Crispin frowned, wondering if the man was a bit mad. "I am afraid I do not follow, sir."

"Napoleon's army has been making use of a new, numerical cipher for several months now," Sir Robert elaborated, and he did not sound mad at all but utterly lucid. "The intelligence officers on the Peninsula have been unable to break the cipher. Dispatches discovered in the possession of captured or killed French soldiers have been sent to me so that I may solve it. Jacinda was aiding me before coming here to you as governess. It was her notes that ultimately led me to decipher them just this morning, and that is how I know beyond a doubt there can have been no conspiracy committed by you to murder the Marquess of Searle. He is very much alive, Your Grace. According to one of the dispatches I read, he is being held prisoner by the French."

The familiar confines of the salon swirled before him as he struggled with the knowledge that Sir Robert had just imparted. "But that is impossible. Morgan was taken by *El Corazón Oscuro* and murdered. I witnessed the aftermath with my own eyes. I saw the pools of his blood, the hand containing his signet ring all that remained."

"The marquess is alive," Sir Robert repeated. "He is a captive, and from what I was able to glean, he has been tortured in an effort to gain information about our forces. But the Spaniards did not kill him that day, Whitley, and neither did you conspire to have it done. I know that now, and I shall go to the Foreign Office with the proof myself."

Incredible. Impossible.

Morgan was... alive.

His brain whirred, calculating and assessing everything Jacinda's father had just told him. One face struck him. "The cipher you just cracked was numerical, Sir Robert?"

The elder man nodded. "You are not to speak a word of this to anyone. I should not even have divulged this much to you. Indeed, I would not have done so had not my conscience weighed upon me so heavily for my part in this disaster."

"There were ciphers hidden in a locked drawer of my study desk," he said, the jagged shards of the truth piecing together in his mind. "Someone planted them there. But they were nothing but random letters, no numbers to speak of."

Sir Robert's expression was grim. "It is as I feared, then. Kilross created a cipher for Jacinda as a test before sending her here. It was alphabetical, based on one of the old French ciphers no longer in use. I believe the earl has a vendetta against you, Your Grace."

It would certainly seem so. But why? And how? Crispin did not even know the man. "We are in agreement on that, sir. As to your daughter... I am keeping her confined in her chamber, under guard."

Red surged to Sir Robert's pale cheeks. "You are keeping her a prisoner?"

Shame assailed him. How quick he had been to think her false. How easily he had turned his back upon her, so caught up in his own selfish grief. "I shall take you to her, Sir Robert. She is free to leave with you, this very morning should she wish it."

Damnation, but he hoped like hell she did not wish it. The thought of her leaving Whitley House... leaving him... it left him aching as if his flesh had been torn open by the stab of a bayonet. Furious as he had been over her betrayal, he still had not allowed himself to contemplate the notion of her being anywhere else.

He cleared his throat against the violent surge of emotion threatening to choke him. "Follow me, if you please, sir."

In uncomfortable silence, he led Sir Robert to the second floor. But when they reached Jacinda's apartments, the door was ajar, and there was no sentry stationed outside. Heart hammering in his chest, he broke into a run.

Crashing into her chamber, he found the guard sitting on his arse on the floor, rubbing a knot on his head with a wry expression. "I am sorry, Your Grace, but she claimed she saw a rat. When I came inside to have a look, she knocked me over the head with something."

Jacinda was gone.

Damn it all to hell.

Panic clawing at him, he began a cursory inspection of the room, stopping when he discovered the neatly folded missive on her writing desk bearing his name. He tore it open, the panic growing tenfold as he read the content.

"Where the hell is my daughter, Whitley?" Sir Robert demanded from the threshold.

"She has gone after Kilross herself," he bit out hoarsely. "We have to find her."

For if anything happened to her, he would never forgive himself.

"Mrs. Turnbow." The Earl of Kilross rose at her entrance to his study, odious as ever, bearing an expression that was equal parts surprised and smug. He offered her an abbreviated bow. "You have arrived with ample time to spare. I trust you have the ciphers and their translations?"

"Yes," she said agreeably, fixing her most saccharine smile upon him. An eerie calm settled in her bones. Finding her way to him as a female traveling unaccompanied had been no mean feat. But she made it there, and she knew what she needed to do. "Of course, my lord."

His smile deepened as he gestured for her to take a seat opposite his desk. "Seat yourself, madam. I expect this accounting shall take some time. Tell me, where did you locate them?"

Jacinda crossed the soft carpet, but instead of taking the chair he had indicated, she remained standing, extracting a packet of letters from a pocket she had sewn into her spencer. "I found the ciphers in His Grace's desk drawer, tucked between the pages of his journals."

"This is most excellent," he said, holding out his hand impatiently. "Deliver them now, Mrs. Turnbow, and I shall return some of your father's vowels to you in exchange."

She ought not to be surprised a man who would attempt to incriminate another would also renege upon his promises. Biding her time, she played along, dropping the packet of letters into his hand. "Only some of the vowels, my lord? But you promised all of them would be restored to us. I have found the ciphered missives as you required."

"So it would seem, but it took you far longer than I anticipated, and I find myself unwilling to part with such a sum so easily." He paused, his stare dropping to her bosom. "Perhaps, as a widow, there is another means by which you can offer repayment."

She had an inkling or two of how she might repay the villain, but she had a suspicion it was not anything like what he had in mind. She gritted her teeth. "What I meant to say, my lord, is that I found the missives precisely where *you* left them."

He stilled. "My dear Mrs. Turnbow, I cannot fathom what you mean by such a statement."

"Yes," she charged, allowing her contempt for him to show at last. "You can, because you are guilty and you know it. You fashioned these supposed ciphers yourself and made certain they were hidden in the duke's study where I would find them."

He laughed, but it rang false and hollow. "What a fanciful imagination you have. Would that the Duke of Whitley was the hero everyone hails him as, but the truth is, he is a traitor and he needs to be punished for his sins."

Her protective streak longed to fly at Kilross and scratch his eyes out for the cavalier manner in which he would condemn Crispin, a kind and good and brave man who had fought nobly for his Crown and country. Who had loved his friend like a brother. Who deserved so much better.

But she forced herself to maintain her poise. "Would you like to know how I am certain you are the author of the ciphered missives, my lord?"

His expression soured. "I cannot say I would. Your delusions are entertaining at best and insulting at worst, Mrs. Turnbow. You have given me the evidence I required, and we shall settle the remainder of your father's debt in due time."

"You transposed the words," she continued, ignoring him.

He raked a haughty brow. "I beg your pardon?"

"*Full fathom five thy father lies,*" she repeated, for she knew the Shakespeare by memory. "*Of his bones are coral made; Those are pearls that were his eyes: Nothing of him that doth fade, but doth suffer a sea-change into something rich and strange.*"

"Brava, Mrs. Turnbow," he said coolly. "Perhaps you have a wish to tread the boards. I shall not object, but only after I am finished with you, naturally."

Anger roared through her, but she persisted. "That is the correct order of words which I recited to you just now. However, the very first cipher you gave me as a test transposed 'rich and strange to 'strange and rich.' It stayed with me, for it not only ruined the rhyme but was incorrect. How odd, then, that all seven of the ciphers I translated were marked by the same confusion of word order."

He stared at her, his gaze dark and fathomless. "Your conjecture proves nothing."

Her lip curled with disgust she could not subdue. "On the contrary, my lord. My conjecture proves everything."

"It will be your word against mine, my dear," he said, a note of smugness entering his voice. "You have already so foolishly provided me with the proof of Whitley's guilt."

"Have I?" she asked innocently.

His face darkening, he tore open the first folded paper from the small stack she had given him. An inhuman growl of pure rage emanated from his throat. He moved to the second, and then the third.

"I am afraid you shall find them all the same, my lord," she said sweetly. "Blank. For that is the evidence of the Duke of Whitley's guilt, represented on the page. There is none."

"You simple-minded whore!" Slamming his fists on his desk, he stood, skirting it until he was so near, she could smell the stale scent of his sweat.

She stood her ground, refusing to cower. "Why do you seek to destroy him?" she dared to demand.

The earl grabbed her hair, jerking her head back with such force, that tears blurred her eyes. He snarled into her face, crowding her with his body. "Why do you seek to save him? Have you been warming his bed? Is that what this show of defiance is about?"

"He is the sort of man you could never be," she taunted, needing to drag the truth from him. Needing his confession. She would endure anything, accept any pain or debasement, if it meant getting the answers she needed so she could help Crispin. "Perhaps you are jealous of him? It must be difficult to watch a man of his looks and talent, to hear him praised as a war hero. To know every woman wants him and every man wants to be him."

He jerked her hair again, his face twisting. "He is the devil's spawn, the same as his brother before him, and he deserves his fate."

Blinking away the tears clouding her vision once more, she continued, certain she was on the right course. "What has his brother to do with this?"

"Everything," Kilross bit out, his other hand clamping on her neck. "His bastard-of-a-brother destroyed my sister. He ruined her and tossed her away as if she were worthless. She died birthing his bastard, and he did not even have the grace to stop carousing and drinking on the day she was laid into the earth."

His fingers tightened on Jacinda's throat, as if he were choking the life from the former duke instead of her. "You wanted revenge upon Whitley's brother?" she choked out, desperate to keep him talking.

"The whoreson died before I could mete out the punishment he so richly deserved."

It all made sudden, horrible sense. Crispin's wastrel brother had ruined the earl's sister without compunction. In the absence of someone to blame, Kilross's horrible need for vengeance had settled upon Crispin instead.

"Let her go, Kilross."

The deep, familiar voice made her hair stand on end. Relief and love swirled through her.

Crispin was there.

But she did not have a moment to rejoice or even wonder how or why he had found his way to her with so much haste. Because the earl spun her about and hauled her against him, his arm hooking around her neck so tightly, she could scarcely breathe.

There he stood on the threshold of Kilross' study, a lone, menacing figure. His expression was grim, but he did not even allow his gaze to settle on Jacinda. He was intent upon the earl.

"Your quarrel is with me," Crispin continued, slowly making his way into the chamber step by step, hands raised in a placating gesture.

"Stop right there," Kilross ordered in a growl she felt rumble against her back. His arm tightened. Something cold, circular, and metal pressed to her temple.

A gun.

Dear God.

Crispin stiffened, his eyes flicking to hers at last, and she read the distress there before he looked away, keeping his face an impassive mask. "How do you suppose the murder of an innocent woman will aid you in your quest for vengeance, Kilross?"

"She is your whore, is she not?" Triumph gilded the earl's voice. "Why else would you be here if it were not so? But perhaps you make your decision, you ought to know just how duplicitous she is. Not a scant five minutes before your unexpected arrival, she gave me *everything* I wanted."

There was no doubt as to what Kilross implied. He was suggesting she had not only betrayed Crispin but had willingly given herself to the earl. Struggling to find her breath, she beseeched Crispin with her eyes, trying to convey what she could not say.

Robbed of air, she mouthed the words.

I would never betray you.

I love you.

He nodded, the only sign he had taken note of her desperate attempts to communicate with him. "Let the lady go, Kilross. Face me on the field of honor if you must."

"I do not wish to duel you, Whitley. I want to see you suffer."

The conviction in the earl's tone had not wavered. He was set upon his revenge, and he would not settle for anything less. But Jacinda was not about to surrender. She was no meek miss, and she was not about to allow Kilross to harm anyone she loved. The time to act was now.

In a burst of action, she stomped his foot and elbowed him in the gut with all her might. The force of her blows made his grip upon her go slack, and she took advantage, twisting away from his grasp. As she made a dash for freedom, a gunshot echoed through the chamber.

Terror unfurling, she looked back at Kilross to find him crumpling to the floor, red spreading over his chest. She pressed a hand to her heart and looked back to Crispin to discover he was not alone. Father had joined him, and it was his pistol, held in his shaking hands, and not Crispin's, that had discharged, a small curl of smoke emerging from the barrel.

Somehow, Crispin and Father had saved her. Together. Her heart thudded at the sight of them, the two men she loved above all else, standing together. And only then could she allow the relief to wash over her. Only then could she accept what she saw before her.

It was over. Kilross was dead.

The room seemed to spin about her then. Shock descended. Darkness claimed her, and she fell headlong into it.

CHAPTER TWENTY

C RISPIN HAD NEVER before played the role of suitor. Indeed, the notion had not once entered the realm of his thoughts. He did not attend Almack's. He did not pretend to drink orgeat. Nor did he eschew the waltz. When he kissed, he always used his tongue, and when he loved a woman... well, bloody hell, he had never loved *any* woman until one flame-haired siren had swept into his study one day.

Now, he could not imagine living his life without her at his side. It had taken him a few days to get his affairs in order. Engaging in an unmitigated amount of caution lest any hint of scandal taint Jacinda, he had kept his distance from her until the inquiry into Kilross's death was at an end. That had been completed yesterday, and Crispin wasn't about to spend another day without knowing that she was his. With her father's approval, and with a special license in hand, he was en route to his destination, prepared to court her like a lovesick swain.

Because a lovesick swain was precisely what he was. But he was not alone as he arrived at Jacinda's father's modest townhome far from his own Grosvenor Square address. No indeed, his sisters had accompanied him.

The minxes had insisted, and in truth, he knew Cin harbored a tender place in her heart for the two hellions. If bringing them along might further his cause, he was not above bringing them to her.

As their carriage came to a stop, he gave each hoyden a careful, stern stare. "You are both to be on your best behavior this morning. I am in love with Miss—" here he caught himself, for in the wake of the revelations that had unfolded, he had come to know that Jacinda was not an unwed miss at all, but instead, a soldier's widow. "Ahem, with *Mrs.* Turnbow."

"Of course you are," Nora said, rolling her eyes with a dramatic flourish. "Con and I have known as much from the moment you could not stop staring at her and ordering her about."

Had he ordered her about? He did not think it possible. The incident involving the dead mouse returned to him then, and he could not help but to smile as he recalled her defiance. Only later had he learned she had forced Con and Nora to dispose of the thing. And he silently applauded her for it.

"Quite silly of you really, going on and keeping us in suspense without courting her in the slightest," Con added with an eye roll of her own. "But now that you have recognized the error of your ways, we would dearly love to have a new sister, and there is no one we should like better than Miss... er, Mrs. Turnbow."

Yes, she was perfect for him in every way. Perfect for them.

He could only hope that she felt the same way.

"Either way," he continued, undeterred, "I will thank you not to ruin this for me."

He, Con, and Nora were ushered into the modest brick affair by a smiling house maid, who directed them to Sir Robert's study, where Mrs. Turnbow could be found. She was seated alongside her father, head bent over a sheaf of papers, quill in hand. Her fingers were ink-stained, her brilliant sunset hair was confined in an artless bun, she wore a simple gray morning frock, and he had never seen a more beautiful sight.

"Mrs. Turnbow," he greeted formally, offering her his most elegant bow.

Flanking him, Con and Nora dropped into proper curtsies.

There, he thought with an absurd surge of pride. This wild Ash-forth clan—or rather what remained of it—could be respectable when the situation merited it.

Jacinda stood, surprise evident on her lovely face as she, too, dipped into a curtsy. With a wink, her father rose as well, sketching a bow.

"Crispin," she greeted, a frown furrowing her brows. "Forgive me, Your Grace. What are you doing here?"

He held out the bouquet of hothouse flowers he had come armed with. "For you, my love, and I hope this time you shall not crush them into my chest and then discard them on the floor."

An adorable flush stained her cheeks as she came forward and took the flowers, burying her nose in them for a moment before glancing back up at him. "Thank you. They are lovely."

"Not as lovely as you," he said quietly, forgetting for a beat that they were not the only occupants of the chamber.

Then Con giggled, and he felt the tips of his ears go hot. Why the devil had he brought the minxes along, anyway? He cast a warning glower in his sister's direction.

Con blinked innocently. "What? I did not even say a word."

"But if she were to say anything at all," Nora interrupted with a serene smile, "she would say we do hope you will be our sister, Mrs. Turnbow. Indeed, we should like nothing better."

"And not just because you bake the most divine sweets either," Con added. "Though, to be sure, it is most appreciated."

Crispin ground his jaw. "Devil take it, you two."

Sir Robert cleared his throat. "Perhaps Lady Constance and Lady Honora might like to sample some of the Portugal cakes Jacinda made earlier this morning."

"Portugal cakes? Oh, my yes, do let's, Nora," Con said happily.

Sending a look of gratitude to Sir Robert, Crispin waited until his sibling interlopers had been shepherded from the chamber and the door helpfully closed behind them before turning back to Jacinda. She watched him with a cautious expression, her warm sherry eyes unreadable, the flowers still clutched in her hands.

"What my sisters were attempting to say, albeit with a notable lack of aplomb, is they are in desperate need of a sister who will watch over them and keep them from sliding down the stairs on salvers." He took a step forward. "And I am very much in need of a wife who will love me in spite of all my faults and scars. Who will not hesitate to give me a dressing down when I deserve it. Who is braver than I could ever be, and kinder and lovelier and my better in every way."

Her lips parted. "Have you forgiven me?"

"There is nothing to forgive, my love." He did not stop until her skirts pressed against him, until there was noting separating them but the bouquet he had brought her. "You did what you had to do to protect yourself and your father."

Unshed tears glistened in her eyes as she searched his gaze. "But I deceived you. I should have come to you, revealed everything. Mayhap then we could have stopped Kilross sooner."

"No." He shook his head slowly, banishing her protests. "There was no other way for it to unfold, Cin. The important thing is his machinations are over and you are safe from harm. That is all I care about."

"I am so very sorry, Crispin." Her lush lower lip trembled.

He pressed a gloved thumb there, stilling the tremor. "As am I, darling. I should have believed in your love. I should have known you would never betray me. Do you forgive me for doubting you? I swear to you it will never happen again."

She kissed his thumb. "As you said, there is nothing to forgive. We have both wronged each other in our own ways. I thought you never wished to see me again."

"You are all I want to see, now and forever," he vowed, taking the bouquet from her and settling it upon her father's desk so he could take her into his arms. "I love you, Jacinda Turnbow. My heart is yours if you will have it."

"I love you, too," she whispered. "So much it hurts. My heart is yours as well. Forever."

"Will you marry me, Cin?" he asked. "Be my duchess. Spend all your days and nights at my side."

"Yes." A gorgeous smile stole over her face, and it was like the sun breaking free of the clouds after a storm, light and transformative, glowing and bright and beautiful. "I would be honored to be your duchess."

He could not wait another moment to claim her lips. Their kiss was open-mouthed and starving, laden with promise. She tasted of tea and Jacinda, and nothing had ever been more delicious on his tongue. "Thank God," he muttered against her mouth, pressing their foreheads together. "I was terrified you would not want me."

"There will never be a day when I do not want you, Crispin Ash-forth. I love you so much it hurts." She kissed him, long and slow and sweet.

He caught her around the waist and spun her around and around until they were both breathless and laughing and dizzy. Joy burst in his chest like a volley of cannon fire. "I feel the same way, my darling. What do you say to the notion of getting married today?"

Her warm eyes blazed into his, her smile soft. "I would like nothing better."

EPILOGUE

J ACINDA SURVEYED HERSELF in the looking glass, taking in her elaborate coiffure and how it showed her bold red locks to perfection. Her gown was pink, all the better to complement her hair, and it hugged her form, celebrating her figure in a way that none of her old gowns had dared. At her neck, she wore the Ashforth diamonds. Her ruby and diamond earbobs were new, commissioned by Crispin himself, matching the breathtaking collar that wreathed her throat.

She had been the Duchess of Whitley for three months now, and at times, she still could scarcely believe it was real. That she had married the one man she loved above all others. That they had defied the odds against them to find their happiness, together as one.

"You are so bloody beautiful it hurts to look upon you, Duchess."

Jacinda turned to her husband, feasting her eyes upon the sight he presented in his navy coat, crisp cravat, and buff trousers. With his tall, lean form outfitted to perfection, she could not help but stare. A surge of heat pooled between her thighs. "As are you, Duke."

"How do you feel, darling?" He drew her to him gently and kissed her as she loved best, hot and hungry and open-mouthed, as if he could not get enough of her.

"I feel well enough to attend Duncan's wedding," she assured him when their mouths parted at last and she was breathless, a fresh ache of need building inside her. She supposed it would always be thus between them—fierce and all-consuming. And she would not have it any other way.

Thankfully, the sickness that had been plaguing her in the mornings had seemed to subside in the last few days. This morning, she felt no nausea at all. Instead, she felt nothing more than deep, abiding happiness. Not just contentedness, but the swelling sensation she was precisely where she was meant to be, in the arms of the man who owned her heart.

"Mmm." Her husband's mouth settled upon the hollow behind her ear, driving her mad. "I still cannot countenance Duncan is about to be wed."

Nor could she. The raffish gaming hell owner's abrupt nuptials had come as a surprise. As had his choice of bride. All London was abuzz with the news, as it was not every day that one duke's bastard wedded another duke's daughter. The scandal sheets were rife with speculation and caricatures calling it the *mésalliance* of the age. For Duncan's sake, Jacinda hoped he would find the same love and passion with his new wife she and Crispin had found together.

"Much has changed," she said softly.

Father had taken up residence in Whitley House, and Con and Nora were getting on famously with their new governess. Nary one dead rodent had been hidden in recent months, nor had any impromptu sledding sessions occurred down the main staircase. Crispin's nightmares had grown far less frequent and pronounced, and word had recently reached London the Marquess of Searle had been liberated from the enemy forces holding him captive.

"I can think of one change more than others that pleases me the most." Crispin's hands, large and gentle and strong, came between them to cup the slight roundness of her belly through her gown. "I cannot wait to meet my flame-haired daughter. She will be as willful and stubborn and intelligent and beautiful as her mama, I know."

She could not suppress her smile as she covered his hands with hers. "Or you shall have a dark-haired son who is as wonderful, honorable, witty, and handsome as his father."

"Daughter or son, of one thing I am certain." He kissed her throat, inhaling deeply as if he could not get enough of her scent, and continued his slow caress of the place where their child grew. "I am the most fortunate man in the world."

Her love for him rose within her, coalescing with need. It had been a mere two hours since he had last made love to her in the earliest strains of the morning, and still she wanted more.

She kissed his ear, catching the shell between her teeth and giving it a naughty tug that made a groan rumble deep in his throat. "And I am the most fortunate woman in the world, my love."

"Minx," he said as his wicked mouth found hers once more. Framing her face in his palms, he kissed her deeply, his tongue toying with hers.

An answering sluice of need ran through her. Her busy fingers found the fall of his breeches, and she cupped the long, hard length of him. "Oh, dear," she whispered against his lips. "I do not think you ought to attend Duncan's wedding in such a state, Your Grace."

He grinned down at her, his pale gray eyes burning with the promise of pleasure. "What do you propose to do about it, Duchess of Depravity?"

She freed one button, then another. "I do believe we have an hour to spare before we are required elsewhere. Do you think it ample time in which I can ravish you, sir?"

"Bloody hell, woman. There is *always* time for that."

"And that," she said with a grin of her own, "is just one of the many reasons why I love you."

His mouth came down upon hers, voracious as ever. "God, I love you Cin," he murmured when their lips parted once more. He scooped her up into his arms then, carrying her to the bed. "Now let my ravishment commence."

About the Author

Bestselling author Scarlett Scott writes steamy Victorian and Regency historical romances with strong, intelligent heroines and sexy alpha heroes. She lives in Pennsylvania with her Canadian husband, their adorable identical twins, and one TV-loving dog.

A self-professed literary junkie and nerd, she loves reading anything but especially romance novels, poetry, and Middle English verse. When she's not reading, writing, wrangling toddlers, or camping, you can catch up with her on her website. Hearing from readers never fails to make her day.

LINKS:
Website: www.scarlettscottauthor.com
Facebook: facebook.com/ScarlettScottAuthor
BookBub: bookbub.com/profile/scarlett-scott
Instagram: instagram.com/scarlettscottauthor
Pinterest: pinterest.com/scarlettscott
Twitter: twitter.com/scarscoromance

Made in the USA
Columbia, SC
06 April 2020

90510713R00169